Wing of Madness

I could feel his stubble against my skin and the heat of his mouth. A delicious watery ripple slid down my spine. Jim brought his mouth to my palm, kissed it, then released it. He let it go reluctantly and with tender care, as if my hand was a bird he was releasing into the wild, unwilling to let it go yet certain it deserved its freedom.

'Does your pussy need stroking yet?'

'It's needed stroking for ages, as a matter of fact.' Though my voice was calm my insides were boiling like lava. Jim didn't answer; he just looked at me. His eyes moved over my face like fingers, exploring every curve.

'Downstairs you were prepared for me to set you alight . . .'

'I'm already burning, Jim. Can't you feel the heat?'

Time seemed to slow down. I could hear my own breathing and quiet laughter as someone walked along the corridor. A car pulled up outside and a door slammed. I could even hear the soft tick-tick of Jim's wristwatch.

'I'll tell you what. At the weekend I've got to go to London. I've got a few boring things that I need to do, but they shouldn't take long. I'd like it very much if you'd come with me. If you come, then our journey together will begin.'

Wing of Madness
Mae Nixon

BLACK LACE

Black Lace books contain sexual fantasies.
In real life, always practise safe sex.

First published in 2007 by
Black Lace
Thames Wharf Studios
Rainville Road
London W6 9HA

Copyright © Mae Nixon 2007

The right of Mae Nixon to be identified as the Author of
the Work has been asserted in accordance with the Copyright,
Designs and Patents Act 1988.

www.black-lace-books.com

Typeset by SetSystems Ltd, Saffron Walden, Essex

Printed and bound by Mackays of Chatham PLC

ISBN 978 0 352 34099 3

For my friend
David Smith
With respect, gratitude
and, above all,
love

1

'Take off your trousers.' His voice was quiet, yet the authority was unmistakable. Under my shirt, my nipples peaked.

We drove through busy London traffic. Rush hour. The streets were turning to gridlock and it was the kind of baking hot day that always turned the capital into a lethargic, gritty nightmare.

I was still tipsy from lunch. Who was I fooling? It wasn't just the wine; the last few hours had been intoxicating. I hardly knew if I was on my head or my heels. But the one thing I knew with unshakable certainty was that I belonged to Jim.

The engine hummed. I unclicked my seat belt. I raised my bottom off the seat and pushed my trousers down until they pooled around my ankles.

I was naked from the waist down. My knickers were already in his pocket. I'd taken them off in the cramped toilet of the restaurant and handed them to him at the table, my cheeks blazing with shame and excitement.

The leather seat felt clammy against my skin. I could hardly breathe.

'Open your legs. Spread them wide.' Jim's voice conveyed demand and arousal in equal measure. Knowing that my obedience turned him on gave me a bravery that was totally out of character. I let my legs fall open. My knee rested against his thigh. The contact made me want him even more, yet he kept his eyes focused on the road, his hands on the wheel.

A blast of cold air from the air conditioner cooled my crotch, making me more conscious of the damp and heat there. I waited for instructions. I longed to touch myself. In truth, I wanted him to pull over and take me in the back seat as rush-hour traffic thundered by. But he was in control now and both of us knew it.

He reached over and touched my leg. My breath caught in my throat. His fingers tapped out a dance of desire against my inner thigh. He ran a trembling fingertip across the swollen ripeness of my clit. I moaned, tensing my legs and arching my back. Jim withdrew his hand slowly, raised it to his lips and licked his fingers clean.

'Put your feet up on the windscreen.'

I stepped out of my trousers, slid my bottom to the edge of the seat and raised my feet, pressing my soles against the windscreen. Steamy imprints began to appear and disappear like warm breath on a mirror.

'Touch yourself, Claire. Make yourself come.' Jim reached down and undid the button at the top of his fly.

My head was halfway down the backrest. My nape was damp against the leather. I ran my fingers along the length of my pussy, spreading the moisture. I ran my finger around the edge of my clit. I was panting hard, breath hissing out between clenched teeth.

The car snaked through London streets, making slow progress. A couple of lads in a white van honked their horn and cheered. As we pulled up beside them, the driver rolled down his window and half-stood up in his seat to get a better look.

'Open your shirt. Show them your breasts.' Jim's voice was husky and breathless.

I unbuttoned my shirt and reached behind to unhook my bra. I pulled it up, releasing my breasts. Humiliation burnt my face yet I pulled my shirt wider and thrust out my chest. My nipples were swollen and dark. The cold air made them tingle. The driver clapped and put his hand on his crotch. Behind him, horns hooted as the lights turned green. As we accelerated away he shouted after us: 'You've given me the horn.'

I turned my attention back to my aching crotch. There was a hot ball of pleasure at the base of my belly. My nipples prickled with delight.

I could hear Jim's ragged breathing. We stopped at a junction and he looked at me. The hunger in his eyes made me tingle all over. My fingers moved between my legs. My bottom stuck to the seat. Traffic rumbled. Somewhere in the distance I could hear the urgent wail of a siren.

The ball in my belly had intensified and spread. I was trembling, alive with tension and pleasure. I locked my legs at the knees and raised my bottom off the seat. My nipples were on fire. My fingers moved with a rhythm of their own. I rocked my hips.

The tension in my gut focused and broke. I cried out; a deep animal groan that was so visceral and wild I could hardly believe it had come out of my own throat. My feet pressed against the glass. My legs quivered and shook. Jim's eyes, sharp with excitement, flicked between me and the road.

The car stopped and he pulled on the handbrake. Jim reached into his pocket and pulled out my knickers. He leant across and wiped my pussy dry. He soaked up all the moisture, making sure he had missed nothing.

'I'm keeping these as a souvenir.' He smiled. 'We're home now. Do you want to sort yourself out?' He put my underwear back into his pocket and turned off the engine.

As we crossed the road to his house, we saw a dead blackbird lying on the tarmac. Its bloodied body was squashed and mutilated yet one wing had remained completely intact. Caught by a gust of wind, the wing began to flap in parody of flight. The breeze ruffled the perfect feathers, making it seem as if the wing belonged to a living bird moving with conscious thought in spite of its flattened body.

Neither of us could look away. There was something both grisly yet wonderful about it, which filled me with tenderness and regret, as though the urge to soar and swoop could transcend even death. Yet, the fruitless flapping also seemed pointless and wasted, a metaphor for life. I held Jim's hand and stood in the middle of the road, watching the dead bird's wing beat with futile beauty.

A month earlier, I'd never have behaved with such abandon. But that was before I met Jim. Sometimes you don't know how much you want something until it falls into your lap and you realise you've longed for it all your life. Only that longing has got buried somehow, hidden and stuffed down so far that all that's left is a vague sense of unease.

Jim wasn't even my type really – he seemed too handsome, too perfect – but the instant we met there had been something about him that got to me. At forty, he was five years older than me. He had the sort of tall, broad-shouldered, upright physique that seems designed to look good in a suit and he knew it. He appeared to have a vast collection of expensive suits and he wore shiny shoes and proper shirts with cufflinks.

He moved with a sort of effortless, loping elegance which seemed sophisticated, urbane and powerfully masculine. Something about him reminded me of an old-fashioned movie star, like Cary Grant in his prime or Connery's Bond.

His brown hair was expensively cut and fashionably tousled. He had the kind of face you normally only saw between the pages of *GQ* plugging aftershave or expensive wristwatches. The tiny creases visible around his eyes were his only flaw but, rather than aging him, they just made him look distinguished. And those eyes were what intrigued me most. Blue and twinkling with intelligence and playfulness, they made his face seem lively and open.

He was staying at my sister's hotel in Oxford and came into the bar when I was helping out. He was polite to me, but never paid me any particular attention. And, as far as I was concerned, he was just another customer I had to keep happy for a few hours.

But after a week of enforced company, he began to intrigue me. He obviously wasn't a salesman like most of the clientele yet he clearly wasn't a holidaymaker. His language and manners were straight off the polo field yet, according to him, his background was humble.

Though he was friendly, even charming, towards the other guests he always seemed to hold some part of himself back. He'd coax someone to share their deepest secrets yet he never once revealed anything important about himself. On more than one occasion, he'd been asked where he'd grown up and, each time, his answer had been 'I haven't yet.'

He was very free with a kind of emotional disclosure that people mistook for openness and sharing but essentially revealed nothing. He'd admit to getting an erection the first time he'd seen Donatello's *David* in Florence, or being moved to tears when he'd read *Jane Eyre* as a child but real facts and locations were a currency he didn't trade in.

I asked Colin, my brother-in-law, how long Jim had been staying and learnt he'd been with them since the spring and paid his considerable bill once a week in cash. According to Colin, he was a businessman taking a year's sabbatical from the office to do some travelling and that was as much as he knew. I still didn't fancy Jim at this point, but my interest was piqued.

One night, I turned up for my shift behind the bar to find Jim in conversation with an American couple, Candy and Irving. They were discussing differences between British and American English: sidewalk and pavement, vest and waistcoat, that sort of thing. The couple clearly found him charming

Jim leant over the bar and called to me, 'Bring us another round, please, sweetheart.'

I was busy with another customer so I called back, 'I'll be with you in a moment.'

'That's another one, Irv.' Jim patted him on the back. 'When an Englishman says "momentarily" he means "for a moment" yet to a Yank, it means "in a moment". And don't get me started on "fanny", we'll be here all night.'

'You know what Bernard Shaw said –' I put their drinks on the bar '– we're "two nations separated by a common language".'

Jim looked at me as if he was seeing me for the first time. He smiled and his eyes crinkled with genuine warmth. 'And get one for yourself, please.' He handed me a twenty-pound note.

When I came back with the change, Irving was talking about the big account his advertising agency had landed. His wife turned her eyes towards the ceiling and gave a mock yawn.

'Come on, honey. Jim doesn't want to hear about your work. And neither do I. We're on vacation.' Candy's tone was conciliatory but the edge of boredom in her voice made it obvious she had long ago tired of the subject.

'You remember what Anthony Burgess said about advertising, I'm sure?' Jim winked at Candy.

'No, I don't think I do.' Irving scratched his head, trying to remember.

'It's "the rattling of a stick inside a swill bucket".' Jim swirled the brandy in his glass for emphasis.

Candy laughed.

'Actually, you're wrong.' I put my hand on Jim's arm. 'It was George Orwell.'

He turned to look at me. 'Yes, now I think of it, you're right. I must say, you're very well read for a barmaid.'

'I teach English at Somerville. I'm only helping out while my sister's on maternity leave.'

'Really?' He smiled at me again and this time I saw something new in his eyes. A hint of recognition and interest, perhaps, and even respect.

A few days later I arrived for my shift early so I could get things properly organised. I was putting away the clean glasses when I became aware of Jim standing at the bar watching me.

'When you're ready, Claire, I'll have a glass of red wine.'

'Do you mind if I put these away first? It'll get busy in a while and I'll never get the chance.'

'Of course. Go ahead.'

As I reached up to put the glasses on the shelf above the bar Jim watched me, his eyes focused on the front of my shirt. I gave him a mock stern look but he just smiled and carried on.

When I'd finished putting the glasses away, I poured Jim's wine and put it down on the bar in front of him.

'Would you like one yourself?' He opened his wallet.

'Thank you. I'll have a mineral water.'

'Do Colin and Bernadette ever let you have a day off? After all, it hardly seems fair to have to spend your entire vacation working here when you should be enjoying your time off.' He pocketed his change.

'Actually, this is my last week. Bernie's coming back to work, so I'll have plenty of time for relaxation from then on.' I poured myself a glass of Perrier.

'I'm glad to hear it. I'd like to take you out to lunch, to help get you in a holiday mood.' Jim took a sip of his wine, but his eyes never left my face.

'I'd like that. But I'm working two shifts a day until Friday.'

'Perhaps Saturday lunch, then?'

'I'd like that.'

'Shall I meet you here about twelve?'

Things got busy after that and I didn't have time to talk to Jim again until after I'd called time. The bar gradually emptied but Jim didn't move.

As I emptied ashtrays and put glasses into the washer, Jim leant on the bar watching. I could feel his eyes on my body as I moved around the room. I could feel a little shivery tingle shoot up my spine and then spread to my face. I know it sounds crazy, but it almost felt as though Jim's fingertips had touched me. Inside my bra, my nipples went hard.

Though it's never been my nature to show off to a man, I found myself doing just that. When I bent to wipe a table I made sure he had a clear view of my bottom or cleavage and I moved languorously, deliberately exaggerating my movements and every so often looking straight at him. He watched me work and, though I was too far away to see his eyes, I could see his smile of approval and admiration.

When I'd finished, I walked back to the bar with the bin full of ash in one hand, a dirty cloth in the other. As I approached the bar he got off his stool and walked around to the other side of the counter.

'You look like you could do with a drink. I'm sure Colin and Bernie won't mind if we have a quickie after hours. What can I get you?' He rested both hands on the bar and smiled at me in perfect imitation of a genial landlord. I couldn't help laughing.

'Isn't that what I'm supposed to say?'

'There's nothing wrong with a little healthy role reversal. You should try it sometime.' Jim looked me straight in the eye as he spoke, a slight smile on his lips. A warm tingle of pleasure crept up my throat and over my face.

'I'd really love a coffee, but you'll probably need me to show you how the espresso machine works. I'll just put these cleaning things in the kitchen then I'll do it.'

Jim intercepted me and carried the things into the kitchen himself. I took the opportunity to wash my gritty hands in the sink behind the bar. When he reappeared he pointed to a bar stool and gave me a stern look. I sat down.

He operated the espresso machine as if he'd been doing it all his life and put two cups down on the bar, before pouring us both a couple glasses of brandy. He'd even remembered to put one of the little caramel biscuits we always serve with coffee on each saucer. Then he came back round to the customers' side and sat down at the stool next to me.

The bitter coffee warmed and revived me. I drained the cup and tore open my biscuit's cellophane wrapping. As I ate my biscuit I watched Jim biting into his. He half closed his eyes and his face expressed such pleasure that I almost felt as though I was intruding on a private moment. I felt like a voyeur, yet I couldn't stop. When I finally looked away, I realised I'd been holding my breath.

'What kind of food do you like? I'm thinking of doing a picnic for Saturday.' He drained his cup.

'I'm not fussy. I'm very easy to feed. I love food as a matter of fact.'

'I like that in a woman. I can't tell you how disheartening it is when you take a girl to dinner and all she does is push the food around the plate. I love a woman with a hearty appetite for all things. Don't you agree?' He swirled the brandy around in his glass.

'Broadly speaking, though obviously I prefer men.' I took a sip of my brandy.

'I'm delighted to hear that. I've never understood why women put up with us, but I've always been eternally grateful that they do.'

'I know it's popular to think men and women are different animals – Venus and Mars and all that – but I've never really believed it. Underneath it all men have exactly the same feelings and anxieties as us women.'

'Of course we do. And, I'll tell you a secret –' he leant in close and lowered his voice '– I've always considered myself to have a very strong feminine side.'

'Is that code for "I want to borrow your knickers"?'

Jim laughed. He laughed easily; it was one of the first things I'd noticed about him. And when he did, he seemed to lose his worldly-wise persona and become transformed, for a moment, into the boy he must once have been.

'Oh, I'm enormously interested in your knickers, I assure you, but you need have no fears about me stretching them. A last nightcap before bed?' He held up his empty glass.

'I'd better not. I've got to drive home, after all. In fact, I'd better get moving soon.' I drained my glass.

'I'd rather assumed that you stayed here when you were working.'

'No. I have a house in Jericho. Not that I'm seeing much of it at the moment.'

'Really? I lived in Jericho when I was a student. Down by the canal. There was no central heating and, if you wanted a bath, you had to put fifty pence in the meter and wait hours for the tank to heat up. But I was happy there.'

'I didn't know you'd studied in Oxford.'

'There are a lot of things you don't know about me, Claire.'

'That sounds rather mysterious . . .'

'Perhaps.' He was smiling, his eyes sparkling with mischief and challenge.

'I've been watching you these past few weeks . . . well, you've just admitted you're rather mysterious. You can hardly blame me for being curious.'

'You know what curiosity did to the cat, Claire.' Although he was smiling, his eyes were unreadable.

'You obviously delight in being enigmatic.'

'Look at it like this. An enigma is a riddle. Something to decipher, discover and ultimately to conquer. Doesn't that sound like fun to you?'

'You make yourself sound like a crossword puzzle. One of those very cryptic ones you have to be a professor of English to solve.'

'Meaning that you think you'll be able to crack my code?'

'Maybe.'

'I'll tell you what, Claire, let's play a game of truth . . . three questions each.'

I looked at him for a long moment. 'I think I'll need a drink for that.'

Jim went round to the other side of the counter. He poured us both double brandies and put the money in the till. He sat back down.

'Ladies first?'

'OK.' Faced with the opportunity to get the facts I'd been so hungry for, my mind went blank. I took a mouthful of brandy and swallowed it, relishing the heat's slow transit through my body. 'Where did you grow up?'

'Reading.'

'Beer, bulbs and biscuits, isn't that what they say? I think that's all I know about Reading.'

'They do say that. And, as a matter of fact, my father worked for Huntley and Palmers. Only pushing paper around in the accounts department but at least he wasn't on the shop floor like his mum and dad.'

'I'm surprised. Most people would assume you'd been born with a silver spoon in your mouth.'

'Not at all. I've been lucky. I've come a long way. My mum cleaned people's houses to make extra cash. They were poor but decent. They had solid values but, if I'm honest, there wasn't a lot of love in the house. They had me late in life and I never really felt as though they wanted me.'

'That wasn't so difficult, was it?'

'Not yet. Ask me another.'

He looked calm enough but I thought I could detect a slight tightness of the jaw and the ghost of tremor in the hand holding his glass.

'Have you ever been married?' I took a sip of brandy. 'Or perhaps you still are?'

'I was married for more than ten years. Happily, I might add.'

'Children?'

He shook his head. He was smiling but I thought I saw a hint of regret in his eyes. 'You see? I'm not that mysterious really. You've got one question left. What's it to be?'

'Tell me about your proudest moment.'

He smiled. 'That's easy –' Jim's mobile phone trilled in his pocket. He stood up to retrieve it and looked at the display. 'Sorry, I've got to take this. Excuse me.' He walked across the bar and out the door.

I watched him through the glazed partition. It was obvious from his body language that he was agitated and angry. A scarlet spot had formed on each cheek. He paced up and down talking animatedly into the phone. After several minutes he snapped it shut and dropped it into his pocket. For a moment, he stood there, his mouth set into a hard line and his eyes unfocused. When he realised I was watching he smiled at me and came back into the bar.

'Sorry about that.' He sat down. 'Where were we?'

'Trouble at work?'

'Storm in a teacup. Nothing to worry about ... Let me think ... my proudest moment. It's got to be the day I got my degree. Dad was dead by then but seeing Mum's face as I picked up my BA was wonderful.' Jim ran his fingers through his hair. It was a simple gesture, yet I sensed it was intended to distract and delay. He folded his arms. 'Is it my turn now?'

Though his tone was light I sensed that the phone call had unsettled him and he was glad the spotlight was no longer on him. I took a slow swallow of my brandy.

'I'm ready.'

'What's your earliest memory?'

I didn't even have to think about the answer. 'Falling asleep in my pushchair. It was hot; I remember the sun beating down on my bare legs. It must have been summer, I suppose, so maybe I was about a year old.'

Jim smiled. 'Do you have other brothers and sisters? That's not one of my questions, by the way, it's a supplementary.' Jim got up and refilled our glasses. As he slid mine across the bar to me I noticed it was a double.

'You bet. Four brothers and a sister ... We had a typical Irish Catholic upbringing, I suppose. Mass on a Sunday, confession, fish on Fridays ... most of my Catholic friends grew up with a sense of guilt and a profound hatred for the smell of incense.'

Jim leant over and put his head close to mine as if he were about to tell me a secret. 'All the girls I know who were bought up Catholic are thoroughly depraved. Does that apply to you, do you think?'

'I'm familiar with the theory ... I've never quite been able to stop being a good girl but maybe there's a deep seam of wickedness that I've never expressed.'

I took another sip of my drink, feeling its warmth slip down my throat.

'And it's that part of you I'm most interested in getting to know.' Jim met my gaze. His eyes were a particularly vivid blue like the sea on holiday postcards. They were the kind of eyes you looked into rather than at and, as I returned his gaze, I feared for a moment I might drown. I saw in Jim's bottomless eyes a kind of recognition and understanding that was as inviting as it was frightening. His gaze didn't waver. Finally, he spoke. 'Second question. What made you choose the academic life?'

'Oh, I don't know ... It chose me, really. I was offered a scholarship to a Catholic boarding school. I missed the family terribly at first but, eventually, when I went home for holidays, I realised I no longer fitted in. They were proud of me, I knew, but we didn't know each other any more. So the academic life became my refuge and my salvation. I went on to university and after that I did my doctorate. Teaching seemed the only logical next step.'

'But you enjoy it?'

'Oh, I love it. Helping young people to appreciate books I love is a privilege and an honour. These kids are motivated, they're hungry for it and they're like sponges, soaking up everything I have to offer them.'

'That's how I felt when I first went to university. For a working-class boy like me, it was another world; one that my parents wouldn't even have been able to imagine. In some ways, I feel I've lived a charmed life.'

'You talk as if it was over, Jim.'

He shook his head. 'Perhaps it is.'

There was a sort of wistful expression on his face that I couldn't read. I wouldn't call it sadness exactly, more as if he was remembering an old, yet still painful memory.

'OK. Now you've got one question left. Make sure you don't waste it.'

'Let me see . . . I know – this is a good one. I want you to tell me about your most intense experience. The most powerful moment of your life.'

The moment he said it, I knew the answer, yet I wasn't sure I wanted to share it.

'I hope you're not going to back out now, Claire. I'd be very disappointed.'

I looked him straight in the eyes and began to talk. 'When I was at college I had an affair with an older man. He was thirty and when you're nineteen that seems enormously mature. He was the first real man I'd ever been to bed with – before that they'd all been boys.'

'Tell me more.' His lips were slightly parted and, for the first time, I noticed that his mouth was unusually full and sensual for a man. His blue eyes glowed.

'Funnily enough, he was called Jim too.'

'Really? I like him already.'

'I can't tell you how different Jim was from the lads

I'd been with before. He respected me. He liked me and, more importantly, he saw – really saw – who I was and made it OK for me to express it fully. Especially in bed. He encouraged me to tell him what I liked and he really cared about my pleasure. He wasn't just waiting for me to come so that he could have his turn.'

'I told you I liked him.'

'You knew that if you asked me about my most intense experience it would be a sexual one, didn't you?' I drained my glass.

He shrugged. 'People say I'm easy to talk to. But go on, you can't stop now.'

'One day Jim and I were making love. I don't know if it was because we'd spent all day doing it and my body was full of sexy hormones but I started to tingle all over and I knew that if we kept doing it I was going to come. The thing is, I'd never come from penetration alone before. I told Jim and he promised he'd keep going until I got there.'

Jim's face was a foot from mine. He never took his eyes off me. 'The earth moved, I hope?'

'The universe moved, Jim. I saw stars. I mean it – I literally saw stars. Then I burst into tears. It was … heavenly.'

'It sounds like it.' He leant close once again. I could feel warm brandied breath on my face. When he spoke, his voice was almost a whisper. 'I love it when I fuck a woman to tears. I watch her face as she loses control and when she comes it tips me over the edge and I explode inside her like a bomb. It's at those moments that I feel most intensely myself.'

As Jim spoke, my skin began to tingle all over. His warm scented breath on my face felt like the most intimate of caresses. As I breathed, I could feel my nipples rubbing against the fabric of my bra. I felt a warm flush creep up my throat. I picked up a beer mat from the bar and fanned my face.

'I need another drink after that.'

Jim nipped behind the bar and refilled our glasses. 'You'll be over the limit, surely, if you have another?' He sat down.

'I think I already am. I shouldn't have had the last one really. I'll call a taxi when I'm ready to go home.'

Jim took a long swallow of his brandy. 'Tell me, Claire, what do you fantasise about? I bet you've got a sexual fantasy that you've never even dared to speak about.'

'What makes you think that?' I sipped my drink.

He shrugged again. 'We all have. Surely you're not shy of telling me about it after all we've shared this evening?'

'I think you've run out of questions. Or is this another supplementary?'

'It's called communication. I'm curious.'

His big hands cupped his glass, making it seem unnaturally small. His manicured nails tapped the surface, making a gentle drumming noise. I took a long slow swallow of brandy for courage then set my glass down on the bar.

'I dream about ... Do you know, I'm not really sure I even have a name for it? I fantasise about letting the man be in charge. I dream about doing whatever he wants me to do. I don't mean having no say or no choice or not being respected; I don't want to be a doormat or a victim. I just want to give myself to him totally, sexually. To be his to use.'

Jim was smiling. He took a sip of brandy and, when he lowered his glass, his lips glistened in the light. 'How do you feel now that you've shared your fantasy?'

'Oh I don't know ... sort of liberated, lighter.'

Jim laughed out loud. 'Unburdened, perhaps? So confession really is good for the soul.'

'And how about you, Jim? I showed you mine, now it's your turn to unzip.'

'Well –'

Before Jim could respond there was a bang behind us as the bar door swung open. A drunken resident stumbled in. Seeing Jim and I at the bar his eyes lit up.

'You're open. How about a large G & T before bed?' The drunken guest walked across the room towards us, moving with a deliberate, if slightly swaying, gait. I got up to intercept him.

'I'm sorry, Mr Porlock, we're closed. Mr Hyde and I were just having a chat. But there's a mini bar in your room if you'd like a nightcap.'

Mr Porlock's face crumpled. He looked around and began to pat his pockets. 'The fact is, my dear, I think I've lost my key and there's nobody at reception.'

'I'll get the master key and let you in.' I turned to Jim. 'I won't be long.'

When I got back Jim had put our empty glasses in the washer and had turned off the lights behind the bar. As he saw me come into the room he climbed off his stool and walked over to me.

'Time to turn in, I suppose. Are you sure you'll be all right getting home?'

'Yes, I'll call a taxi from reception. Thanks for clearing up, Jim.'

'It was the least I could do after leading you astray.' He put his hand on my forearm. His fingers were soft and warm and his touch made my heart beat a little faster.

'Did you lead me, do you think? Maybe I was already astray.'

Jim laughed. 'I hope to find out very soon.'

'You do realise that you've avoided answering my question, don't you?'

He nodded and smiled. 'Perhaps I'll answer it on Saturday. Or, perhaps, you already know the answer. Good night, Claire.' He leant over and kissed me on the cheek and walked away. As the door to the bar swung closed behind him I could still feel the tingle of his stubble on my face.

2

A few days later I was manning the reception desk. It was probably my least favourite job because it involved long hours of boredom punctuated by periods of frantic activity. I was halfway through my shift when I saw Jim coming down the stairs. He was wearing a suit I'd never seen before in conker-brown linen with a cream silk shirt, open at the neck. He looked devastating. When he spotted me he smiled and raised a hand in greeting. I smiled back, delighted to be distracted from the monotony.

He was halfway to the desk when the telephone rang. I shrugged in apology and picked it up.

'The Feathers Hotel. How may I help you?'

'I'm trying to locate a friend, Mr Powney. I believe he may be staying there.' The man's voice had a strange raspy edge to it and the kind of working-class Estuary accent that half of England seemed to speak these days.

'Let me check for you, sir.' I leafed through the register. 'No, I'm afraid we have nobody of that name staying here.'

'Are you sure? Only his father's been rushed to hospital and I need to get in touch with him. Maybe he's moved on but left a forwarding address? I'm sorry to push but obviously it's urgent.'

I covered the receiver with my hand and mouthed 'sorry' to Jim. I checked bookings for the previous eight weeks.

'No, I'm sorry. We've had no Mr Powney registered here.'

'Thank you very much for your help.'

'You're welcome. I hope you find him.'

'So do I.' He hung up.

When I looked up from putting the phone down Jim face was dark with anger.

'What's wrong?'

'Who was that on the phone?'

'I don't know, he didn't say. He was looking for someone but he's not staying here. What's the matter? Your face looks like thunder.'

'Someone named Powney? What did he say?'

'That Mr Powney's father's been taken to hospital.'

Jim's whole body looked tense. His nostrils flared as he breathed and his mouth was hard. 'What did he sound like?'

'He sounded ... I don't know ... Cockney maybe ... southern anyway ... and sort of hoarse – half whispering. Jim, what's this about? Is it something to do with you?'

He turned and walked out of the building.

I didn't know what to think. When I'd described the man's voice it had obviously meant something to him. And who was Mr Powney? Was that Jim's real name? No other explanation made sense.

I'd known there was something mysterious about him; why did he choose to live in a provincial hotel when he clearly had the money to live in luxury? What sort of business did he have and why had he distanced himself from it? Then there was the phone call the other night which had upset and agitated him. But it hadn't occurred to me before that there might be something sinister behind the secrecy.

If he was living under an assumed name he must be

hiding something, but what that might be I couldn't imagine. I spent the rest of my shift trying to make sense of Jim's behaviour, coming up with one fabulous scenario after another. Perhaps he was a criminal mastermind on the run, or maybe he was involved in industrial espionage or some shady business activity like arms trading. But I was letting my imagination get out of hand. I gave myself a stern talking to and tried to think of more plausible explanations. Perhaps he was hiding from an ex-wife after his money or was recovering from a breakdown or bereavement. But even these more prosaic explanations didn't account for his odd behaviour.

Towards the end of my shift Jim entered the hotel. He headed straight for me. He stood patiently while I dealt with a resident's query about guided walking tours of Oxford and waited until the guest was out of earshot before he spoke.

'Claire, I've come to apologise. What must you think of me?'

'I'm glad to see you looking calmer anyway.'

'Yes, I did get rather upset. I'm sure you must have found the whole thing very confusing.' He smiled as he spoke, but somehow it didn't reach his eyes.

'You can say that again.'

'You see, I have a close friend called Powney and it's a very unusual name so naturally I wondered if it might be my friend the caller was looking for. And when you said his father had been taken ill I was very concerned.'

'And was it your friend?'

'Yes, I'm afraid it was. You see, I know the family and I've grown quite fond of his dad so I just rushed off to find him and it never crossed my mind how strange that might appear to you.'

'Very strange. I didn't know what to think.'

'Well, now you know and I hope you can forgive me for my rudeness.' His contrition seemed genuine. His brow was creased in concern and his eyes were serious.

'Forgiven and forgotten.'

'I knew I could rely on the Catholic in you to pardon my sins.'

On Saturday morning I got up early to get ready for our date. As I moved around the house I felt distinctly unsettled. There was a hard little knot of tension under my ribs and my hands seemed to have grown clumsy. I almost dropped the milk as I put it into the fridge and my orange juice slipped out of my hand, breaking one of my favourite glasses.

I'd been a clumsy child – not because I lacked co-ordination but because, most of the time, I'd been mentally elsewhere. I was a solitary, bookish little girl who preferred the invented world of novels and my own imagination to reality. After I went to boarding school, I retreated into the realm of the imaginary even further.

I read voraciously, consuming books like junk food, always hungry for more. I wandered through life like a sleepwalker, absorbed and distracted by the world in my head and barely present in the reality other people seemed to prefer. At times of stress, this distraction and the resulting clumsiness returned. Spilling my juice was a sure sign something was wrong.

Jim and I had chatted often over the past few days but had never again reached the same level of intimacy. Our conversations were tinged with a little hesitation on my part; somehow I'd never quite bought his pat explanation about Mr Powney.

I was convinced Jim was lying to me or, if not lying, deliberately obfuscating. He seemed happy enough to discuss the past because that was safely distant and he could put any spin on it that he chose, but he was cagey and evasive about the present.

But, in spite of my concerns, there was something about the way Jim looked at me and the quiet authority in his voice that seemed to reach deep inside of me. I felt that he could see my thoughts, my secrets and my shame. When he looked into my eyes, it was as though he was reaching inside of me, drawing out my true nature and holding it up for me to see.

No wonder I was afraid. That was why I'd broken the glass and why my hand shook as I poured boiling water into the cafetière and why my breakfast stuck in my throat like stones. I climbed the stairs, went into the bathroom and stepped into the bath, surrendering to its perfumed embrace, and closed my eyes.

When I walked into the lobby of The Feathers, I spotted Jim immediately. He was sitting with his back to me reading the *Guardian*. Light glinted off the lenses of a pair of fashionably slimline reading glasses. I'd never seen Jim wearing spectacles before and I thought they made him look both scholarly and vulnerable, as if the flaw of poor eyesight somehow highlighted his human frailty.

As I watched Jim it struck me this was the first time I'd had the chance to look at him in the way he'd often looked at me. I'd grown accustomed to the feel of his eyes on my body. And, to tell the truth, I'd grown to enjoy the secret little shiver that crept up the back of my neck like fingertips whenever I became conscious of it. But I'd never had the chance to look at him in the same way.

I felt like a voyeur. I let my eyes linger, discovering every plane and curve of his face, learning each mole and blemish like an explorer staking a claim. I felt both ashamed and aroused. My cheeks burnt and my breath caught in my throat.

I walked over and tapped on his shoulder.

Jim was parked behind the hotel. I don't know why, but I hadn't expected him to own a car. Somehow it seemed too permanent and settled for the rootless, nomadic lifestyle he appeared to lead. It was a brand-new Range Rover with leather seats and polished wood interior and I knew it must have cost a bomb. Another clue, if I needed one, of Jim's financial standing.

'You know, I had the strangest feeling when I was reading, like someone breathing on the back of my neck, and I couldn't shake off the feeling that I was being watched.' He looked into my face as he spoke and the directness and intensity of his gaze made me feel that he already knew the truth.

'I can't tell a lie. I stood for a couple of minutes looking at you reading. I'm not sure why. Do you mind?'

Jim laughed, softly. 'Of course not. But I'm much more comfortable with the arrangement when it's the other way around.'

'Didn't you tell me that you believed in role reversal the other day?'

'Yes, I did. How did it feel?' Jim looked at me with the same directness and focus that he had used a moment before and, once again, I knew I couldn't lie.

'It feels rather wicked actually. I've never realised before what power the voyeur has.'

Jim nodded. 'A voyeur can turn something completely innocent into pornography and yet his victim may not even know, let alone co-operate.'

'Unless he or she is an exhibitionist.'

'Aah! Another favourite subject of mine.'

Jim drove out of the city. We sped through fields and farmland. We hadn't seen another car for miles and it was easy to believe that our air-conditioned cocoon existed in some private universe which contained only the two of us.

We turned off the road and drove down a country lane totally overhung by trees, like a verdant tunnel. We moved slowly as the lane was windy and only wide enough for a single car. Inside our green chamber, where light was muted and dappled and even sounds seemed somehow muffled and distant, my sense of pleasurable isolation grew.

We turned down a narrow rutted track and parked beside a fence. As we stepped out of the car, I could smell the warm bread aroma of sun-baked grain and the sharp scent of manure. On the other side of the fence was a path leading away from us and disappearing between a copse of trees.

'It's lovely, Jim. After being cooped up behind the bar this seems like paradise.'

'We've got a little walk ahead of us, but it isn't far.' Jim opened the boot.

'Let me give you a hand.'

Jim handed me a folded picnic blanket and a leather holdall. He put two cool boxes on the ground, closed the boot and locked the car.

'Now we just go over this stile and along that path.' Jim stepped over the stile in a single stride. He extended a hand to help me. I stepped down with a little hop and almost overbalanced. It was a brief ungainly moment but it reminded me of the underlying cause of my clumsiness and I felt my face grow warm and my heart thump in my chest.

Jim led me into the woods. Under the cover of the trees it was cool and dark.

'It's lovely in here – like being in a green cathedral.' I looked up at the tall treetops.

'That's a beautiful way of putting it. I discovered this place when I was a student. A lecturer I was having an affair with introduced me to it.'

I looked at him expecting to see the wicked grin that would tell me he was teasing but, instead, I saw a level, honest gaze.

'You had an affair with a lecturer?'

Jim shrugged. 'Doesn't everyone?'

'Not these days. It's illegal for one thing.'

He laughed. 'Claire, you're so law abiding. It's time you learnt that an illicit pleasure tastes just that little bit sweeter.'

Before I could answer, Jim stepped up his pace and strolled off ahead of me. I followed him along the narrow path. Twigs crackled underfoot. Birds twittered overhead.

Jim led the way down a slope and we found ourselves on the banks of the river. He put down the cool boxes and leant against a gnarled tree trunk, waiting for me. When I arrived beside him my summer dress clung to my back and my long hair was damp against my nape. Jim took the blanket from me and spread it on the ground and we sat down.

'This is a lovely place, Jim. It's so quiet and secluded.'

'Not that secluded, really. There's a pub half a mile in that direction –' he pointed along the bank '– so civilisation is on hand if required. I hope you're hungry. And, more importantly, thirsty.'

Jim unzipped the holdall and took out two champagne flutes. He opened one of the cool boxes and brought out a bottle of cava and opened it. The cork made a soft pop as he pushed it free with his thumbs and the bottle exhaled a puff of vapour. He filled our glasses, took a sip from his own then set it down carefully on the ground.

From the holdall, he produced plates, cutlery and white linen napkins, then began to unload the cool boxes. There were two loaves of ciabatta, a packet of butter, olives, tomatoes on the vine, hummus, salad and several paper-wrapped parcels tied up with string.

'I just love this sort of food. What's in the parcels?'

'This one is venison pâté and these two are cheese.' He began to unwrap them. 'A beautiful ripe Camembert and a piece of Dolcelatte – I hope you like blue cheese.'

'I love it. And Dolcelatte is my absolute favourite.' I watched as Jim cut the Camembert in half. Its ripe golden interior began to ooze and bulge like a pregnant belly.

'Did you know Dolcelatte is really unripe Gorgonzola?' Jim leant close and spoke softly as if he were sharing the most intimate secret.

'Really? I didn't know that.'

'Somehow that makes it all the more special, I think. You have to eat it at the perfect moment of voluptuous ripeness before it tips over into harshness.' Jim was fiddling with the food as he spoke, putting the cheese and pâté on plates and opening cartons, but the intimacy of his tone belied the casual activity.

After the meal, Jim produced a fresh fruit salad and crème fraîche from the cool box and a second bottle of cava. When we'd finished eating I was feeling distinctly tipsy and the heat was beginning to get to me. I lifted my damp hair off my neck and pressed my cold wine glass to my forehead.

'I wish I'd brought something to tie my hair back with. I'm roasting under here.'

'You've got lovely, thick, heavy hair haven't you? It was one of the first things I noticed about you.'

'Thanks, but I've always hated the colour.'

'Nonsense. It's beautiful. Strawberry blonde, don't

they call it? Though I've always thought it was more of a gentle peach colour. Or like the sun on ripe corn. Scoot over here.' He parted his legs and patted the blanket between them. I crawled across the blanket and sat down in the V of his legs.

I could feel his body heat through his trousers and the soft bulge of his crotch against my buttocks. I surrendered to his body's gentle captivity. He leant forwards and began to comb my hair with his fingers. His fingertips brushed my scalp and, instantly, a warm pleasurable tingle began to spread through me.

I felt him parting my hair and dividing it into sections then a soft tugging sensation as he began to cross one section over another.

'You're plaiting my hair? How did you learn to do that?'

'Keep still. It's a French plait. It'll get the hair off your face and keep you nice and cool. I'll fasten the bottom with a piece of this string. I used to do it for a woman I knew.'

'You're an endless source of surprise, Jim. Did she have nice hair? Was it your wife? What was her name?'

'And you're an endless source of questions.' He plaited my hair silently for a few moments, pretending he wasn't going to answer. I loved the gentle tugging as he worked with my hair and the sensation of his fingers on my scalp. 'Her name was Adriana and her family were Italian so she had that almost black, thick, wilful hair that Mediterranean women have.'

'I hate her. I bet she had that effortless Italian sense of style as well.'

'Yes, she did as a matter of fact. But you have no reason to envy her, Claire.'

'Meaning?'

'Stop fishing for compliments. Meaning you're every

bit as beautiful as she was, but in a wholesome, pale, Irish way.'

'That's just the problem. I've always wanted to be sultry, but it's very difficult when you've got freckles.'

Jim laughed. He finished the plait and picked up a piece of string. 'Don't be deceived by appearances. That sort of woman might look hot and passionate but it's all for show. There's no fire burning in the grate to keep a man warm at night.' He fastened the string around the end of my plait and tied it in a bow. He laid a warm hand on each of my shoulders and kissed me on the back of the neck. His warm breath on my nape and the reassuring weight of his hands made me tingle.

'Thank you. That's much cooler.'

Jim hadn't moved. He sat with his hands resting on my shoulders, leaning forwards slightly so that his chest pressed up against my back. I realised that he'd completely avoided telling me if Adriana was his wife, yet somehow, leaning with my back against his warm body, it didn't seem to matter.

Overhead, the birds sang. Somewhere on the water a duck quacked. A sculling boat slipped along the river, silent but for the cox's shouted orders.

'You're beginning to go pink. Let me put some sunscreen on you, otherwise you'll burn.' He rummaged in the holdall, found a tube of cream and began to rub it into my shoulders.

'You thought of everything.' My voice sounded dreamy.

'I'm just well prepared. And you know what they say: "Chance favours the prepared mind."' His strong hands moved against my skin.

'Who said that?'

Jim was rubbing the cream into my chest. His hands

moved slowly and his fingers dipped tantalisingly under the top of my dress.

'Louis Pasteur, I think.' He tossed the tube of cream back into the bag and slid his hands slowly down my slippery arms until he was holding my hands. He wrapped his body around me, drawing in his legs to hold me tight. I felt his breath against my neck then his hot mouth. I gasped.

Jim's mouth slid along my neck, eliciting a wave of shivery delight which almost took my breath away. Under normal circumstances, I'd have objected to such personal liberties. Perhaps it was the wine, or the location, or the intimacy engendered by proximity and Jim plaiting my hair, but I just couldn't rouse sufficient energy to resist.

He wrapped his arms around my body and pulled me closer. As he was still holding my hands, this meant that we both ended up hugging me. Something about his firm grip on my hands and the way our limbs intertwined made it feel as though mine had fused with his and I was being held in a tender, endless embrace by four strong arms. Jim's mouth moved over my skin, slowly exploring from the tip of my shoulder up towards my ear.

'You're full of questions, aren't you?' He spoke between kisses.

'You keep saying that.' Jim's mouth felt silky against my sun-warmed skin. 'I've always had an inquisitive mind. Anyway, you don't answer unless you want to. I still don't know what sort of business you run. And I haven't forgotten that you managed to avoid answering one of my questions the other night.'

'I was wondering when you'd bring that up.' Jim spoke right against my ear, then nibbled on the lobe. His breath warmed my skin and made me tingle.

'And now you have your answer.'

'Even though you still don't have yours? Is that what you mean?' Jim put his face against my hair and I heard him inhale deeply.

'Let's just say you seemed only too pleased to take advantage of Mr Porlock's unscheduled arrival.'

'It wasn't my intention to avoid answering. But he did rather ruin the mood.'

'Well, he's not here now.'

Before he had a chance to reply, there was a sudden noise of drumming water and I looked up to see heavy rain falling on the river, disturbing its glassy surface and making it dance. Under the canopy of the tree branches we were relatively sheltered, but it didn't take long before rain began to penetrate our refuge. A big drop landed on the back of my neck and trickled down my spine under my dress.

We began to pack the remains of our meal away. When we had finished, we both stood up and Jim folded the blanket and stuffed it into an empty cool box. We were standing under the tree, growing progressively wetter. The sudden rain had lowered the temperature and I was already beginning to shiver.

'I think we'll have to make a run for it.' Without waiting for an answer, Jim picked up the cool boxes and sped off in the direction of the car.

When we reached The Feathers, Jim pulled up beside my car and turned off the engine.

'I had a lovely time, Claire. Thank you very much.'

'So did I.'

'Before you go, I'd like to give you this.' Jim opened the glove compartment and took out a wrapped gift. 'It's a book – *The Ages of Lulu* by a Spanish writer called

Almudena Grandes. I hope you haven't read it.' He handed it to me.

'No, I haven't. Thank you.'

'It's about a girl's relationship with an older dominant man. I hope you find it ... inspiring.' Jim leant over and kissed me. He lingered for a moment, kissing me with slightly parted lips so that our warm wet tongues met and mingled, then he pulled away.

I climbed out of his car and walked over to my own. As I unlocked the door, it struck me that we'd forgotten to arrange another meeting. I went back over to the Range Rover and tapped on the glass. The electric window slid down with a soft hum and Jim's face appeared in the gap.

'Give me your mobile phone number so I can call you during the week.'

'You don't need it. After all, it's not as though you don't know where to find me.'

The next day, I went to The Feathers for Sunday lunch with my sister. When I arrived she was sitting in the kitchen in tears surrounded by uncooked food. She was bouncing the baby on her lap as he bawled, his face screwed up and red.

'What's up?' I went over and took the baby.

'Ollie kept my up all night with colic. I'm exhausted.' She tore off a sheet of kitchen towel and wiped her face.

'Where's Colin?'

'Working. We've got two staff off sick. I'm sorry about the meal, I wanted it to be really special.'

'It doesn't matter. Why don't you go and lie down for a couple of hours while I get it ready?' I stroked her hair.

'What about Ollie?'

'I'll take care of him. Now go and lie down.'

'Are you sure? He can be a handful.'

'I'm sure. Go on, get some sleep.'

I gave the baby his bottle then settled him down in his bouncer where he instantly fell asleep. I put the joint in the oven and turned my attention to the half-prepared food. When Bernie woke up the meal was almost ready and Ollie was still sleeping contentedly.

'You're a miracle worker.' Bernie bent to look at the baby.

'It's easy when you're not sleep deprived and still getting over the trauma of childbirth.'

'Maybe. It smells delicious. I'm starving.'

'Let's eat then.'

After the meal we sat on the sofa with Ollie on a cushion between us. He seemed fascinated by the brace-let I was wearing and he pulled on it with his little hands, trying to bring it to his mouth.

'You'd make someone a wonderful wife, Claire.'

'You sound like Mum.'

'Sorry. But it's been ages since you had a man on the scene, hasn't it?'

I shot my sister a look. 'Not that long. You make me sound like an old maid.'

'Believe me there are times when I'd happily swap with you.'

'You don't really mean that. Give up this little fellow? I don't think so.'

'Isn't there anyone on the horizon?'

'Well ... no not really ... I had lunch with someone yesterday.'

'And you didn't mention it? Tell me everything.'

'Not much to tell.'

'Who is it? You're a dark horse. You've been working here for weeks and you've never breathed a word. When did you even find the time to meet someone?'

'I met him here, actually.'

'Who? A guest?'

I nodded. 'Jim Hyde.'

Bernie's excitement seemed to evaporate. 'Mr Hyde? Oh, Claire . . .'

'Now you really do sound like Mum. What have you got against Jim?'

'Well nothing, I suppose. He's handsome enough and a real charmer but there's something a bit . . . oh, I don't know . . . a bit vague about him, a bit secretive. I mean, what's he doing here? He's clearly got money; he could afford to stay anywhere. And do you know what he does for a living because I don't and I've asked him several times. Did you know, he insists that the chambermaid makes an appointment to clean his room?'

'No, I didn't know that.'

'You've got to admit it's a bit odd. I think he's hiding something.'

'Why can't you just be happy for me? Why do you always have to pour cold water on my dreams?' I extricated my bracelet from the baby's grip and got up.

'Talk about overreacting. We're not twelve any more, Claire. Grow up.'

'I will when you do.' I picked up my handbag and headed for the door.

I thumped down the stairs, pounding out my anger with my running feet. Crossing the reception area, I collided with Jim. He put out his hands to steady me.

'Whoa. Where's the fire?' He stroked my upper arms. I could feel his body heat seeping into my skin, calming and soothing me.

'Upstairs . . . I've just had a row with my sister.'

'Come and have a drink. It'll calm you down.'

'OK.' I allowed Jim to lead me into the bar. He sat me down at one of the tables and went off to get our drinks.

A few minutes later he came back with two glasses. He set one down in front of me and sat down.

'It's brandy. Is that OK?' He sipped his drink.

'Perfect.' I took a long swallow.

'So do you want to tell me about it?' He smiled at me, his eyes full of concern.

'It's nothing really. Bernie and I have always rubbed each other up the wrong way. I'll ring her tomorrow and apologise.'

'A touch of sibling rivalry? I'm an only child. I've always been jealous of large families.'

'Really? I always envied people like you. At least you get attention when you're an only child. You can't be forgotten or overlooked. And you never have to wear your sister's hand-me-down clothes.'

'Attention yes, but that's the problem. You're the culmination of all their hopes and dreams; their success as parents depends on you so, if you let them down . . .'

'I've never thought of that. But you haven't let yours down, surely? Just look at you. I bet you made them proud.'

He shook his head. 'I wouldn't be so sure.' He sipped his brandy then set it down on the table and looked into it, avoiding my eyes. 'But why don't we change the subject? What shall we talk about?'

I looked at him. His handsome face seemed serious and somehow wistful. He fingered his glass, turning it round and round on the table in front of him.

'It seems as if life is conspiring against us finishing our conversation. First Mr Porlock and then the rain.'

'And you'd like to finish it?'

'Wouldn't you?'

He looked at me for a long moment, then nodded. 'I've barely been able to think of anything else. So, go on, do your worst. No – wait a minute – I think I might need more alcohol for this bit.' He drained his glass. 'Another?'

I nodded. He went to the bar and came back with two more brandies. I finished my first drink and moved the glass aside.

'As I recall, we were speaking about my submissive fantasies.' It was the first time I'd ever really named my desires, let alone spoken the words out loud and it felt distinctly strange and, I must admit, rather exciting. 'And I asked you about your own fantasies.'

Jim took a slow mouthful of brandy and tilted his head back, eyes slitted. I watched his Adam's apple bob as he swallowed. 'I've always considered myself a dominant man – in life as in the bedroom. But more than that –' he leant a little closer and lowered his voice '– I think it's the man's job to make his partner's fantasies come true, no matter what they are, and that has led me down many paths I would otherwise never have explored.'

'Such as?' I took a sip of my drink.

'Well, let me see ... one of my ex-girlfriends was quite a masochist so we bought a riding crop. And my wife, though I'm sure she'd never have described herself as submissive, loved it when I held her down and fucked her in the arse.' He looked over to me as he said this, gauging my reaction to the crudity. Though I had no intention of telling him, the dirty words made my skin prickle and my heart beat faster. 'She quite got off on the humiliation but, the funny thing was, afterwards she'd always deny enjoying it and claim she only did it to please me. But fantasies are like that, aren't they? If they're at all transgressive we can never quite shake off the sense of shame that prevents us from owning them.'

'I know exactly what you mean. Would you believe I actually found it quite difficult just now saying out loud that I had submissive fantasies?'

Jim reached over and touched my arm. 'Of course I do. Thank you for trusting me.' He took another sip of his brandy. 'But why don't you tell me a little more about them. What do they entail exactly? Bondage? Humiliation perhaps? Pain even?'

I looked at him. He held his glass between both hands. Jim was right, I reflected as I took a delaying sip of my drink, it wasn't easy to shake off a lifetime's habit of shame. But just because it was habitual, didn't mean it was valid.

'All of the above, really. I've always had a thing about spanking but I've never done it with a partner – as a teenager, I used to do it myself with the back of a hairbrush. I like the idea of being restrained while naked. Or maybe not naked; I fantasise about being made to dress up – corsets, stockings, impossibly high heels, that sort of thing. And somehow, in my fantasies, the clothes themselves become a form of bondage. Does that make sense?'

Jim had turned his body towards me and was leaning forwards, his face inches from mine. My heart was thumping so hard I almost expected to be able to see it move beneath my dress. I was goose-pimply all over. He nodded. 'Perfect sense.'

'I want to be his plaything, his toy. I want him to call me dirty names, to be his to use for pleasure or punishment, whichever he chooses and I really don't care which of them it is. All that matters is serving him.'

Jim's sea-deep eyes never left my face. On the table, his hands seemed tense, poised on the edge of movement.

'These things you've shared with me, Claire – do you

think you'd like to try them in real life?' Jim's voice was soft and uncharacteristically tentative.

'Yes, I think I would.' I looked into his eyes. 'With the right partner, of course.'

'With the right partner, anything is possible. And the only limit is our imagination.' Jim's steady gaze was a blatant challenge I found hard to ignore.

3

I didn't see Jim for a more than a week after that because I was busy with all the jobs at home I'd had to put off while I was covering for Bernie. I'd arranged to have new carpet laid in my study and decided I might as well take the opportunity to decorate the room before it was fitted. I spent three days dressed in old clothes at the top of the ladder and my evenings soaking in a hot bath trying to wash paint out of my hair.

When the study was finally complete I decided I could procrastinate no longer and it was time I got back to work on the book on the modern novel I'd been writing intermittently for eighteen months.

I easily got back into the swing of working and really enjoyed the process of writing. I loved the challenge of trying to express myself clearly, succinctly and elegantly and found myself working long into the night, only stopping when my back began to protest that I'd been sitting in front of the computer too long.

In fact I slipped back so easily – hungrily almost – into the academic life that I began to realise how much working at the hotel had worn me down. Coming home night after night with my feet aching and my eyes gritty from cigarette smoke, too tired to do anything other than fall straight into bed, had disconnected me from who I really was. The sheer exhaustion of the long days and late nights had turned me into a robot, navigating through life on autopilot.

But the one bright spot on my narrow horizon had

been Jim. He alone, it seemed, saw who I really was. He responded to the academic in me as well as to the woman and his open admiration of both was arousing and exciting. It was flattering, of course, but more than that, seeing myself through Jim's eyes was both powerfully erotic and self affirming.

As I went to bed about a week later I spotted the book Jim had given me on the bedside table. I picked it up and began to read.

I'd intended to browse the book and read a few pages before going to sleep but I was halfway through before my drooping eyelids finally compelled me to stop. I instantly identified with Lulu, a young girl who fell in love with Pablo, a much older friend of her brother's. He was a mysterious, charismatic figure – a poet and political activist in Franco's Spain who had served a prison term for his outspoken views. He saw in Lulu a dark bottomless sexuality that needed only to be awoken.

Jim had known it would speak to me, that I would find resonances in the story and characters and echoes of the fantasies I had shared with him. As I read of her initiation into womanhood, in which Pablo shaved her pussy bare with a razor blade before taking her virginity, I felt a shiver of excitement and longing so powerful that, for a moment, I'd considered getting in my car and driving over to the hotel to beg Jim to re-enact it.

That had been Jim's intention, of course, and I wasn't so naïve that I didn't realise it. He had known that the combination of beautifully crafted words and dark fantasies could not fail to reach me. Yet, I didn't feel manipulated. If anything, I felt respected and understood.

In the morning I woke up with the characters running through my head. Their restless sexual energy had got under my skin. I lost concentration so many times I had to abandon my work on the book but when I tried watching daytime telly I was twitchy and unsettled.

It was as if the book had awoken the Lulu inside of me and, tired of confinement, she was demanding her freedom. And along with that demand came a pitch of sexual arousal so extreme that it was physically painful. My skin felt sensitive and alive. My nipples were permanently hard and the moisture between my legs flowed so freely that the crotch of my panties was soaked through.

Well, this was an itch I knew how to scratch. I'd spent much of my adolescence with my hand between my legs, learning the complex language of my body with the same enthusiasm and dedication I applied to my studies. I learnt a different touch for each of my moods, a special caress for every day of the week. And I discovered that orgasms could be different too. From the celebratory, cathartic release that occasionally brought me to tears to the slow burn that began as a gentle ripple and ended in an extended climax which I felt from my toes to the roots of my hair.

At boarding school they'd drummed into us that failure to curb fleshly appetites would put us on the fast track to hell. At first, I'd confessed my sins to the tremulous and slightly deaf old priest who came once a week to listen to our catalogue of transgressions and usually earned an act of contrition and half-a-dozen Hail Marys. But the next week, there I was again, having to own up to the same shameful act.

In the end, I'd made a private deal with God even though I knew that having the audacity to think he might enter into such a sordid arrangement was a sin in itself. I wanted to be a good girl, a good Catholic – I really did. The only problem was, it felt so damned good. So one Sunday afternoon – and that was another sin, if you weren't supposed to work on a Sunday I was pretty sure wanking was twice as bad – I set God a challenge.

I was in bed with flu in the sickbay while the rest of the school was at chapel and I decided to pass the time by doing what I loved most. As I reached my climax, both hands clamped over my hot pussy and my aching nipples rubbing against my starched nightie, the church bells in the village began to ring. A tumbling, triumphal peal that seemed to celebrate my release and, at the same time, make me feel thoroughly ashamed.

As the bells continued to peal and my climax subsided I had an idea. My parents had named me after St Claire because I was born on her feast day. When enemy soldiers had planned to raid her convent she'd prayed to God to protect the nuns in her care. And God had answered her. Not just by protecting the convent, but literally. A voice had spoken from the heavens.

Catholics prayed to God for a specific intervention all the time. We lit candles for the sick, we even paid to have Masses said. If God was prepared to intercede for the price of a beeswax candle or a Mass card, I reasoned, why wouldn't he answer me? So I got on my knees beside the creaking iron bedstead.

The lino was cold and hard under my knees. The air smelt of disinfectant and polish and, as I closed my eyes to pray, I could have believed myself in a nun's plain cell. I prayed as hard as I knew how for God to send me a sign. I even made it easy for him; if he didn't want me to do it any more, all he needed to do was to stop it from feeling good. If touching myself still felt good I'd take it as a sign of his approval.

I had no proof that he'd heard me. The clouds didn't open. There was no lightning and no booming voice. Yet, when I next fingered myself, a few days later back in the dorm while the other girls slept, it had felt as good as ever and I knew I had my answer.

Over the years, God's failure to intercede had somehow transformed in my mind from disinterest to approval. I came to view masturbation as a celebration of my own body and, somehow, of life itself, each tingle, flutter and throb representing a syllable in an extended prayer.

What would Jim make of my pact with the Almighty, I wondered? He'd have approved of my audacity, I was sure. And if there was one other soul on earth who could relate to the notion of an orgasm as a sacred offering it would be Jim.

As I wandered from room to room, unable to settle because of my tingling nipples and a hard knot of tension at the base of my belly that refused to go away, I experienced an epiphany as profound and pure as the one I'd had in that bleak sickroom all those years ago. It wasn't just God who wanted me to masturbate, it was Jim.

The book had been intended to arouse me – that had always been obvious. But it was also a message, a promise and a blueprint. Responding to the arousal the novel had created would be my first step on that journey and my first surrender to him.

I raced up to my bedroom, stripped off my clothes and climbed onto the bed. I closed my eyes and lay still, focusing inwards. I could hear the laughter of my neighbour's children as they played in their paddling pool. In the distance, a lawnmower droned its insect buzz. A bird twittered away in the cherry tree. I could feel the air against my body and the cool cotton of the duvet beneath me. The breeze caressed my nipples like ghostly fingers, hardening them. I brushed their tips with my thumbs and the contact made me shiver.

I flicked my nipples with my thumbnails. It felt good. They swelled and hardened. Little pinpricks of pleasure radiated out from my nipples. A slow shiver slid up my spine. My crotch was liquid and warm.

I rolled the engorged buds between thumb and forefinger, pinching and pulling, stretching them out. I gasped out loud as sensation flooded over me. Goose pimples rose on my skin. I was tingling all over.

Jim had known the book would make me want to masturbate. Did he lie awake at night picturing me doing it? Did he wonder what caresses I used to arouse myself? Did he hope I would think of him while I did it and wonder if Lulu's story had given me a taste for the perverse?

I imagined him standing at the bottom of the bed as I pleasured myself, saying nothing and never touching me, but totally engrossed and unable to look away. Perhaps, when I'd finished he would take out his cock and wank himself to an orgasm. Then he'd put it away, zip up and leave, never even having spoken to me.

Jim's imagined indifference aroused me all the more. I wanted to put on a show for him, even though he wasn't really there. Part of me wondered if, like God, to whom my adolescent orgasms had been dedicated, he might not be omnipotent. I wanted to give him a spectacle he would never forget. I would be filthy, depraved. I'd come until I was sweaty and trembling then I'd come some more, offering him, like prayer, my orgasm.

The tips of my nipples were on fire, burning and prickling with divine pleasure. My breathing had grown rapid and shallow. The fine hairs on the back of my neck were erect and sensitive. Between my legs moisture welled.

I reached down and stroked my clit with one finger. I sighed in relief. My crotch ached with frustration and arousal but I wanted to make it last. I gave my clit a final caress and withdrew my hand.

I pinched my nipples harder, rolling them between my fingers, increasing the pressure until the pleasure blurred into pain. It hurt, certainly, but somehow the pain was experienced as the most exquisite pleasure.

I loved to do this, to ride the line between pleasure and pain and, occasionally, to cross it. I'd learnt that, when I was aroused, the distinction between those two opposites seemed to blur and merge. Both were experienced as extreme, intense sensation which took my breath away and made my legs go weak.

I opened the drawer of my bedside cabinet and located several toys and a bottle of lube. I got up and fetched my hairbrush from the dressing table and threw it onto the bed together with the matching mirror. I got several silk scarves from my wardrobe and arranged all my implements on one side of the bed then lay back down.

I studied the row of objects, trying to decide which of the motley collection would produce the stimulation I desired. I wished I owned some proper bondage equipment: gags, cuffs, blindfolds. I made a mental note to look on a sex toy website next time I was online.

But, as I looked at my selection of items, their very ordinariness made them seem all the more perverse, as if I was subverting their mundane domestic functions in the service of my own kinky needs.

I picked up the hairbrush and ran its stiff bristles experimentally over my right nipple. I gasped as they rasped over my already sensitised flesh. I rubbed harder, scrubbing the bristles against my nipple. It burnt and stung but, underneath it all, the pleasure was intense and continuous.

I brushed my left, more sensitive, nipple. My skin reddened and my nipple hardened and grew. Slow watery shivers slid up and down my spine. I imagined Jim, sitting beside me, holding me down with one strong hand while his other dragged the brush over my eager nipples.

I loved the thought of being helpless before him, being bound and gagged and unable to resist. Not that I'd want to. I sat up and grabbed one of the silk scarves. I tied one end round my left ankle and the other to the corner post of my brass bed, then did the same with my other ankle.

I'd never been properly restrained before and, even though I'd done it to myself, the excitement was extreme. My nipples were taut and swollen, the duvet beneath me was damp and creased and my entire skin was goose-pimply and sensitive.

I could picture Jim standing at the bottom of the bed, arms folded, smiling softly to himself at my predicament, waiting to see what I'd do next. Perhaps he'd select a scarf and hand it to me, silently indicating that I should gag myself, increasing my bondage and my helplessness further. I picked up another scarf to use as a gag, but realised it alone wouldn't be very effective.

Glancing around the room for something to put into my mouth, I spotted my discarded knickers on the carpet. I reached to pick them up but, with both legs tied to the bed, I couldn't quite reach them. I lay flat on the bed and managed to reach them by stretching out my hand. I screwed them up into a ball then stuffed them into my mouth and tied the scarf tightly over the top. I closed my eyes.

I moved my legs, testing my bonds. The bed creaked but the scarves held fast. The knots dug into my ankles. The balled-up knickers soaked up my saliva and made my mouth feel dry. As I breathed in I could taste a faint tang of my own sexual juices.

I'd never felt so alive, so aroused. I picked up the brush and rubbed it across each nipple in turn. It was incredible. Every pore seemed alive with pleasure and sensation.

I couldn't help moaning and I imagined Jim smiling to himself and letting out a soft private laugh.

My crotch ached. I longed to touch it, but I didn't want to rush. The longer I waited the bigger my eventual orgasm would be. I found my fat eight-inch dildo in the pile of toys and slid it into my hungry pussy. I sighed as it slid home. It's cold metallic intrusion felt nothing like a cock, yet it was completely satisfying.

Then I picked up the lube and spread the cold gel thoroughly over my finger. I slid down the bed so that I could bend my knees, tilted up my hips and pressed my lubricated middle finger up against my arsehole. I pushed it slowly in, millimetre by millimetre, moaning appreciatively as it entered me.

When it was fully inside me, I took the mirror and positioned it between my legs, angling it so that I could see both the dildo and my finger inside me. I'd always enjoyed using a mirror to look at my aroused pussy and, today, I could almost imagine that what I saw in the mirror was Jim's viewpoint.

I visualised him bending over to get a closer look of the dildo inside me. My pussy was red, swollen and glistening with moisture and lube. My openings were stretched wide and, when I tensed my muscles, the dildo in my pussy twitched as if it had a life of its own. I imagined Jim laughing as I performed the feat and asking me to do it again.

As I contracted my muscles around the dildos every nerve ending tingled with pleasure. I could see my clit, swollen and dark, begging for attention. But I wasn't ready yet. I wanted a banquet with many courses not a quick snack. If I listened to my body and took my time, I knew that I would come several times before I was finished.

I dropped the mirror and pinched my nipples. I let out a deep visceral groan. They burned, throbbing with heat and pleasure. I picked up the mirror and looked at my reflection.

I could see my chest rising and falling as I breathed. There was a faint sheen of sweat along my cleavage. My nipples were dark, engorged with blood. A slow cold shiver slid along my spine.

In my mind, Jim made a twisting gesture with one hand, then folded his arms expectantly. Slowly, I twisted one nipple. I looked down and saw my nipple stretch as I continued to twist. It burnt with sensation, excitement and incredible pleasure. My crotch ached. The bed creaked as I pulled against my bonds.

My nipple tingled and throbbed. The sound of my heavy breathing seemed amplified and urgent under the gag. The trapped breath felt moist and warm inside the scarf. I dropped the mirror and began twisting both nipples, one after each other. I gasped out loud. Pleasure, pain, excitement had somehow all got mixed up and confused. I didn't think I could tell them apart any more. All I knew was that it felt incredible and I needed to come.

Reluctantly I released my nipples. I reached down and spread my lips and circled my clit with one trembling finger. My burning nipples seemed alive. My muscles gripped the dildo and my finger as it moved in and out. I vaguely registered that the scarves were digging into my ankles but I didn't care.

With my eyes closed, I could easily visualise Jim witnessing the finale to my self-abuse. I could almost hear the floorboards creaking as he walked around the bed to get a better view. I could hear the soft swish of his trousers as he moved, hear his excited breathing.

I was rubbing my clit in earnest now. I was on heat. My body ached for release. Every nerve ending was alive and working overtime.

My hand was clamped between my legs, spreading my pussy. My fingers slipped against the wet flesh and, from time to time, I'd reposition them, stretching my lips wide. If I got it right, the tension of my spread lips created an extra frisson of pleasure in my taut clit. I pulled myself apart, using one finger to tease my eager button.

In my mind, Jim sat on the edge of the bed near my feet and leant close to my crotch. I could almost feel his warm breath on me and I imagined him deliberately blowing on my aching pussy, then laughing softly to himself when I responded. I became wanton, spreading my lips wide and working my clit frantically.

The bed creaked. The scarves cut into my ankles. I was covered in sweat; my hair clung to my face. My nipples throbbed and burnt. My whole crotch tingled with excitement and anticipation. I was groaning and gasping under my silken gag. Sweat trickled into my eyes. The pleasure built and built. My whole body was rigid and trembling.

I imagined Jim's breathing growing hoarse and throaty as he watched me. The bed creaked under his weight. I felt his eyes burning into my flesh.

I could hear a woman making short urgent sobs and realised the sounds were coming from me. I was coming. The first, I knew, of a series of ever-growing orgasms. I gasped and sobbed as the first wave crashed over me like a flood. My legs thrashed, but were held fast by the scarves.

Somehow the bondage seemed to intensify my excitement and I began to come again, slightly stronger this time. It surged through my body like a rush. My nipples ached and throbbed. Every millimetre of my skin was tingling and sensitive. The roots of my hair prickled with pleasure.

The iron bedstead banged against the wall behind me. Springs creaked. The duvet beneath me was rumpled and damp. My face was wet under the gag. I was coming continually now, like the tide rushing in. I bucked and writhed, my legs held open by the scarves at my ankles. I was gasping and screaming so hard that it hurt my throat. I was no longer in control. Not a rational, thinking being, but a body – a mass of nerve endings responding instinctively to a natural force it was powerless to resist.

And it was all for Jim. I pictured the look on his face as he watched me surrender to the moment. Was his cock hard and uncomfortable inside his trousers? Did he long to touch me? Did he ache to climb between my legs and satisfy himself? And, when he finally touched me, would I come even harder knowing that it was my wantonness that had so aroused him?

I let out a low deep moan as the final huge orgasm gripped me. My breathing was shallow and rapid. My body shook, my chest heaved, tears wet my face. It went on and on and on, surging through my bloodstream like a drug.

Blood thumped in my ears. I was tingling all over, sobbing, screaming, crying. And as I reached the final peak and my whole body quivered with helpless pleasure, I heard myself call out his name.

4

It was twenty minutes before I trusted myself to get up. I was trembling, breathless and covered in sweat. I was still experiencing little aftershocks of orgasm, which were as exhausting as they were pleasurable. Several times I sat up to untie my ankles but had to lie back down again because my head was spinning. I was exhausted and drained. I closed my eyes and relaxed back against the damp duvet.

I don't know how long I slept, but when I woke up I was cold and uncomfortable. The sweat had cooled on my body, chilling me, and the scarves were digging into my ankles. I raised myself up on one elbow, experimentally. No dizziness this time, but I still felt slightly unreal, as if I'd drunk a glass of wine too quickly. I sat up and untied my ankles with trembling hands.

I stood under the shower, letting it tumble down over my head, hoping that the cleansing water might purge my mind and bring me some clarity. Though what I'd just done had been a solo act of masturbation it had felt as intense and intimate as if Jim had made me come with his own fingers.

I'd been in no doubt as I came that doing so was my first act of submission to him, that he had wanted me to do it. I still believed that, but as I stood under the shower, leaning against the tiles for support, I no longer felt so certain that he had been the instigator. As the water crashed over me I felt the same sense of sinfulness and self-delusion I'd had as a teenager in the days before I'd reached my deal with God.

I was pretty sure that giving me the book had been a deliberate, even cynical act of manipulation but I was responsible for my own feelings and, if I was to do it for real, I had to be clear about my motives. They were my desires, my needs and my fantasies and, while Jim had provided the mirror in which I had been able to see them, I was the only person who could be held accountable for choosing to release them.

Fantasies couldn't hurt you. They were safe and contained and reassuring and, if they frightened you from time to time, you could comfort yourself with the notion that they weren't real anyway. But when you set your fantasies free and made them flesh there was no telling where they might end. As Jim had said, the only limit was our own imagination and mine had always been overactive.

I turned off the water and stepped out of the shower. I reached for a towel and roughly dried my hair. If I was to take the next step I needed to be certain that I was ready to give myself fully to Jim and to allow him to make my sexual choices even though I still knew little that was tangible about him. Not because he wanted it, but because I did.

I waited until evening to call Jim, though it had taken every ounce of self-control I possessed. Apart from anything else, my post-orgasm glow had lasted for hours and I'd somehow felt that ringing him in that mindset would put me at a disadvantage. He could have suggested anything and I'd have said yes.

Nevertheless, when I picked up the phone and dialled the number of The Feathers my hand was shaking and I could feel my heart pounding in my chest. The receptionist informed me that Jim was in his room and put me straight through.

'Jim Hyde.'

'Jim, it's Claire.'

'Claire. Good to hear from you at last. How are you?'

'I'm fine, thanks. But I've been busy decorating my study and having a new carpet laid. Then I thought I ought to do some work on my book, or it would never get written. I haven't had a moment...' My voice sort of petered out. I was babbling and we both knew it. 'But never mind all that. I'm sorry I haven't called before. I haven't been able to stop thinking about you.'

'Thank you. I've missed you too. How about dinner tomorrow night?'

'I'd like that, Jim.'

'Good. I'm going to take you to one of my favourite places, a hotel. It's a short drive away in the Cotswolds. Bring an overnight bag. After a few glasses of wine I'll be over the limit so we might as well take advantage of their hospitality. And bring something dressy to change into because it's rather posh. I'll book us a room each so you needn't worry about your virtue.'

'I assure you I'm not worried about my virtue. Quite the opposite.' Though I didn't say so, I was glad Jim had made it clear he was booking two rooms. I didn't want to be railroaded into spending the night with him. When it happened – and I now had no doubt that it would – I wanted it to be my own free choice and not the result of proximity and circumstance.

'Meaning you're worried about your vices?' Jim laughed softly and I could picture his blue eyes crinkling. 'I think we're going to have fun, Claire.'

'I'm looking forward to it.'

'Me too. Are you all right? Only, you sound a little ... I don't know ... different somehow.'

'I'm fine. A little tired perhaps.'

I gave Jim my address and we said goodbye. I'd offered to pay for my own hotel room, but he wouldn't hear of it. One of the first things I'd noticed about Jim had been his thoughtless, almost profligate generosity. He bought drinks for others or invited them to dinner for no other motive than that doing so gave him genuine pleasure. He never seemed to expect, or even want, the kindness to be reciprocated. Though it was obvious to me that he could easily afford to do so, I'd met enough wealthy people working at the hotel to know that there's no direct link between financial security and generosity. In fact it was my experience that the well heeled were often penny pinching and mean spirited.

There was nothing about Jim, I realised as I sat with the phone in my lap, that was parsimonious or frugal. Everything about him was writ large: his laugh, his appetite, his kindness. The only thing, it seemed to me, that he guarded closely were his secrets and I was scarcely in a position to hold that fault against him. I cherished my own secrets like jewels, piling them up like treasure. I could hardly suggest that Jim had no right to do the same.

Tomorrow night seemed intolerably distant. Having made my decision, waiting seemed unreasonable and outrageous. But then, I'd never had any patience. I'd even pierced my own ears with a bodkin and a cork as a student, because the jeweller was closed for lunch.

I was tempted to spend the 24 hours before my meeting with Jim flat on my back, living out, in fantasy, the desires I hoped we would make real but, somehow, I felt it would be too easy.

More than anything I feared that if I tamed the beast within me like I always had I might bottle out at the last moment and I couldn't afford to let that happen. I would resist the easy release of orgasm and meet Jim with my desires unconfined. With all that pent-up want and hunger boiling away inside me like a fever I could not fail to surrender to it. And the one thing I knew with unshakable certainty was that I must surrender.

Jim's favourite hotel turned out to be the Lygon Arms in Broadway, which I knew by reputation but had never visited. I knew it was frequented by the rich and famous and had a price tag to match and, as our bags were carried into reception by a liveried footman, I couldn't help feeling relieved that I hadn't insisted on paying for my own room. The thought was quickly followed by a stab of guilt and shame at my own spectacular lack of generosity and the boundless extent of Jim's.

We were shown to our rooms and, as the footman opened the door for me, I did my best imitation of a woman who was used to the luxury and even slightly bored by it. The room was like something from a stately home, which you gazed at from the wrong side of a rope barrier, with a four-poster bed, oak panelling and oil paintings on the walls.

I unzipped my bag and carried my toilet things through to the en-suite bathroom to check on my make-up. We'd agreed to freshen up, change and meet in the Great Hall restaurant in twenty minutes. I put on some fresh lipstick and brushed my hair and went back into the bedroom to change.

When Jim had suggested I dress up for the occasion I had instantly thought of the red silk dress I'd bought for a Christmas party then chickened out of wearing. It scooped low in the front, revealing far more cleavage than I normally displayed, then skimmed my hips before flicking out in a fluted hem.

As I zipped it up and turned to look at myself in the

full-length mirror I couldn't help smiling at what I saw. I might look like a Hollywood vamp but inside I felt like a nun dressed in her wedding gown ready to become the bride of Christ.

As I walked downstairs to meet Jim my stomach was fluttery with nerves. The Great Hall had a barrelled ceiling, stags' heads on the wall and a minstrels' gallery. Jim was sitting by the window and, as I approached, he stood up and pulled out my chair.

'You look beautiful. I took the liberty of ordering you a gin and tonic.'

'Thank you.' I sat down.

'That dress really suits you. The colour makes your pale skin look like porcelain.'

'Thanks. I've never worn it before, but this seemed like the right occasion for it. And you look very nice yourself. There's something about a man in a well-cut suit that always gets me excited. A suit is so masculine, isn't it? Designed to show off a hard body and broad shoulders and cut to make a man look that shape even if nature hasn't made him that way.' It was my nerves talking but if Jim noticed his face gave nothing away. I picked up my drink and took a sip, making a supreme effort to stop my hand from shaking.

'I know what you mean. There's something old-fashioned and elegant about a good suit. Wearing one somehow makes me feel confident, makes me stand a little straighter. I always feel a little like Richard Gere when I wear a suit, but I don't flatter myself that anyone else makes the comparison.'

I laughed. 'No ... you do ... I know what you mean. You look well groomed and graceful. Is that a Trinity tie you're wearing?'

'Yes, I did my degree there. Didn't I mention it?'

We both knew he hadn't mentioned it. I had no doubt

that he'd worn such a recognisable tie with the deliberate intention of allowing me the satisfaction of believing I'd solved a great mystery.

The waiter arrived and handed us menus. I chose duck rilettes to start followed by roast saddle of venison and Jim selected foie gras and fillet of beef. When our starters arrived, Jim offered me a mouthful of his foie gras, holding out his fork to me with his other hand cupped underneath it to catch any drips. The pâté was rich and soft. I liked it so much I asked him for more and he laughed delightedly and cut me another slice.

'That's delicious, Jim. I don't really approve of the way they make foie gras, but it tastes so divine that all my animal rights indignation just dissolves.'

'It's their destiny, Claire. A foie gras goose is born to be force-fed and slaughtered. Our lives may not be so short or brutal, but we aren't that different really. We're born, we toil and then we die and, if we're lucky, we manage to squeeze a bit of pleasure between the two.'

'True, but nobody rips our livers out and makes them into pâté after we're gone.'

Jim put down his cutlery and imitated Hannibal Lecter reminiscing about the census taker and the nice Chianti and I burst into laughter.

'Not usually, you're right. But eating each other is much more ecologically sound.'

'Maybe, but if they make it compulsory I think I'll turn vegetarian. Did you read about that German bloke who advertised for a man on the internet who wanted to be eaten?'

Jim nodded. 'Yes, an odd fetish I agree, but I think I understand what's behind it.' He took a sip of wine.

'I can't say I do. I mean, there's some logic in eating the corpses of your dead comrades if you're in a plane crash or trapped up a mountain, but killing someone just for the purpose of eating them. That's perverse and abnormal.'

'Look at it this way. Have you ever loved somebody so much that you wanted to be with them always? Now close your eyes and imagine there was a way that the two of you could have become one being, one soul – for ever. Don't all of us long for that? It's the most natural, the most ancient impulse on earth. And if two people wanted it enough is it such a leap to imagine that they might decide to eat each other?'

'It's an interesting idea.'

'It's the ultimate act of surrender, when you think about it. What do you think, Claire? Are you tempted?' Jim was gazing into my eyes. His voice was low and seductive and his description so erotic that my nipples had hardened under my dress and my cheeks had grown hot.

'You make it sound almost appealing. Remind me never to turn my back on you.'

The waiter appeared and topped up our glasses before clearing away our plates. If he'd overheard any of our conversation his inscrutable, deferential expression gave nothing away.

'And you're a Catholic – isn't that what the Sacrament is all about? The blood and body of Christ? The Pope clearly sanctions cannibalism in certain circumstances. It's a holy act of surrender to God and, when that man in Germany ate his friend, who's to say it wasn't exactly the same thing?'

'Maybe, but you've got to admit it's a bit bloody strange.'

'It's extreme perhaps, but then so are our tastes to some –' Jim's mobile phone rang and he retrieved it from his inside pocket and looked at the display to see the identity of the caller. 'I'm sorry, but I have to take this, it's business. I won't be a moment.' He got up and walked out of the restaurant.

5

I took advantage of Jim's absence to visit the ladies'. While I was reapplying my lipstick a woman came in and went into a cubicle. As she closed the door our eyes met in the mirror and I recognised a look of undisguised envy and curiosity.

I wasn't accustomed to being on the receiving end of such looks, though I'd seen many women looking at my sister Bernie with the same expression in their eyes. She was naturally pretty in an earth mother sort of way and pregnancy and parenthood had seen her blossom into a head-turner. But now, looking at myself in the mirror, I saw a tall striking woman with hair the colour of a cornfield and skin like porcelain and wondered why I had never seen her before.

Jim hadn't returned when I got back to the table so I sipped at my wine and looked around the restaurant. Most of the other diners were middle aged and well heeled. The woman I had encountered in the loo came back and sat down beside a fifty-something man with silvery hair and the ruby, swollen nose of a dedicated drinker. She was clearly much younger and I suspected she was a second, trophy wife and I couldn't help wondering what, apart from his money, they could possibly have in common. I was so involved in looking at them that I didn't notice Jim come back into the restaurant. By the time I spotted him he was almost at our table.

'Sorry about that. It was a business problem. I hope you don't mind.' He sat down.

'Of course not, though I still don't know what sort of business you have.'

'I'm in the service sector. Clients expect a personal touch and, though my staff are all perfectly competent, some clients still insist on speaking to me. But let's forget about business. We're here to have fun.'

I picked up my glass and took a long slow swallow of wine. 'It's obvious you're being deliberately mysterious but what I can't work out is what your motives are. At first I thought you had something to hide, something criminal or shameful perhaps. But now . . .'

'You're not so sure?'

'I'm beginning to feel that you just enjoy secrecy. It's a way of keeping me interested and . . . I don't know . . . having power over me.'

'Interesting. And do you like the feeling of being in my power?' Jim leant close to my face. His lips were on the edge of a smile.

'If you maintain the right not to answer I don't see why I should be expected to respond to that.'

Jim laughed. 'There's no need, Claire. Your face gave you away.'

The waiter arrived with our main courses and, for several minutes, we ate in silence. Jim ate with obvious enjoyment. As he cut into his fillet of beef I could see the blood running. He ate another mouthful and wiped his lips with his napkin.

'Food is such a wonderful invention, isn't it? Sometimes I think it's almost as good as sex.' I dipped a piece of bread into the sauce on my plate.

'Only almost? You can have a perfectly satisfying meal alone. You can hardly say that of sex, can you?'

'I won't hear a word said against masturbation, we've been intimate friends for as long as I can remember.'

Jim picked up his glass. 'I'm shocked, Claire. Isn't self-abuse one of the sins that cry to heaven for vengeance? I thought you were a nice Catholic girl.' He sipped his wine. 'But tell me –' he leant close and looked directly at me '– when was the last time you did it?'

'I can't remember.' I kept my voice deliberately casual.

'Come on.' He lowered his voice until he was almost whispering. 'After all we've shared together, surely you can tell me that?'

'What about you? Why do personal revelations always have to be one-way traffic?'

Jim laughed. 'OK. In the spirit of sharing ... I did it this morning in the shower. Your turn.'

'Yesterday.'

'When, where? I need details.'

Jim's eyes were shining with excitement, curiosity and something else I couldn't quite read.

'In bed, in the middle of the afternoon.' I was determined to look him straight in the eye, even though it took all my self-control. 'If you must know, it was the book you gave me that put me in the mood.' That was as much as I was prepared to reveal.

I saw the flicker of triumph in Jim's eyes and, for the first time, realised what it was I had seen in them a moment ago: power and a desire to control.

'So you liked the book?'

'Yes, I did. It's poetic, intelligent and very compelling.'

He nodded, holding his wine glass between both hands, swirling its contents. 'Yes, that's what I liked about it. It's wonderful to be able to discuss books with someone. It doesn't happen often in my line of work.'

I opened my mouth to speak but Jim's mock stern expression made it clear that any discussion of his line of work was off limits.

'What's your favourite novel, Jim? I always think you

can tell a lot about people from the books on their shelves, but since I've never seen your shelves . . .'

'Let me see. There are so many.'

The waiter came to take away our plates. 'Would you like to see the dessert menu, sir?'

'We certainly would, thank you.'

We selected our desserts and the waiter left. Jim topped up our glasses with the last of the wine.

I took a sip and allowed the aromatic liquid to slide down my throat.

'While you make up your mind, I'll tell you about my favourite novel. It's just got to be *Lolita*.'

'Yes, that's high up on my list too. His prose is so rich, so clever. It's just joyful to read, a real journey into language. And, of course, obsessive love and transgressive desire . . . they're things you can relate to, aren't they?'

'I suppose so, I hadn't thought of it like that . . . I can't wait to hear what your favourite novel says about you.'

'OK . . . I know, *Moby Dick*. Now, do your worst, Dr Freud.'

'That's easy. It's all about power, obsession, being driven by a compulsion that defies logic.'

'That's right. And when you think about it you can see lots of parallels with *Lolita*. Ahab's obsessive focus and need consumes him almost to the point of insanity.'

'And both obsessions ultimately end in destruction.' I took a sip of wine and laid the glass down carefully on the white tablecloth. A tear of ruby liquid trickled down the stem and discoloured the virgin linen, soaking into the absorbent fabric and spreading like a bloodstain.

'And is that where you think our journey will end, Claire? In destruction?'

I shook my head. 'No, I hope not. Quite the opposite, in fact. I hope it leads to . . . oh, I don't know . . .

enlightenment if you like. Though, in a way, that does mean that destruction of my old life is inevitable. I have to allow my old life – the old Claire even – to burn to a cinder then rise, phoenix-like, from the ashes.'

'That's a very beautiful image. And in that red dress you almost look as though you've walked out of the flames.'

Before I could respond the waiter brought our desserts and laid them down with a flourish. When he'd gone I dipped a fingertip into the chocolate sauce on my plate and sucked it clean.

'That's what scares me most, I think. Letting go of my old life. I know it's never been what I wanted but at least it's safe and familiar and I know how to do it. And nobody chooses to voluntarily walk into a fire, do they?'

'I understand. But I'll be there to keep you safe. So you just have to ask yourself one question. Do you have the courage to walk into the flames?'

I looked at him. Though I could see kindness and warmth in his eyes, I couldn't quite read him. It was like there was some part of himself he always held back and it was that part of him I was most eager to know even though I was as nervous of it as I was intrigued. But then, I was an expert in holding aspects of myself in reserve. In fact, the other Jim had once joked that half of me was perpetually closed to the public. It was time to open the door a chink. I took a sip of wine.

'Have you got a match?'

Jim reached across the table and laid his hand on top of mine. 'Good girl. Now, let's eat the divine desserts. Do you want to try mine?'

When we'd finished our meal Jim suggested we have our coffee and brandy in his room. We walked up the stairs side by side and he caught my elbow, slid his palm sensuously down my forearm and took my hand in his. As we went down the corridor I looked up at Jim and smiled and he winked at me. He unlocked the door and held it open for me.

'Wow. The last time I saw a room like this I had to buy a ticket.'

'It is something isn't it?' Jim closed the door. 'It's extravagant I know, but I enjoy a little luxury from time to time. I hope your suite is comfortable?'

We sat down by the fireplace.

'It's more than comfortable, it's fabulous. Thank you very much, Jim.'

He waved the thanks away with the back of his hand. 'You know people are always saying money doesn't make you happy?'

'I've always thought that was sour grapes. After all, only people who haven't got any say it, don't they?'

'Exactly. But it's true, in a way. Having money, leaving it in the bank and counting it to see how rich you are, that only leads to misery. But spending it on what you want and sharing it with others can bring a lot of happiness.'

'I'll have to take your word for that. Most of what I earn goes on the mortgage. I've never had the opportunity to live like this. It's a long way from the way I was brought up. Seven of us living in a poky flat above a shop.'

'I know what you mean. When I was a kid we lived in a two-up two-down, very basic. Maybe money doesn't buy happiness but it certainly gives you more choices.'

There was a knock on the door.

'That will be our coffee.' Jim got up to answer the door and the waiter set the tray down on the table between our armchairs.

We drank in silence for a while, though the stillness was anything but relaxed. My stomach was flipping like a fish in a net and I could hear blood pounding in my ears.

Jim had put a CD on low and Miles Davis's swooping, urgent trumpet seemed to accentuate the mood. Jim picked up a truffle from a saucer on the tray and popped it into his mouth. I watched as he licked chocolate dust off his fingers and I realised how much I wanted him to touch me.

I could still remember the sensation of his warm confident fingers massaging suncream into my shoulders and then his hot breath on my skin, prelude to a kiss. My stomach had lurched and my nipples peaked when he had kissed my neck and thinking about it now produced an identical reaction. I drained my cup and set it down on the tray and selected a truffle.

'Delicious,' I murmured contentedly.

Jim smiled and put down his cup. 'I'm not quite sure whether you're referring to the chocolate or the view. You've been staring at me for the last five minutes.'

'Have I? A cat can look at a king – though I've never entirely understood what that means.'

'Me neither, though I can't tell you how flattered I am by being compared to a king.'

'If the crown fits . . . Does that mean that I'm the cat? All hiss and claws?'

'Doesn't sound like you. You're more of a pussy, I think – sleek and sensual and purrs when stroked.'

'Is that supposed to be an innuendo? A pussy that likes to be stroked?'

Jim shrugged. 'If someone asks me for an innuendo, I'm always prepared to give them one.'

'I love it when you make me laugh. It's such an appealing quality in a man. My sister always says that any man who can make her laugh is halfway to her bed.'

'Interesting, though I must confess I'm more interested in your bed than Bernie's.' Jim picked up the saucer and offered me the last truffle.

I took the chocolate, bit it in half and held out the other half for him. He leant forwards and took it into his mouth. He held my wrist and slowly, sensuously sucked the powdered chocolate off my fingers.

I could feel his stubble against my skin and the heat of his mouth. A delicious watery ripple slid down my spine. Jim brought his mouth to my palm, kissed it, then released it. He let it go reluctantly and with tender care, as if my hand was a bird he was releasing into the wild, unwilling to let it go yet certain it deserved its freedom.

'Does your pussy need stroking yet?'

'It's needed stroking for ages, as a matter of fact.' Though my voice was calm my insides were boiling like lava. Jim didn't answer; he just looked at me. His eyes moved over my face like fingers, exploring every curve.

'Downstairs you were prepared for me to set you alight . . .'

'I'm already burning, Jim. Can't you feel the heat?'

Time seemed to slow down. I could hear my own breathing and quiet laughter as someone walked along the corridor. A car pulled up outside and a door slammed. I could even hear the soft tick-tick of Jim's wristwatch.

'I'll tell you what. At the weekend I've got to go to London. I've got a few boring things that I need to do, but they shouldn't take long. I'd like it very much if you'd come with me. If you come, then our journey together will begin.'

'And if I don't?'

'Did you think I'd never want to see you again? I like you, Claire. I want to have you in my life, but if you want us to remain friends and nothing more, I'll respect that.'

'And you won't mind?'

'I'll be heartbroken, I assure you. You're a beautiful, compelling and dangerous woman and I want to get to know you as completely as possible. But if you decide that isn't what you want I'll respect that and I'm already far too fond of you to want to lose you altogether.'

'Thanks.'

He leant forwards and lowered his voice. 'But it's taking every ounce of self-control I possess to resist a very powerful urge to drag you into the bedroom. I want to know every millimetre of your body. I want to go to sleep with the sweat of our lovemaking drying on our skin and I want to wake up with the aroma of your hair in my nostrils.'

'It sounds lovely.' My nipples had hardened. The fine hairs on the back of my neck were erect and tingling.

'It sounds divine. But I'm just enough of a gentleman to wait until you're sure. Though I think you'd better go back to your room now before I prove myself a liar.' Jim stood up and held out his hand to me. I took it and got to my feet and allowed him to lead me to the door.

He cupped the back of my neck in his hand and kissed me. His lips were hot and coffee bitter. Beard stubble scratched my skin. I closed my eyes.

He ended the kiss. Looking straight into my eyes, he took my hand and pressed it to the front of his trousers. I could feel his erection straining under the thin fabric.

'That's what you do to me, Claire.' He opened the door. 'See you tomorrow.'

'Goodnight, Jim. And thank you for not having me.'

'Don't worry, my right hand and I will both have had you before you're even back in your room.'

'Ditto, though I think I'm inclined to wait until I'm actually in my room so as not to frighten the other guests.' I turned to go but Jim caught my wrist.

'Actually, I think it would be better if you didn't. That way you'll be all steamy and excited on Saturday.'

'OK, I will if you will.'

Jim shook his head. 'I'm not the one who likes following orders.' He brought my hand to his lips and kissed it.

I looked at Jim. My stomach felt fluttery. I was light-headed and my legs had gone wobbly. 'All right. I promise.'

'Now, go to bed and – don't forget – leave your cunt alone.' Jim held the door open for me.

6

Back in my room, I stripped off my clothes and got ready for bed. I was under the covers with the light out inside five minutes but, as I lay there in the dark, I knew sleep wouldn't come.

I had hoped the booze I'd consumed over the past few hours – more than I usually drank in a month – would quickly bring the welcome oblivion of sleep. But the snug, sedative cocoon had already begun to wear off, leaving in its place throbbing temples and wakefulness.

Maybe I would have found it easier to sleep if I hadn't been so completely furious with Jim. Though it wasn't the first time I'd heard the word 'cunt' in the context of my own female parts, I had to admit it had shocked me. Sometimes it's the only word that will do, but it belongs in the bedroom between lovers. Said in the exaggerated formality of Jim's hotel drawing room, it seemed as out of place and offensive as a turd on the coffee table.

I knew he had been playing with me all evening, a subtle game of tag in which he always seemed to be one step ahead. His need to demonstrate his control over me seemed as obvious as his attraction to me and, much as I wanted it, I couldn't quite help resenting the manipulation. I was terrified and he knew it so why did he insist on making it so hard for me?

I got up and went into the bathroom. I drank two glasses of tepid water straight down, too thirsty to wait for the tap to run cold. In the mirror, I could see that my eyes were dark rimmed and I was deathly pale. My head was still throbbing and I felt dizzy. I found some aspirin in my toilet bag and swallowed them down. Back in the bedroom I picked up my watch and saw that it was after two and I hadn't had a single wink of sleep.

I climbed under the covers and my hand reached automatically for my crotch. Masturbation was nature's sleeping pill and, though it was definitely habit forming, you didn't need a prescription for it. My fingers had found the groove between my lips and were beginning to tease the margin of my clit when I remembered that Jim had forbidden it and I pulled my hand away guiltily, as if he could see what I was up to. Reluctantly, I pulled my nightie down and closed my eyes.

Next morning, I covered the dark circles under my eyes with concealer and applied blusher to counteract the pallor of my cheeks. Jim was already at the table when I went down for breakfast, dressed in a dark-blue suit and silk shirt the colour of a summer sky. My heart seemed to give a little flutter when I saw him and a slow shiver slid down my spine. As he saw me enter, he stood up and pulled out my chair for me.

'You look quite beautiful, this morning.' He handed me my napkin.

'Oh it's purely artifice, I assure you, paint and powder. I'd have been down ten minutes ago but it's taken me that long to cover up my eye bags.'

'Do you know that whenever I give you a compliment you find away of dismissing it?'

'Do I really? It's another Catholic thing, I think. Pride is a sin, don't forget.'

We ordered cooked breakfasts and coffee and went off to choose some fruit and cereal from the buffet.

When we got back to the table the coffee had arrived. Jim spooned sugar onto his bowl of porridge then dipped a slice of bread and butter into it. He ate like this for a while, dipping the bread into the bowl, getting a little heap of warm porridge onto it and bringing it to his mouth.

I was intrigued. He obviously noticed me looking because he smiled at me and I could almost swear I saw him blush a little. He wiped his bowl with the last piece of bread.

'Have you never seen anyone eat their porridge that way before?' He popped the bread into his mouth.

'No, I haven't. Is it a childhood thing? Like eating your shepherd's pie with a spoon because it reminds you of the nursery? I must admit I do that at home when there's nobody looking.'

'Do you? How sweet. Actually, it's a prison habit. It's rather uncouth, I know, but I've grown to like it.'

'Are you serious?'

'Maybe. Does it matter, anyway?'

I opened my mouth to speak but Jim shot me a mock stern look that told me any further questioning was futile.

As I entered the lobby to meet Jim after breakfast he was standing beside the exit talking into his mobile. He waved in greeting when he saw me then pointed at the phone and mouthed 'Sorry'.

I walked over to an armchair and sat down. I tried not to eavesdrop but my natural curiosity overcame my scruples and I found myself straining to listen. Jim was standing with his back to me so I only caught fragments of the conversation.

'No ... I told you yesterday ... why don't you listen

to me? Of course I do ... You know I do ...' He sounded exasperated and patronising, as if he was talking to a child or an idiot.

It certainly didn't sound like a business call. I never spoke to my colleagues or boss like that. It sounded personal, intimate almost; the way you'd talk to a family member. Or a lover.

I felt the blood draining from my face. It couldn't be? He'd told me he was divorced. Could he have lied? Maybe they'd argued – it would explain why he was living at The Feathers.

My heart was racing. There was a strange hollow feeling under my ribs and I was light-headed. Surely it couldn't be true? I'd cast him in the role of Moriarty when all along he'd merely been an adulterer?

Jim ended his call and turned to face me. He smiled. 'Sorry about that. Are you ready?'

I stood up. 'Who was that on the phone?'

Jim picked up my overnight bag. 'No one, just business.'

'Business? That's not how it sounded to me.'

'How did it sound?' Jim was smiling.

'Like ... like you were talking to a lover.' I looked into his eyes but they were unreadable.

'Don't be ridiculous.' He turned and began to walk away.

Furious but anxious not to make a scene in the hotel I followed him through the exit and out onto the drive. He opened the boot and tossed in my bag.

'How dare you walk away from me.'

'Claire, please don't be angry with me. I'm sorry if I upset you.' He closed the boot and came over to me. 'I'm not seeing another woman. You are the only woman I'm interested in.'

In his eyes I saw concern and contrition.

'So who was on the phone?'

'It was a business call,' he said, looking away. 'Shall we get moving?'

There was never any real doubt that I'd be waiting for Jim in The Feathers' lounge on Saturday morning. I was mildly unsettled by Jim's prison revelation and his refusal to talk about the phone call but the more I thought about things, the more confused I became. Under pressure, I always resorted to the comfort of logic and reason but those old friends could not help me now.

I told myself that I'd decide at the last moment, making my choice based on desire and not logic but I found myself spending so much time fantasising about it that I knew I'd never be able to live with the regrets if I didn't do it.

I set the clock for eight o'clock, but I was awake long before that. I ran a bath and shaved my legs and armpits while it was filling and, on impulse, lathered up my crotch and in a few short swipes of the blade I was completely hairless. I usually kept my pubes trimmed short, so it was a fairly easy job. When I was finished I looked at myself in the full-length mirror and, with my hairless mound and my pale curls tumbling around my shoulders, I thought I looked like Eve in the Garden of Eden in a medieval painting I had once seen. How apt, I reflected, since like Eve I was just about to lose my innocence.

After my bath I opened my bedroom curtains and the light came flooding in. It was already a baking hot day. Marigolds danced in my garden below and a sparrow ruffled its feathers in the bird bath. I selected a pair of cream linen trousers and a fine cotton sleeveless blouse. Underneath I put on my best silk underwear. Even if Jim never saw it, wearing nice underthings always made me feel a little bit special; a cheeky little secret I was keeping to myself.

I dried my hair with the diffuser attachment, so as not to disturb the curls, then scrunched in serum to make them glossy and bouncy. Normally I dried my hair straight, pulling it cruelly with the brush then flattening it with ceramic irons.

I'd grown up hating my curls, believing they made me look too Irish and unsophisticated. While I'd developed a better relationship with my wayward hair in adulthood, I still felt I looked more grown up with straight hair. Today, however, curls seemed appropriate. If I looked young and unsophisticated, so be it. The likeness to Eve that I had seen in my bathroom mirror was proper and natural.

When I arrived at the hotel Jim was already waiting for me, even though I was more than half an hour early. He smiled when he saw me and crossed the room to intercept me.

'You've obviously never learnt that the lady is expected to be fashionably late.' He kissed me on the cheek, his warm hand resting on my naked upper arm. It was the briefest of kisses yet I felt it all the way to my toes; a Mexican wave of tingles that almost took my breath away.

'I was worried that if I was late you might not wait for me. And anyway, I couldn't sleep.'

'Me neither. I was like a kid headed for Disneyland today. I woke at the crack of dawn my stomach aflutter with excitement. And then when I opened my curtains and it was another beautiful day I thought it must be an omen. You look lovely this morning. I don't think I've ever seen your hair like that. You remind me of Ophelia in the painting. She's reaching up to pick something from a tree overhead, her curls tumbling all the way down her back like yours. Is it Rosetti?'

'Arthur Hughes, I think.'

'Of course, you're right. But let's get moving, we mustn't waste this fabulous day.'

We headed for the car.

'How do you feel?' Jim took his hand off the steering wheel and patted my leg.

'Like you, I suppose. Excited mostly.' We were speeding along the A40 with the sunroof open.

'Only mostly? What else?'

'Well, nervous obviously and a lot of other things I'm not sure I could name. Like I've suddenly been plopped down in a foreign country; I don't speak the language and I haven't even got a map.'

'It might seem like an uncharted wilderness to you but you've forgotten one important element. You have me – your trusty Sherpa and native speaker.'

'I hadn't forgotten, thanks.'

'But you're still scared?'

'Wouldn't you be?'

Jim didn't answer immediately, he drove with both eyes on the road ahead. The only sign that he'd heard me was his fingertips tapping thoughtfully on the steering wheel.

'Yes, I suppose I would be. But you have nothing to worry about. You're far too precious for me to let anything bad happen to you. It might be challenging, it might be difficult but I promise you will always be safe.'

'I'm not worried about my physical safety, Jim. I'm expecting pain and restraint and all that – in fact I'll be highly disappointed if there isn't any. But the other night in the hotel when I couldn't sleep I realised that, in letting go of my past, I'll be letting go of my identity in some way. Does that make sense?'

Jim nodded. 'Of course it does. That's what makes your gift so valuable to me. And, in return, my gift to you is to keep you safe, physically, spiritually, whatever it takes.'

'Trust me, I'm a pervert?'

'Something like that. But you do trust me?'

'Completely . . .'

'Completely? I thought I heard a but.'

'Not a but as such. More an ambiguity. I do trust you completely or, believe me, I wouldn't be here. But I'd feel a lot more comfortable if you weren't so bloody mysterious all the time.'

'I see. And are being mysterious and being trust-worthy mutually exclusive?'

'No, not at all. I've thought about it a lot. I can trust you, I know that.'

'You can.' Jim smiled at me. 'Why don't we try some-thing? If I asked you to do something for me, would you do it?'

'Of course.'

'You haven't heard what it is yet. Call it a first step in our journey. Are you sure you're ready?'

I nodded my assent because, frankly, I didn't trust my voice not to quaver. My nipples peaked and my skin went tingly.

'For the rest of the day if I ask you to do something will you obey me no matter what it is?' Jim glanced at me, his blue eyes shining.

'Yes I will.' My heart was thumping so loud I was sure Jim must be able to hear it. My breath seemed to have caught in my throat and every nerve ending in my body seemed alive and tingling. Jim said nothing, but he treated me to a delighted smile that brought on another bout of palpitations.

'I'm going to turn down this lane. I need a pee.' Jim steered the car off the main road and drove for about half a mile. The lane was wooded on either side and, as we drove, the trees grew thick and dense. Jim stopped the car. He climbed out, gesturing for me to do the same. He took my hand and led me into the woods. Twigs and dead leaves crackled under our shoes as we walked. It was cool and moist under the umbrella of tree branches and I could hear birds twittering. A few hundred yards into the woods he stopped and turned to me.

'You're still sure you want to do this?'

'Yes, I'm sure.' I felt tingly and weak. My face was hot and I knew my cheeks would be pink. My nipples were swollen and uncomfortable inside my bra and I swear my legs were trembling.

'Good. Now I want you to walk over there.' He pointed.

I walked over to where he was pointing, negotiating the uneven ground with difficulty. I turned to him for confirmation that I was in the right place and he gestured for me to move to the right. I eagerly complied.

'Turn your back to me. That's right. Now, I want you to pull your trousers and knickers down to your ankles and bend right over for me. Head on your knees.'

I hesitated for a second but I didn't even think about disobeying him. I pushed my clothes down my legs so enthusiastically that they got tangled and stuck and it took me a moment to get them all the way down. I could feel the cool air on my naked skin. I'd never felt so exposed or so alive. I bent over slowly, my hands braced against my shins and all the blood rushed to my head.

'Open your legs a little wider, I want to see your pussy.'

I obeyed, spreading my legs as wide as I could without taking my trousers off. I dangled my head, gazing at the stretched, virgin gusset of my own panties. The ends of my hair dangled on the ground and I knew that when I stood upright I'd have leaves and pieces of bark stuck in it. I imagined him feasting on the sight, drinking in every detail. My legs were trembling visibly now and, for a moment, I feared they might fail me.

'Lovely. I can see it now, all plump and delicious. Reach round with your hands and spread it for me. I want to see if you're wet.'

I did as he asked, reaching round with trembling hands. I was already slick and slippery and it took me a few seconds to position my fingers. When I'd got a good grip I pulled myself open, holding it wide for him.

'Ahhh,' Jim exhaled – a long, slow breath that signalled his appreciation more eloquently than any words. 'Just as I imagined. Glittering, rosy and moist. Now, I want you to pull your cheeks apart for me so that I can see your other hole.'

I used both hands to hold my buttocks apart. I had to bend my knees slightly, otherwise I risked falling over. I shuffled my feet around, repositioning them more stably. I pressed my fingers between my buttocks, into that secret dark crack. I pulled my cheeks apart, revealing the puckered rosebud. My thigh muscles were taut and trembling. My crotch was tingling. I was covered in goose pimples.

I heard him lower his zip behind me and I imagined him manipulating his cock. Did he feed it through the slit in his underpants or did he pull them down and lift it over the top? Did he hold it in his left or his right hand or did he, like I knew some men did, prefer to use both?

Was he cut or uncut? Was it thick and veiny or long and purple? Did his balls dangle down underneath or were they already hard and tight, signalling his arousal? I strained my ears, waiting for the sound of his urine hitting the ground but all I could hear was a bird singing overhead and the distant rumble of traffic.

Perhaps, I thought, he was having trouble pissing because the sight of my naked arse, so wantonly displayed, had made him aroused. I imagined it growing thick and hard in his hand, full of piss and heat. I was panting. Though my breasts were squashed up inside my bra my nipples were hard and sensitive.

Behind me, I heard the unmistakable noise of Jim urinating and, in my excited state, the mundane sound seemed like the most erotic and personal of gifts. I stretched my cheeks apart even further, exposing myself. I felt a trickle of moisture run down between my lips. I heard him zip up and walk towards me.

My whole body was taut and trembling. I was dizzy and hot. Jim bent down behind me and I felt his hot breath on my exposed arsehole. He pressed a wet finger against the dark wrinkled eye and I gasped and almost fell over. Jim reached out a hand to steady me. He placed a warm hand on each of my hips and I felt his mouth on me. He laid a chaste brief kiss on my secret opening then stuck out his tongue and licked.

His hot wet tongue probed and danced and I let out a long slow grunt of pleasure and surprise. He lapped at my hole for several seconds, lavishing it with attention, exploring every wrinkle, crease and pucker. I was tingling all over. My legs felt weak.

He put the pointed tip up against the opening and

pushed it inside, making me gasp. He ran his tongue slowly backwards and forwards, then gave my hole a final kiss. I felt his fingertip slowly tracing the length of my pussy, then dabbling in the pooled moisture. My crotch prickled with pleasure. My nipples were rigid. There was the unmistakable sound of a finger being sucked clean and a satisfied smack of the lips.

'I'll wait for you back at the car.' He got to his feet and walked away. I straightened up carefully, conscious that it was likely to make me dizzy. I stumbled over to a nearby tree, my clothes still around my ankles, and leant on it for support until the dizziness past. It took me several minutes before I felt composed enough to dress myself and walk back to the car.

When I reached the road, I saw Jim already in the car, waiting for me with the engine running. When he saw me, he leant over and opened the passenger door for me. As I buckled myself in, Jim glanced over and smiled at me.

'Your hair's full of leaves, Ophelia.'

The rest, as they say, is history. We went to Covent Garden, wandered around the various stalls and shops and Jim surprised me by buying a pair of expensive earrings I'd admired. We ate lunch at the Rock Garden. It was here that he'd asked me to take off my knickers in the toilet and bring them back to him at the table. He'd made me flirt outrageously with the waiter, telling me to undo another button and then another. From time to time he'd fingered me under cover of the tablecloth, then laid my palm against his straining crotch.

On the drive home he'd made me strip and masturbate, even asking me to flash my tits at the two lads in the white van. We'd arrived back at his house late in the afternoon. As I waited on the path for him to open the front door it struck me that I had no idea what was going to happen to me and that not knowing was precisely what made it so appealing.

7

Jim's house was in the fashionable enclave of Hampstead Garden Suburb which had been built in the 1930s in the art deco style. The exterior was an impressive expanse of white walls and picture windows. On the flat roof there was a glass sunroom; its gleaming panes twinkled in the sunlight.

It was the kind of house you often see in seaside resorts pointing majestically seawards. Their elongated shapes and proportions have always reminded me of ocean liners and I knew this resemblance was intentional. In those days, ocean cruising was the height of chic, representing luxury and excess and these bold houses were built as a tribute to that lifestyle.

I don't know what sort of place I'd expected Jim to live in but the reality took me rather by surprise. It was so singular and so firmly rooted in its era that it seemed somehow out of keeping with the middle-class values he chose to present to the world.

I'd have expected a rambling Victorian house with cast-iron fireplaces and stained glass in the front door, or a Docklands flat with a spectacular view and furniture straight out of Habitat. But, seeing his house, I understood its attraction immediately. It was original and striking and unapologetic. Its identity and its statement were clear. Love it or loathe it, you could never ignore or overlook it.

Jim opened the door for me and I stepped inside. There was a chrome and glass table against the wall at the foot of the staircase. Beside it was a sculptural metal and canvas creation which I instantly recognised as a Marcel Breuer Wassily chair.

He took me on a brief tour of the ground floor. The living room ran the entire depth of the house with full-length windows and French doors opening onto the garden at the rear. The carpet was a pale silvery grey and the walls throughout were white. He had obviously chosen furniture to match the house; there was an Eames recliner by the French doors, an open book resting on it with a pair of reading glasses folded on top.

He had mixed authentic deco pieces with an eclectic selection of modernist furniture to create a space that was soothing, uncluttered and homely. Two armchairs faced the flat-screen television which, together with the stereo system, were the only concessions to the twenty-first century.

Jim led me through the house without comment, holding my hand and taking me into one room after another as if his home were a museum and I a paying customer. I drank it all in conscious that I was in Jim's territory and, while that put me at a disadvantage, it was also a valuable clue to who he really was. Having been starved of personal information until now, it seemed to me that every tiny feature might have significance.

Jim led me back into the hall. He turned to face me. He stroked my cheek and bent his head to kiss me. It was the briefest of kisses yet my nipples stiffened and my scalp tingled.

'I've been desperate to see you naked all day. Will you undress for me?' His voice was soft and slightly husky. He sat down in the Wassily chair.

A wave of watery shivers slid down my spine. I only hesitated for a moment. I turned to face him and began to unbutton my shirt, my fingers clumsy and disobedient. It took me far longer than usual to get it undone. I slid it off my shoulders and down my arms, conscious of Jim's eyes on my body.

I pushed my trousers down to my ankles then bent to unbuckle my sandals and, when I straightened up to step out of them, I felt dizzy and slightly drunk. Heat and tension were spreading between my legs.

I hoped that Jim liked the underwear I had so carefully selected. It was cream silk with a pattern of tiny rosebuds. Reaching behind me, I undid my bra and my nipples immediately stiffened as the cool air hit them. Dropping my bra on top of my other clothes, I stood in front of Jim fully naked for the first time.

I was covered in goose pimples. My breathing had grown shallow and rapid. I could feel heat burning in my cheeks. Tension throbbed in my belly.

My shaved pubes suddenly felt like a mistake, as if I'd unintentionally denied myself even the limited concealment of hair. My crotch felt unprotected, announcing my gender and my arousal.

My nipples were standing out hard and dark. I was tingling all over. The hairs on the back of my neck were erect and prickly, making me feel as though there were fingertips gently trailing up my nape.

Jim's eyes roamed unhurriedly over my body. They lingered over my breasts, taking in every detail. When he looked at my crotch I could swear I saw a faint smile as he realised I had shaved myself. Though his eyes gave nothing away, I could see the bulge of his erection. Heat and excitement welled between my legs.

I was practically trembling by now, and it took every ounce of self-control to stand still. I looked straight at Jim, hoping that my eyes would convey my desire and determination. I loved his eyes on my body. My nipples were painfully erect and my crotch was tingling.

'I think it's time I showed you my bedroom.' He took my hand and led me upstairs.

Jim's room was minimally furnished, just the bed and two bedside cabinets and a window seat upholstered in cream silk.

The bed dominated the room. The black cast-iron railing at its head extended at least six feet up the wall and gave the place a gothic look. A matching curtain rail hung above the window supporting dramatic flowing drapes which were so long the bottoms pooled on the carpet like a silk waterfall.

Jim sat me down on the bed. My nipples were swollen and sensitive, my crotch aching. He knelt on the carpet in front of me. He dipped his head and sucked on my nipple. I gasped.

I could feel his warm breath on my skin. His mouth was hot and soft and wet. My nipples tingled with delicious pleasure. I could hear the blood throbbing in my ears.

Jim gave my nipple a final nip and I tingled all over. He sat up, resting a hand on each of my knees.

'Remember when you said you were expecting pain and humiliation? Are you ready to put your money where your mouth is?' He stroked my thighs.

My insides seemed to turn to liquid. I felt a warm rush of excitement crash over me like a flood. My heart was thumping.

'Is the Pope Catholic?'

Jim slid a hand between my legs. His fingers found my clit and my whole body shuddered. He smiled.

'Just checking to see if you're excited as I am. Look.' He got to his feet and rubbed his erection with the heel of his hand. 'I'll be back in a minute.' He left the room. I heard him walking along the landing. A door opened and I listened to him moving around in the room next door. I was rigid with excitement and anticipation. My scalp was prickling. I heard Jim's feet approaching down the hall. The bedroom door opened and he stepped inside. 'Close your eyes.' His voice was a hoarse whisper.

I instantly obeyed. The sound of my beating heart seemed to fill the room. I heard him walk over, then a soft thump as he dropped something on the bed. He knelt in front of me and laid one hand on my shoulder, hot and heavy. A ripple of pleasure and satisfaction shot through me so violently I almost collapsed.

'I'm going to blindfold you. OK?' His hand stroked my hair.

'Yes, I understand.' My voice sounded uncharacteristically uncertain.

'And that's what you want? You're sure.' Jim's fingertip trailed down the front of my torso, between my breasts, and I shivered.

'I want it more than you can possibly imagine.'

'I doubt that's true, but I know what you mean. You see, what makes this arrangement so perfect and balanced is that I want it –' his fingertip circled my breasts and I had to hold onto the bed frame for support '– just as much as you do. And I want you to know that while it isn't me sitting there naked and trembling that's exactly how I feel inside.' He bent and kissed my neck. His mouth was hot and his stubble scratched my skin. I arched my back and sighed.

Almost immediately his lips were gone and I felt the blindfold's downy interior pressed to my eyes. I could feel Jim buckling it behind my head and the creaking sound told me that it was made of leather. The inside was padded and lined with something soft and velvety.

He buckled it tight and I realised that I was completely blind. For a moment I was alarmed, then Jim ran a finger down the length of my arm and I realised that, with no vision to guide me, every touch was magnified and intense.

I heard Jim get up and open the window. He moved around the room unhurriedly. He opened and closed a drawer, then walked over to the bed and dropped something onto the quilt.

Deprived of my vision my senses were hyper alert. I could detect the far-off rumble of city traffic and a distant piano playing. I felt as if I could feel every fibre of the carpet under my feet and each individual hair on my head. It seemed as though the air in the room was composed of individual pinpoints and I could feel them pricking my skin, sensitising it. My own breathing sounded deafening and Jim's, too, seemed unnaturally loud.

My crotch was aching and hot. My nipples were rigid. Jim knelt behind me and began to fasten something around one ankle. It was soft and slightly scratchy inside and, like the blindfold, it creaked as he buckled it, telling me it was leather.

'Is that too tight?'

'No. What is it? I can't work it out.'

'Leather ankle cuffs, sheepskin lined so they don't dig in. They're connected by a short chain.' He pulled on it. 'So you can hobble about but not really walk.' He began to fasten the cuff around my other ankle. Cold prickles of pleasure moved up my neck and over my scalp.

When he'd finished buckling the ankle cuffs, he fitted a similar pair to my wrists. Now I was completely powerless, unable to run away or defend myself. A shiver of excitement and anticipation shot up my spine like electricity.

'Now I want you to stand up and take a step forwards.'

I got up and shuffled forwards experimentally, testing the length of the chain between my ankle cuffs. It was no more than six inches long, just enough to allow me to shuffle around but progress was slow. I hobbled forwards.

I strained my ears for any clue as to what might come next. I could hear Jim's feet on the carpet as he moved about and the sound of clothes rustling. His shallow breathing betrayed his arousal and, in my helpless state, that knowledge seemed like a lifeline and a caress. Every footfall and movement felt like a declaration of love. I felt a fingertip running along my spine and sliding down the cleft between my buttocks. It was the briefest of touches, over almost as soon as it had begun, yet I shivered all over and my nipples tingled.

I was wound up with anticipation and arousal, my thigh muscles trembling uncontrollably. My hair was sticking to my body with sweat. I was holding my breath, listening for clues. I heard the bed creak as Jim sat down.

'Turn round ... that's right. Now I want you to bend over my knees.'

I put out my hands, feeling for his legs. I shuffled back a little to get into a better position, feeling clumsy in my shackles. When I lowered myself over his lap I realised he had undressed. I could feel the hairs on his legs and his body heat. He reached between our bodies to adjust himself and I felt his erection jabbing into my side.

My hair fell forwards over my face. Blood rushed to my lowered head, making me feel even dizzier.

'Are you going to spank me?' I could hear the hunger in my own voice.

'What do you think?' He held me onto his lap with one hand and began to stroke my bottom, running his hand over the sensitised skin, and I began to tremble.

He rubbed my buttocks with his hand, warming it. I was tingling all over. My crotch was hot and tight. He massaged my skin, kneading and pinching it. His hands slid all over my behind, rubbing, stroking and squeezing.

I could feel heat warming my skin and making it glow. I imagined it growing red as Jim handled it. My nipples were tight and prickling, my clit was tingling and sensitive. Shivers slid along my spine.

I could feel the weight of his other hand on my back holding me down and his body heat. His skin was damp against mine. I could hear his breathing, noisy and rapid. I was panting and breathless. I was dizzy and light-headed. My heart pounded.

He rubbed my skin hard, over and over again until it began to burn and tingle. I could feel the strength in his fingers as he kneaded my flesh. His erection jabbed into my side, its tip wet. Heat seeped through me. My crotch ached. My scalp prickled.

He began to tap my bottom so gently that I barely registered the sensation. He patted my behind, gradually increasing the pressure until I could feel the cold rush of air against my skin and, a split second later, the brush of his skin against mine. My thigh muscles began to quiver. I moaned.

I could feel his extended fingers and the flat of his hand as he patted my bottom. My skin tingled and blazed as sensitised nerve endings registered the contact. I could hardly breath. My chest heaved.

He tapped me repeatedly – rapid and gentle like a drum roll, gradually picking up speed. I felt my buttocks wobbling with each slap. My crotch burnt. My nipples were erect and sensitive.

The slaps started to hurt and sting. My skin was on fire, my clit aching and tense. I could hear the slaps now and, somehow, the sound seemed to underline my helplessness and my desire. I was tingling all over, my body trembling. Every touch was delicious torment. If only Jim would touch my aching pussy I knew I would come within seconds.

Jim's erection rubbed up against my side. His skin against mine was damp and slippery. His breathing was noisy and rapid. Every so often he'd let out a little grunt of exertion. I could hardly breathe. My nose was congested from hanging upside down. I supported my weight on my hands, knuckles pressed into the carpet, bracing myself.

Jim spanked me over and over again, stinging slaps that made my flesh tremble and my nipples throb. Heat burnt my backside. My crotch ached with tension.

He delivered slap after noisy slap. I was wound up with excitement, my body rigid. The sensation was incredible: intense, perfect and pure – as if the line between pain and pleasure had grown blurry and vague.

My bottom blazed with heat and pleasure. I was moaning and sobbing. Tears welled in my eyes. My clit tingled. Jim delivered a final thunderous slap that thrust me forwards and took my breath away. He slid his hand downwards and touched my crotch. He slid his fingers slowly along the length of my pussy. He found my clit and I gasped. Jim laughed, softly.

'Can you bend over the bed?'

'I think so.' When I stood up my head swam. I felt Jim catch my arm.

'You're probably a bit dizzy. Wait until it passes. I've got you.'

When it had passed I knelt down and bent over the bed. I supported my weight on my elbows and hoisted my arse into the air. I heard Jim bending down behind me and shuffling to get himself in position. I felt his hands on my hips and his legs against mine. I felt him slide the tip of his cock up and down my wet pussy, lubricating it. I was breathless and hot. My crotch was liquid and tight. My nipples rubbed against the duvet.

He held onto my hips and positioned his cock. I felt his hairy thighs pressing up against me as he leant forwards, using his body weight to enter me. It felt thick and hot, its tip pushed against me. Jim let out a grunt of satisfaction as it began to slip inside.

He held onto my hips, pulling himself forwards as he filled me. Damp hair clung to my face and back. Jim gave one final long thrust and I felt his belly pressing up against my buttocks, his balls slapping my swollen pussy. He circled his hips, rotating inside me, and I began to moan.

The first moment of penetration was intense – a prickly, tingling pleasure as it slid past the muscles and satisfaction and fullness as it hit home.

Jim began to slide in and out. On the in-stroke he slid in deep, pressing his body against mine. On the out-stroke he kept moving until just the tip was inside me, tantalising me before thrusting back in. His movements began to pick up speed. I could hear him groaning and panting. His thighs were slippery with sweat. He felt huge and hard inside me. My skin was alive with pleasure and excitement.

My body was forced forwards on every thrust. My nipples rubbed against the duvet. He was pounding me, his hips moving like pistons. He was grunting and breathing hard. Jim gave one long thrust and let out a deep guttural moan of satisfaction. My clit was tingling, my whole crotch a liquid mass of pleasure.

I felt him twitch inside me, pumping out sperm. He

collapsed over my back and I felt his hot breath on my neck. He kissed me, his lips sliding across my shoulder, cheek and neck, kissing and nibbling me wherever his mouth touched. His body was hot and sweat-slick against my back. Gently he moved my hair away from my face.

'Let me take off the ankle cuffs.' He fiddled with the straps. 'Now the blindfold. Open your eyes slowly because they'll be sensitive, like when you turn on the light in the middle of the night.' He unbuckled the blindfold and tossed it onto the floor. My face felt damp and cold where the blindfold had been. The light shone golden red through my closed eyelids. Jim removed the cuffs on my arms and massaged my wrists for me. 'Now climb on the bed for me and open your legs.'

I obeyed. I spread my legs, resting my feet on the edge of the mattress. He knelt between my legs and leant forwards. His fingertips trailed down the front of my body. I felt my heart flutter, its quickening beat pulsing beneath my breasts as he teased my nipples into tight pink buds. He stroked the soft plane of my belly with his nails. There was a burning ache in my belly. My nipples tingled.

His fingers slid between my legs and brushed my clit. I shivered and opened my legs wider. Heat began to spread through my body. My crotch was aching and tight. I looked down at him. A dark flush of arousal coloured his throat. His eyes were half closed, his lips curved into a contented smile. I reached out and touched his face. I stroked his cheek, followed the curve of his lower lip with a cautious fingertip. I half sat up and pulled his face towards me for a kiss. His mouth was soft and hot. He broke away from the kiss and slid back down between my thighs.

'Hold it open for me, spread your lips with your

fingers. That's it, good girl.' Jim sighed. 'It looks so delicious I feel as though I ought to say grace.' He dipped his head and kissed the inside of my knee. My breathing had grown quick and shallow. I moaned gently, a rush of air escaping through parted lips.

I could feel his hot wet tongue darting against my skin. My nipples were erect and sensitive. His mouth slid along my inner thigh. My heart was pounding. Blood thundered in my ears. Shivers of excitement were sliding up and down my spine. I pulled my lips wide, stretching myself open. Jim ran his tongue along the groove between thigh and pussy and I moaned once again.

His tongue slid lower, finding the cleft between my buttocks. Jim pressed my cheeks apart with his thumbs and worked his tongue around the margin of my puckered hole. I was tingling all over. My nipples were erect and sensitive.

Jim trailed his pointed tongue up my perineum and dipped it into my opening. My whole body tensed. His mouth moved upwards and found my clit. I let out a long deep sigh of satisfaction.

He covered my clit with his mouth and sucked on it, moving his tongue across the sensitive tip. Heat and tension formed at the base of my belly. My thigh muscles began to tremble. I was breathing in short gasps.

I could feel his hot breath on me, hear his excited breathing. He wrapped a hand around each of my thighs and pulled me onto his face. I held my lips apart, creating delicious tension on my clit. I was vibrating with pleasure. My head thrashed against the duvet. My body was covered with sweat. My hair was everywhere: in my eyes and clinging damply to my skin.

He circled the swollen bead of my clit, then lapped at

it with the flat of his tongue. My hands gripped the duvet. My back was damp against the bed. I could hear his excited breathing. His strong fingers dug into my flesh as he held me. Occasionally, his stubbly chin would graze my tender flesh and it felt good: so masculine, so alien.

His open mouth covered me, devoured me. Now and then, he would make a little satisfied grunt and, somehow, this unconscious expression of enjoyment seemed to magnify my own.

The knot of excitement in my pelvis had spread and intensified. I pressed my feet down into the mattress and ground my crotch against Jim's mouth. I was moaning and sobbing and thrashing against the bed. He sucked hard on my clit and my body began to buck. Blood pumped around my body like steam. Heat and pleasure throbbed in my pelvis. I was gasping and panting. Sweat filmed my skin. Damp hair clung to my face.

Jim's mouth was working its magic. His fingers dug into my thighs as he pressed me against his face. He was moaning softly as he licked, little grunts of pleasure and arousal. I rocked my hips, establishing a rhythm.

He held on tight and sucked hard on my clit, drawing it into his mouth and rubbing his tongue over the tip. His mouth was fiery and soft. His breath warmed me. My skin prickled. My nipples were hard and sensitive. I was breathless and sobbing.

I was on the edge. I rubbed myself against him, hips pistoning. My crotch ached, my nipples tingled. Just a few more strokes and I'd be there. My back was arched, my legs taut and twitching. I was practically screaming now. One ... two ... three ... I was coming. Heat and pleasure burst inside me like a firebomb. Jim slid two fingers hard inside me and I howled with delight. He sucked on my clit, riding out my orgasm.

My hair was a tangled mess. I was covered in sweat. Jim struggled to keep hold of me as I thrashed and shook. The waves kept coming, aftershocks of orgasm. Tears ran down my face and into my hair. The duvet beneath me was a damp rumpled mess.

Jim was grunting and panting as he held onto me. The waves of pleasure began to subside, like the tide going out. Taut muscles began to soften. Suddenly my clit became painfully sensitive and I drew back, pushing Jim's face away.

He laughed softly. He pulled down the duvet and helped me to get under the covers. Jim began to undress, sitting on the bed to remove his shoes. I realised that he must have fucked me with his trousers around his ankles hobbled, in a way, as helplessly as I was. He took off his socks and slid his trousers and underwear off. He unbuttoned his shirt and tossed it aside. As he climbed into bed beside me I noticed a mass of red, irregular scars on his belly.

I pushed the covers back to look at them and, though he shot me a look, he didn't resist. There was a long curved scar running from his pubic hair to his ribs. Every half-inch or so it was bisected by another smaller one where his wound had been stitched. It looked like the kind of fake scar kids wore at Hallowe'en and washed off the next day. Surrounding it were dozens of smaller jagged wounds of varying sizes, the biggest in the shape of a star.

'Where did you get those? A difference of opinion in the exercise yard? Another prisoner getting his revenge with a home-made shiv?' I fingered each of the blemishes, running a tentative fingertip along the raised crimson ropes.

'You've obviously read too much Mickey Spillane. For your information, if someone's got a grudge against you in prison they stab you in the arse because the wound bursts open every time you try to sit down. Or, if it's really serious they might slit open your face.' He ran a finger along his cheek from ear to mouth. 'It's called a telephone scar and everyone knows it means you can't be trusted.'

'So where did you get them? It's obviously a bit more serious than an appendectomy. Do they hurt?' I touched the longest scar.

Jim shook his head. 'No, mostly they're numb – nerve damage. For the first couple of years I used to get a lot of shooting pains, like electric shocks, but they don't really hurt any more.'

'Are you going to tell me how you got them?'

'In the army, a long time ago.'

'You were in the army? Where? Ireland? The Gulf?' It was hard to imagine Jim as a soldier. Somehow he seemed to lack the necessary obedience and conformity.

'I told you it was a long time ago.' Jim pulled up the duvet, covering his scars. He wrapped his arm around me and pulled me close so that my head was on his chest. He kissed the top of my head. 'Did you know you've got mascara all over your face? You look like Alice Cooper in a sauna.'

8

When my limbs had come back to life I went into the en-suite bathroom and washed my face, then used Jim's hairbrush to tame my tangled hair. As I turned to leave I noticed a full-length mirror beside the door and I couldn't resist the temptation to see if Jim had left marks on my rear. I turned my back to the mirror and bent over slightly, looking over my shoulder. My buttocks were bright red and glowing. A slow wave of heat and excitement washed over my face. My nipples tingled.

'Stop looking at your war wounds and get back in here, I'm lonely,' Jim's voice called out from the bedroom. I straightened up guiltily and left the room.

'How did you know I was doing that?' I climbed into bed.

'It was a shrewd guess. Why? Do you imagine I'm omnipotent?'

I couldn't help laughing. 'Actually, I have had that thought more than once.'

'Really?' He pulled me close.

I laid my head on his chest and stayed still for a moment listening to his heart beating. 'Do you remember when I told you I had masturbated because of the book you gave me?'

'How could I forget?'

'Well, that wasn't the whole story, but to tell it properly I've got to explain how, as a Catholic schoolgirl, I came to terms with my shameful need to masturbate. Don't laugh!'

Jim's body was shaking with amusement.

I told him about my deal with God and how, over the years, I'd taken the Almighty's lack of intervention as approval and had come to equate masturbation with prayer.

'That's very interesting? But what has it got to do with me?'

'Well, you gave me the book, knowing it would make me want to masturbate.'

'That's certainly what I hoped.'

'And it worked. I was thinking about my deal with God and how my teenage self had come to believe that He actually wanted me to masturbate and it struck me that you did too. And in my admittedly twisted mind it became an act of prayer and surrender to you in the same way as I used to offer my orgasm to God.'

Jim stroked my hair.

'Anyway, I knew you were a lot kinkier than the Almighty so I decided to put on a show for you. I tied my ankles to the bed and used a dildo. I even gagged myself with my own knickers and a silk scarf.'

'I wish I'd seen that.'

'That's the point – I almost believed you could. I wanked myself to a thunderous orgasm imagining you standing at the bottom of the bed, watching it all.'

'I'll have to get you to recreate that for me sometime.'

'Gladly. And at the hotel the other night, you told me not to masturbate but I couldn't sleep and my fingers drifted to my crotch automatically. Then I remembered you'd forbidden it and I pulled them away as if you could see what I was up to.'

'And you must obey your Lord?'

'Exactly.' I stroked Jim's belly. 'Have you ever seen Bernini's statue *The Ecstasy of St Theresa*? She's supposed to be undergoing spiritual ecstasy but, if you didn't know better –'

'You'd think she was having an orgasm. Yes, I've seen it.'

'Right. Nuns are told they must conquer their egos and surrender to a higher power. That's how I felt.'

'I think I understand.' Jim kissed my forehead. 'No one's ever compared me to God before. I'm flattered. Though I'm not quite so sure that He would be.'

We slept after that, curled up in each other's arms. When I woke up it was dark outside and Jim was lying awake, propped up on one arm watching me.

'Do you know, I could see your pulse beating in your throat as you slept.' He touched the spot on my neck with a fingertip. 'There was something so fragile and moving about it. It was absolutely beautiful, almost spiritual.'

'As if you could see my life itself?'

'Yes. That's exactly it. I wanted to touch it – to feel your life under my greedy fingertips – but I didn't want to risk waking you up, so I just lay here watching it throb.' He leant forwards and kissed my throat. 'Are you hungry?'

'I'm absolutely starving.'

'Me too. Why don't you have a shower and I'll nip downstairs and whip up something quick in the kitchen.'

'Is there anything to eat in your kitchen? You haven't been here for weeks.'

'Fortunately I had the foresight to ring my cleaning lady and ask her to leave us a few provisions.' He folded the duvet back and laid a chaste kiss on each of my nipples.

'How very organised of you. I bet you used to be a Boy Scout.'

'Actually I did. A long time ago.'

'Really? You obviously have a secret uniform fetish: the scouts, the army . . .'

'You find it strange that I was in the army?'

'Don't you?'

'Yes, I suppose I do. It's true I have no talent for obedience.'

'No, you prefer to be obeyed.'

'I don't see you complaining.'

I showered and washed my hair and got a nightie out of my overnight bag then went downstairs to the kitchen. Jim was dressed in jeans and a black T-shirt. There was tea towel tucked into his waistband. He had poured two glasses of wine and put a pan of pasta on to boil. I could smell garlic and anchovies. He smiled at me as I walked in and nodded towards the wine glasses.

'Have a drink. Dinner shouldn't be long.'

'What are you making? It smells delicious.'

'Spaghetti puttanesca. I hope you like it.'

'Never had it, I don't think.'

'It means "whore's pasta". The legend goes that Italian whores used to whip it up quickly between clients. It's just garlic, anchovies, capers, olives and tomatoes.'

Jim was slicing black olives on a chopping board. He picked one up and popped it into his mouth then selected another and offered it to me. I watched as he chopped half-a-dozen plum tomatoes, working with the skill and economy of a chef. He wiped his fingers on the tea towel, then picked up his wine glass and took a long swallow. He tossed the diced tomatoes into the pan and gave it all a stir.

'Did no one ever tell you it's rude to stare?' He balled up the tea towel and lobbed it at me.

'Sorry. I know I shouldn't, I just find you fascinating.'

Jim said nothing. He leant against the work surface, his arms spread and his hands resting against the table top. The expression on his face was half apology, half challenge and I could almost believe that his conscious evasions caused him shame.

The kitchen timer pinged and Jim became a whirlwind of activity. He turned off the gas under the sauce and carried the pasta pan over the sink to drain.

'Can you carry our wine glasses to the dining room? I'll be through in a second.'

In the dining room the table was set with white linen and heavy silver cutlery. There were candles in tiny blue glasses dotted around the table and the lights were low. There was a bowl of salad in the centre and the remainder of the bottle of wine beside it. Jim came in carrying the pasta in a serving bowl. He took the seat opposite me and picked up his wine glass.

'Welcome to my home.' He raised his glass in a toast then took a sip.

'Thanks for inviting me. It's really lovely. I'm quite envious. You probably couldn't buy a shed round here for what my house is worth.'

Jim shrugged. 'It's only money. Let's eat.'

After the meal we drank coffee in the living room. Jim put a Chet Baker CD on the player. He made us espressos with a gleaming chrome Gaggia machine and served it in fine bone china cups, which were white and edged with gold leaf.

I looked around the room, noticing details I'd missed earlier. A huge abstract painting hung on the wall by the door, consisting of geometric shapes in monochrome overlaid with swirling, sinuous strokes of scarlet, yellow and blue. A glass table by the window held a sculpture, clearly intended to be a human figure. The face was carved very minimally, only hollows for eyes and lips and curves for cheekbones, forehead and chin. The figure was standing with arms extended and its weight on one foot. It was sinuous and delicate and somehow unresolved, as if he or she was trying to remember something, caught for eternity in perpetual indecision.

I sat in one of the armchairs, my legs crossed under me and Jim sat on the carpet facing me.

'You look particularly lovely this evening, Claire.'

'In my old nightie, with no make-up and my hair all wet from the shower?'

'You've done it again – rejected a compliment.'

'Sorry . . . thank you.'

'The nightie somehow makes you look demure and girlish. Only I know that, underneath the broderie anglaise, there lies the body of Venus and the soul of a libertine.'

'Thank you again. I think.' I sipped my coffee.

'It's a compliment, I assure you. You know that old saying about a woman being a maid in the living room, a cook in the kitchen and a whore in the bedroom? Well, it's not true. Ask any man – we'll all say the same thing. All we really want is the whore. You can hire a cleaner and eat out but finding a woman who's uninhibited, responsive and constantly horny is a lot more rare. Have you finished your coffee? Let me take your cup.'

I handed it to him. 'I know what you mean, but I'm not sure I like being called a whore. It's not the concept I object to, it's the word itself.'

'You don't really like dirty words, do you?'

'No, I suppose I don't. When you told me not to touch my . . . to touch my cunt in the hotel the other night I felt really uncomfortable.'

'I noticed. And yet I'm sure you understood why I chose that particular word?'

'Yes, I think so. You wanted me to understand that

you were in charge. If it was yours, then you could name it. Is that right?'

He nodded. 'Exactly right. When someone asked Casanova why penis is a feminine word in Italian he said, "Because the slave takes its name from its master." You're a creature of contradiction, aren't you? Scratch the surface and your absolutely wanton. You revel in the kinky, the taboo and yet a mere word makes you go all Mary Whitehouse.' Jim slid across the carpet and sat cross-legged at my feet.

'It wasn't the word per se, more the context. It's an intimate word, a title you give it in the privacy of your bedroom –' I shot Jim a look '– or your car. But if you say it over tea with the vicar it can only be calculated to shock.'

'I intended it to shock. You knew that. Whore, cock, cunt and the rest are animal, hungry words and they've got nothing to do with proper behaviour and politeness.' He leant forwards and cupped my calf in his hand, kneading the muscle with his thumb. 'I promise I won't say it in front of your mother, or the vicar if he happens to drop round, but when we're alone together ... You're my beautiful, desirable whore.'

When he said that word I felt a warm glow between my legs and my nipples prickled.

'I rather like the concept, actually. The idea that my only purpose in life is to satisfy you is rather appealing. Somehow it makes me feel irresistibly sexy and ... I don't know ... powerful.'

Jim smiled.

'I'll tell you what –' he lifted my foot and kissed the tip of my toes '– to add a little realism why don't I pay you for it? But, obviously, you've got a lot to learn so you're not worth a great deal. Just pocket change. How does that sound?'

'It sounds utterly degrading and incredibly exciting.'

Jim massaged my other calf, his fingers stroking and pressing gently into the knotted muscles. His palm was hot and soft against my skin.

'So what do you think, now you've dipped your toe into the murky waters of perversion? Do you want to take your towel and run home to mother?'

I shook my head slowly. My cheeks were burning with excitement. My crotch was tingling. Jim brought my foot to his mouth and he kissed each of my toes in turn.

The next morning, we slept late. Jim had opened the curtains before we went to sleep and the sun was spilling onto the bed when I woke. He was curled up behind me, his hand cupping the curve of my belly. He kissed my shoulder.

'Good morning, angel.' He brought his hand up and found a breast. He quickly located a nipple and began to squeeze it between thumb and forefinger. I let out a long sigh of pleasure. I could feel his hardening cock against my buttocks. His mouth explored my neck and the slope of my shoulder. I felt his tongue trailing along my skin, then his teeth as he began to nip me.

'What a lovely way to wake up.' I wiggled my hips, rubbing my bottom against his erection.

A phone began to ring down the hall but Jim didn't move. He lay pressed up against my back, fingering my nipple.

'I expect it'll stop in a minute.'

The phone rang for what seemed like ages, its shrill urgency a counterpoint to my own rapid breathing. Jim had turned me on my back and was mouthing my nipple. The phone stopped ringing. Within a few seconds Jim's mobile began to trill on the bedside table.

'I'm sorry, I ought to take that. It might be the office.' He picked up the phone and flipped it open. 'Yep. Oh no. Did you do what I told you? OK, OK. Hang on.' He covered the phone's mouthpiece with his hand. 'Sorry, I've got to take this. I won't be long.' He opened the door. As he walked out of the room I noticed that he still had an erection.

Jim was on the phone for twenty minutes. I could hear his voice from the study down the hall. Several times he'd sounded agitated and angry though I wasn't able to hear what he was saying. Finally he stopped talking and went into the room next door where, I now knew, he kept his clothes. I heard doors opening and closing and Jim moving around the room. The heaviness of his tread and the slamming doors told me that he was still annoyed. I got up and padded down the hall, still naked. I opened the door just wide enough to put my face through.

'Problem?'

Jim turned to me. He was standing in his boxers and socks, putting on a shirt.

'Yes. Sorry. I've got to go out for a couple of hours; it shouldn't take long. Just something I have to sort out.' He buttoned his cuffs.

'Business? Personal touch required again?'

'Exactly. I am really sorry. I'd planned brunch at the Tower Hotel before we drive back, but we probably won't have time now. Another time, I promise.' He slid his trousers on, then sat on the edge of the bed to put on his shoes.

'No problem. I'm sure I can amuse myself. I'll get some lunch ready for when you come back.' I went into the room and sat down on the other side of the bed.

'I don't think there's much to eat. I hadn't planned on having lunch here.'

'That's OK. I noticed there's a little row of shops in the main road. I'll get something there.'

Jim tied his shoes without looking at me. 'Good idea. Thanks.'

Though his words were friendly enough he seemed distracted and somehow hard. He stood up and put his wallet, phone and keys into his trouser pockets. He bent and opened a drawer beside the bed and took out something metallic and gleaming. As he slid it into his pocket I saw it was a knuckleduster.

'Is that what I think it is? I had no idea you meant that kind of personal touch.'

'It's nothing. Just insurance.' Jim came round the bed and embraced me. I turned my face up for a kiss. He wrapped his arms around me, pressing me against his chest. My naked breasts rubbed against the front of his shirt. He kissed me long and deep and hard; his body was taut and tense though his lips were soft and hungry. 'See you later.' He released me and headed for the door.

Standing in the open doorway he turned and blew me a kiss.

'Take care of yourself, Jim.'

'I'll be all right. It's the other bloke you need to worry about.'

When Jim returned a few hours later he refused to be drawn on what had happened. We ate a quick lunch of pâté and ciabatta then packed up and set off.

We were halfway to Oxford on the A40 when I began to notice that Jim seemed to be looking in the mirror more than usual. I took a look in the wing mirror but nothing behind us seemed out of the ordinary. But something was clearly bothering him. Though he kept up his half of the conversation, he seemed distracted and tense. He was sitting up straight in his seat gripping the wheel tightly. His eyes flicked to the rear-view mirror every few seconds.

'Is there a cop on our tail, or something?' I turned round in my seat to look.

'What makes you say that?' Though his voice was calm, it sounded slightly too loud, as if he were deliberately controlling himself.

'Because you keep looking behind us. Don't tell me you're not insured? Is your tax disc out of date?' I made a show of taking out the disc and looking at it.

'Of course not. I know it sounds stupid, but I'm convinced that silver Lexus is following us. It's been behind us ever since we left London.'

I looked behind us and immediately spotted the car. 'Well, they're probably going to Oxford too. Why would anyone be following us?'

'You're probably right. I'm just being silly.' He smiled at me but his body language didn't change. He was on alert.

My stomach lurched and a hot wave of terror crashed over me. 'Has this got anything to do with the knuckleduster?' I looked at the Lexus again. It was directly behind us, keeping pace. Its gleaming bodywork and darkened glass suddenly seemed sinister.

'Maybe . . . I hope not.'

I undid my seat belt and twisted round in my seat, eyes focused on the car behind us. Its occupants were shadows behind the darkened windscreen. My heart thumped in my chest. The car's indicator lights came on and I saw it peeling off and taking the exit we had just passed.

'They've gone.' I turned to the front and buckled my seat belt.

'False alarm. Sorry to have worried you.' He smiled. He was calm again, his muscles had lost their tension, his hands on the wheel were loose and relaxed

'Do you want to tell me what that was about?'

'No.' He kept his eyes on the road, refusing to look at me.

'No? You're the one who's always talking about trust – why can't you trust me?'

'I do. But there are some things you're better off not knowing.'

'And you expect me to be satisfied with that?'

He shrugged. 'It's probably nothing, anyway. I'm just being paranoid. Sorry if I frightened you.'

Back in Oxford Jim carried my bag into the hall and kissed me goodbye. After promising to call me the next day he dropped a handful of coins on the hall table and let himself out. The coins were mostly copper and a few five pences. I began to count them, sorting them into piles. Altogether there was 65 pence.

9

The next day I looked up the phone number of Eve Randall. We'd met at university and had mixed in the same crowd but had never really been close. Our friendship had deepened when we'd worked together briefly during my first lecturing job at Bristol where Eve had been assistant registrar. She'd taken over as registrar at Trinity a couple of years ago and we'd met a few times intending to rekindle our friendship but it had never really happened. I couldn't remember the last time we'd spent any real time together.

As I dialled her number my heart began to drum and I realised I was actually quite nervous.

'Eve, it's Claire. How are you?'

'Hello. Lovely to hear from you. How've you been? How's the family?'

'I'm fine, thanks. Bernie's had a baby, a little boy.'

'Lovely! She always said she wanted a big family, didn't she?'

'Actually, I think she's rather changed her mind. The agony of childbirth can do that to a person.'

Eve laughed. 'Oh, give her a few years, she'll change her mind. I'd love to chat but I'm on my way out. Did you want something in particular?'

'Yes, sorry, I won't keep you. When you're next in the office can you look someone up for me? Someone I know claims to have done an English degree at Trinity, but I'm not sure he's being straight with me.' I did my best to keep my tone light.

'Sure, of course. Let me get a pencil.'

'Jim Hyde. James William Hyde.' I felt like a quisling.

'And do you know the year?'

'Do you know I don't. He's forty if that helps.'

'Yes, that gives me something to go on.'

'While you're at it, can you check under the surname of Powney as well?'

'Sure. I'm on my way to the office at the moment, as it happens. I'll call you later.'

'Thanks, Eve and we must –'

'Yes, I know. We must get together soon. Got to go.'

As I hung up the phone it occurred to me for the first time that I honestly didn't know what I wanted Eve to find out. If she found him in the records it still didn't tell me if he was a bank robber or a mob boss. And if she didn't then all that meant was that he'd lied about having a degree. Or maybe not even that. He may have changed his name, or studied somewhere else and just told me he went to Trinity knowing it would impress me.

But my attempts to get the truth from Jim had proved fruitless and frustrating; this was the only fact I could actually check for myself. It might not provide a complete answer, but at least it would be a place to start. If Eve didn't find Jim's name on the roll of graduates at Trinity then I'd know that he'd told me one actual lie. Now at least I knew where I should start to look for the truth.

Jim and I arranged to meet a couple of days later for an outing to Canterbury. Jim was due to pick me up at nine o'clock and it was already unbearably hot and expected to get worse. I'd wound my hair into a French pleat, getting it off my neck in the hope of remaining cool. I chose the coolest outfit in my wardrobe: a fine cotton sundress printed all over in scarlet poppies with spaghetti straps and a flouncy skirt.

It was impossible to wear a bra – I'd never liked showing my straps even though it had grown fashionable – and, on a whim, I decided not to bother with knickers either. The old Claire would never have done it, but the old Claire was already beginning to seem like a stranger. With my crotch bare and pussy shaved, I'd never felt so exposed without actually being naked and the mere thought of Jim's reaction when he discovered my little secret hardened my nipples as though I'd just stepped into the freezer.

When Jim arrived I was surprised to see a gleaming new Jeep Grand Cherokee parked on my drive instead of his familiar Range Rover.

'New car?' I ran my finger along the paintwork.

'Yes.' Jim pressed the button on his key ring to open the door. 'I fancied a change. Do you like it?'

I thought he sounded a sheepish. Something didn't ring true.

'Has this got anything to do with you thinking we were being followed the other day? You've changed your car to throw them off the track?' I climbed into the car.

'Of course not. I saw it in the showroom as I drove past and it was love at first sight.' He started the car.

We sped along in the air-conditioned cocoon of the Jeep. The farmland we passed was parched; grass had turned to straw. Cows whisked their tails to keep the flies away.

'I thought we'd explore the cathedral first, then have some lunch.' Jim slowed for a roundabout.

'I'm looking forward to seeing it.'

'You've never been?'

'Never. It's a Protestant cathedral remember. I didn't set foot in a Proddie church until I was eighteen. As far as we're concerned, Protestants are practically devil worshippers.'

'If only the Church of England was that interesting. Canterbury was built by Catholics, remember – by the same masons who built Chartres, did you know?'

I nodded. 'Chartres, I have seen, several times. I think it's the stained glass I love most. When the sun shines it creates a sort of dancing pattern of light on the stone, like a kaleidoscope.'

'And those two spires, the older one simple and plain and the later one with all those curlicues and embellishments.'

'Yes, I always think of that one as the French tickler.'

'Were you tempted to sit on it?'

'Is that what they mean by having a cunt like a cathedral?'

Jim laughed. 'Yours might not be a cathedral – praise the Lord – but whenever I see it I'm overcome with a desire to worship it.'

'I thought I was supposed to worship you.'

'It works both ways. That's the beauty of it.'

We arrived in Canterbury around noon. As soon as we entered the city, the temperature visibly rose. Pedestrians wandered about listlessly, displaying acres of sunburnt flesh. We drove through the medieval city wall and joined the queue for the car park behind a red-faced man in a convertible who kept hooting his horn as if the cars ahead of him were holding him up out of spite.

We passed through the cathedral's ornate Christchurch Gate and paid our entrance fee. It was the first time I had ever seen Jim complain about money but I understood it was the charge itself and not the price that offended him. Inside the building it was cool and echoey. We wandered around reading inscriptions and looking at the tombs of the worthy. We found the spot where Becket was martyred, a simple altar beneath a rugged cross.

Sun streamed through the stained glass illuminating the creamy stone, just as I had seen at Chartres. Feet echoed against the flagstones; people spoke in whispers.

'It's quite lovely. You can understand why it filled medieval man with awe can't you? The sheer scale of it.' I looked up at the vaulted ceiling.

'Yes, and it must have been the tallest building for miles. Can you imagine it towering over the landscape, visible from all over Kent? And, of course, the stone was painted on the inside. It must have been spectacular.'

'Well, I think I prefer it as it is, sort of muted and mystical. It has an atmosphere, doesn't it? Even if you aren't a believer, you feel as though you should whisper.'

'I know what you mean. Let's go and look at the crypt, it's even more special.' He took my hand and led me silently to the stairs that lead beneath the cathedral.

The undercroft was lit mostly by candles. It was quiet and cool and the sound down there had a sort of watery edge to it. There were several chapels in the crypt all with different architecture. Jim read aloud from the guidebook as we wandered around.

'This is the chapel of Our Lady Undercroft. The screen was paid for by the Black Prince in return for a dispensation permitting him to marry his cousin. It's beautiful.'

'Licence to commit incest, as long as you've got enough money. The Church was corrupt in those days.'

'And now it isn't? What is it they say? A Catholic priest is a man everyone addresses as Father except for his children who are obliged to call him uncle. Plus ça change.'

'I suppose so.' We were alone in the crypt. Our echoing footsteps made us feel like trespassers. The flickering candlelight made the stone seem golden and warm.

'And this –' Jim walked over to a pillar, still reading '– must be the central column with the delightfully imaginative carving on the capital. I can't see any carving.'

'It's at the top, it's beautiful.' I pointed.

'Yes. It's lovely down here, isn't it? Tranquil. And it's wonderful having the place to ourselves.' Jim smiled at me. 'Come behind here. Put your hands on the pillar, that's it.'

'I don't think they allow flash photography inside the cathedral.'

He laughed. 'I wasn't planning to take your photo, I was planning to bugger you.' He said the word 'bugger' with exaggerated care, luxuriating in it. He stepped up behind me and flipped up my skirts. 'No knickers! When I saw you were wearing no bra I did hope, but then I thought it was just wishful thinking.' He kicked my feet apart and thrust his hand underneath me, cupping my mound. 'And it certainly is bare, isn't it? Did you do that for me, by the way? I've been meaning to ask.' His fingers worked my clit and I moaned.

'Yes I did. It was an impulse. I was shaving my legs and it seemed like a good idea – like Pablo did to Lulu.'

'Only Pablo got to do the job himself, lucky beggar.'

'Did you want to do it yourself?' My legs began to tremble as Jim fingered me. I leant with both hands against the pillar for support.

'Not necessarily. I'd certainly have made you shave at some point. You just saved me a job.' He slid two fingers deep inside me, making me gasp.

'I aim to please.' I sighed as his fingers rotated inside me.

'Hold your skirt up around your waist.'

I obeyed. Behind me I heard Jim fumbling in his pocket. He fiddled with something for a moment then I felt the unmistakable sensation of icy cold lube being rubbed into my arsehole. My nipples stiffened.

'Oh my God! You really mean to do it.'

'Taking the Lord's name in vain, Claire? How many Hail Marys will you have to say for that? Add sodomy to the list and you'll be on your knees for the next twenty years.' He slid in another finger.

The lube squelched obscenely as he fingered me. It seemed to echo around the silent chapel amplifying its crudity. I leant against the column with one hand, my other holding the bunched skirts of my dress out of the way. Jim's fingers slid easily inside me, making my pussy tingle.

I heard him unzip his trousers and a rustling as he adjusted his clothes. He stepped up behind me. Bracing himself on the pillar with his left hand, he used his right to position himself. I felt it pressing against me.

'God! I didn't think you were really going to do it.'

Jim leant against me and slid forwards. My nipples were stiff; they rubbed against the cotton of my bodice as I moved. Liquid ripples were sliding along my spine. My clit prickled with pleasure. He used his weight to slide home. He slid past my muscles, millimetre by delicious millimetre. I let out a long deep moan as he entered me.

He began to fuck me, sliding slowly in and out. He took his time, easing almost all the way out, then entering me again. With each new penetration, my arousal cranked up a notch. I was panting and gasping, the sound filling the holy space.

I was beginning to sweat, my bodice clammy against

my torso. Jim held onto my hips and fucked me agonisingly slowly as if there was no urgency about it at all, as if there was no risk of discovery.

'Shuffle forwards. You need a bit more support; I can't get a proper grip.' Jim helped me to straighten up and wrapped his arms around me, holding his cock in place. We waddled forwards together, co-ordinating our steps like Laurel and Hardy in a fat man's borrowed trousers. 'That's better. If you stand right up against the pillar I can fuck you as hard as I like without having to worry about knocking you over.'

He pulled down the straps of my dress, uncovering my breasts. His fingers found my nipples and he pinched them, then pulled and twisted them until I moaned.

I could feel his bunched trousers rubbing against the backs of my legs. His balls slapped against my naked pussy on every thrust. He was panting and grunting from exertion. His fingers worked my nipples and they burnt with delicious sensation – pleasure, pain, I couldn't tell them apart. I leant with my arms bent, my hands flat against the pillar.

My hair had begun to come loose, strands falling around my face. I was damp with sweat, my dress sticking to my body. Jim released my nipples and grabbed my hips. He thrust into me, long and hard and deep, jerking my body forwards. My breasts squashed up against the cold stone pillar.

The sound of our excited breathing resonated around the crypt. Candlelight flickered. Jim's hairy thighs were damp with sweat. Clothes rustled as he fucked my arse. He was pounding me now, holding onto my hips and pulling me onto him. His hands were clammy and damp and his fingers dug into me. On each thrust my chest was pressed up against the column, the cold rough stone rubbing painfully against my nipples.

I was on fire. Moisture flowed between my legs. I braced myself against the pillar. Hair fell in my eyes. I was tingling all over. Jim fucked me like a man possessed. The archbishop himself could have come down the crypt's stone steps in his cloak and mitre and Jim wouldn't have stopped fucking me. Being sodomised in this temple to religion seemed at once offensive and holy. A blasphemous sacrament to earthly desire.

Jim grunted and moaned behind me. His cock pistoned. I bashed against the pillar over and over again, my nipples raw and aching from the friction. He began to roar. The sound seemed to inhabit the crypt like a separate entity, an audible manifestation of his animal lust. He held onto me and gave several short thrusts – brutal stabs of the hips that sent me crashing against the pillar.

He was coming. He jabbed his hips, pumping out sperm inside me. My nipples were being grazed by the stone. My hair had escaped its combs and was falling around my shoulders. I could feel Jim's pubes scratching my buttocks as he ground himself into my arse; his balls slapped against my pussy. I could feel his legs trembling. His panting echoed around the crypt, throbbed inside my brain. He pressed himself up against my back, riding out his orgasm.

Behind me I heard the sound of feet on the stairs and the muted hubbub of voices. Jim must have heard it too, but he didn't move. He held onto me long after he'd come, his body flat against mine, his arms around me. His cock softened inside me and plopped out and I felt as though I'd been robbed.

The voices drew nearer but still he didn't move. His

breathing had almost returned to normal. I could feel it, warm and damp against my ear as he exhaled. Damp rumpled clothes, clung to me uncomfortably. His skin against mine was hot and slippery. My sore nipples gained some comfort from their contact with the cold stone.

We heard the voices go into the Black Prince's chantry, the chapel immediately behind us. Though safe in our alcove for the moment it could only be a minute or so before they'd move on.

Jim put his mouth next to my ear. 'You're definitely going to hell now.'

He released me and pulled up his trousers. I walked to the side of the chapel where I hoped I'd be out of the line of sight of anyone coming through the entrance and pulled up my bodice. I straightened my skirt. Jim came over to me and handed me my hair combs, having picked them up from where they'd fallen on the floor. He took my hand and led me towards the door just as a party of Japanese tourists appeared in the entrance.

We joined a guided tour, trailing round with a reverent group of camera-bedecked Americans. Several of them were sporting T-shirts announcing their membership of 'Our Lady Immaculate Catholic Church of Greenville, South Carolina'.

None of them were under seventy and most had skin the colour and texture of tortoises. One particularly wrinkled old woman was in an electric wheelchair, her trembling cadaverous hand operating the joystick. She was breathing oxygen via a discreet tube under her nose, the tank fitted to the back of the wheelchair in a brightly coloured bag which looked more like a fashion statement than a medical necessity.

The tour was led by one of the cathedral's elderly volunteers, though compared to the Greenville crowd she was barely out of nappies. She wore the uniform of the middle-class retired: clothes from Boden and expensively tinted hair intended, but failing, to conceal her age.

She was knowledgable about the building and its artefacts and unfailingly patient with the Americans. We listened to her explain the history of the cathedral, then describe the martyrdom of Thomas à Becket, news of which seemed never to have crossed the Atlantic.

Jim and I lurked at the back doing our best to ignore the 'oohs' and 'ahs' of our companions. My arse was throbbing and my nipples burnt. My crotch was wet and uncomfortable from a combination of arousal and the lube Jim had used. I desperately needed to visit the loo to clean myself up. But, more than anything, I wanted to come. I was walking around in a state of perpetual excitement, longing for an outlet but also, in some perverse self-masochistic way, never wanting it to end.

The tour moved on and we trailed along behind the group. I sneaked a look at Jim, not wanting to give him the satisfaction of knowing I was staring at him again. His eyes were on the tour guide and, though his clothes were immaculate, his face was still red and damp from exertion and a lock of hair had fallen forwards over his forehead.

Nobody would ever know, I thought, that a few moments ago the two of us had been engaged in depravity. No doubt our companions from the States just assumed that we were both pink and sweaty because of the heat of the day. If only they knew. I could just imagine the shocked, uncomprehending, repulsed looks on their wrinkled faces.

Like all Catholics – like me – they'd believe that sodomy was an automatic passport to hell. Lust alone earned that privilege anyway. And what they'd think if they knew we'd compounded our damnation by defiling the house of God, I could only imagine.

That was what I'd found most arousing, I realised, as I stood amongst these elderly faithful – Jim's breath in my ear as he held me and whispered that I'd be going to hell. Quite why the prospect of eternal damnation was so arousing I had no idea but, whatever the reason, I knew that given a choice between it and salvation I'd choose Hades every time.

We ate a lazy lunch with far too much wine. Afterwards, in the loo, I cleaned my damp rear end with toilet paper and washed my face then put my hair up again.

By four o'clock we were both tired and Jim had drunk too much wine to even contemplate driving so we booked ourselves into the Chaucer Hotel and ordered afternoon tea in our room. After a nap and a shower Jim announced he wanted to see the sea so we decided to drive to Whitstable for dinner.

We'd left the car in a multi-storey car park a short walk away. By now, the streets were mostly deserted; the tourists had vanished and the shoppers were long gone. The city's hotchpotch of ancient and modern looked absurd and odd without the people as if, somehow, the thronging masses had given it purpose and meaning. We came to a pub, with customers spilling outside and live music blaring out of its open windows. As we passed by, Jim grabbed me and we danced a few steps to a soaring trumpet rendition of 'Honeysuckle Rose' as customers pointed and cheered.

'I had no idea you were so light on your feet.' I was still breathless from our impromptu dance.

'I don't know if they still do it but when I was at Sandhurst they used to give us lessons.'

'Really? I'd always assumed they just taught you how to kill with your bare hands.'

'That too, but there's more to being an officer than leading the men into battle. There's a lot of politics too. If you can't lead the colonel's lady around the floor in a foxtrot without stepping on her corns you won't get very far.'

'I must say, when you told me you were in the army, I imagined you more as a grunt than an officer.'

'Why? Wrong class?' Jim shrugged. 'I joined after my degree. I wanted to see a bit of the world and I knew it would stand me in good stead whatever I decided to do afterwards. And I haven't done too badly.'

'I learn something new about you every day. I bet tomorrow you're going to tell me you used to be a woman.'

Jim laughed. 'No, all man, thank God. I love women, but I certainly wouldn't want to be one.'

'And I wouldn't want to be a man. Not most of the time anyway.'

'But there are exceptions? I'm intrigued.'

'Yes, when I'm caught short and there's no loo available. Do you know the only thing a man can do that a woman can't?' I paused. 'Pee standing up without wetting his shoes.'

'Actually, I understand you can, if you practise.'

'I've tried. My aim is lousy. Do you think that means I've got penis envy?'

'I don't know why anyone would envy a cock.' We'd reached the car park and Jim held the door to the stairwell open for me. 'It's got a mind of its own, it's got no conscience and it's far too vulnerable to injury. You're much better off with what you've got.'

We tramped up the stairs.

'Normally I'm perfectly happy with what God gave

me. But I must admit I am rather envious of yours today.'

'Why?'

'Because it got to come and I didn't. This is our floor.' Apart from the Jeep and another car beside it, the car park was empty.

'I see.' Jim followed me through the door. 'And you'd like to?' He pointed his keys at the car and pressed the button. The car beeped and its lights flashed.

'I assume that's a rhetorical question.'

We reached the car and Jim opened the door for me.

'You'd have made a terrible nun, you know. You aren't cut out for celibacy.'

'I won't argue with you there.'

He got into the driver's seat. 'Climb into the back. You should just be able to squeeze between the seats, be careful of the gear stick.'

I squeezed myself between the gap and Jim followed. He sat down at one end of the seat and gestured for me to lie down in the remaining space and spread my legs.

'Like this? There's not a lot of room.'

'Why don't you take your dress off first?' Jim sat back like a strip-club customer who'd paid his entrance fee and expected to be entertained.

As soon as he said it a hot wave of excitement crashed over me. I felt something pulling in my gut and, between my legs, heat burnt. I undressed, which wasn't easy in the cramped space, and hung my dress over the back of the driver's seat. I lay back, lifting one leg and resting it along the top of the backrest. I slid my other one between the front seats and rested my foot on the passenger side.

Jim looked down at my naked crotch and smiled. 'For what we are about to receive . . .'

He bent forwards at the waist and covered my pussy with his mouth. He used his fingers to spread my lips and tongued my clit. After a day of enforced celibacy, the sensation was heavenly. I let out a long satisfied sigh.

I looked down at Jim as he licked me. His eyes were closed, an expression of pure bliss on his face. The front of his hair had fallen down over his forehead, making him look boyish and innocent. Somehow the ambiguity of looking like a choirboy but having the heart and soul of a sinner seemed both moving and erotic.

He lapped at my clit, circling it with his tongue. My nipples were erect, standing out against my pale skin like raspberries. Little tremors of tingling pleasure spread out from my groin.

My skin was covered in goose pimples, every hair follicle erect and tingling with excitement. I could feel my pulse beating in my throat and temples. Blood pounded in my ears.

Jim sucked on my clit, flicking his tongue across its tip, making me moan. I reached down and stroked Jim's hair. His eyes snapped open; he looked up at me for a long moment then closed them again.

I began to rock my hips, establishing a rhythm which Jim matched. The sound of my excited breathing filled the car. Already the windows were beginning to steam over. My crotch was tingling.

Jim reached up with one hand and pinched a nipple. I gasped and arched my back. The other nipple received the same attention. My whole body was rigid with excitement. I gripped the edge of the seat and thrust my crotch up at him.

Heat throbbed in my groin. Liquid ripples of pleasure spread through me, making me tingle all over. He pulled on my nipples, pinching them until I moaned. His mouth slid against me, tongue flicking and darting. I ground my crotch against his face.

Sweat filmed my body. The seat underneath me was prickly and damp. Every pore was alive and prickling with pleasure, right up to the roots of my hair. Jim gave each of my nipples a final squeeze, pinching them until I began to gasp. He wrapped his arms around my thighs and pulled me onto his face.

My hips rocked rhythmically, rubbing my clit against his mouth. Every movement of his tongue and lips elicited an exquisite tingle of pleasure which spread through my body like lava.

My head was wedged uncomfortably up against the door. My legs ached from their unnatural position and the upholstery was scratching my skin, but I registered these facts merely as details, sensory input only.

Jim's hair had grown damp and dishevelled. His face was pink and glowing. I gripped the seat, tensing my muscles and using my arms for stability as I rode Jim's face. My nipples burnt. Sensation pumped around my body. A hot coil of tension and pleasure pulsed in my belly. I was bucking and writhing. Jim's fingers dug into me as he held on.

Hair stuck to my face. A strand clung to my lips. Jim sucked hard on my clit and I let out a high little sob of surprise and delight. He did it again, flicking the tip with his tongue, and the sob became a wail.

Tension was building in my groin, accelerating to a pitch. My thigh muscles were taut and straining. My nipples were tingling and tense. Jim's mouth slid against my pussy. He was concentrating on my clit now, teasing the little button with his tongue and lips, sucking on it.

My hips pistoned. I held onto the seat, digging in my

fingers to keep myself stable though my arms ached and my fingers had gone numb. I felt like a violin string, taut and vibrating with a note of exquisite pleasure which grew ever higher.

Jim was grunting and panting. Sweat poured down his face. His mouth moved constantly, sucking and teasing. The air inside the car was hot and moist. Excited animal sounds filled the small space.

The coil of pleasure in my belly focused to a point and I knew I was going to come. I thrashed against the seat, rubbing my crotch into Jim's face, all conscious thought gone. My nipples were burning with delicious pleasure. My clit danced in his mouth.

I was sobbing and wailing, high urgent notes of pleasure and relief. Jim sucked hard on my clit, drawing it right into his mouth and the dam burst. It knocked the breath out of me and made me gasp.

I was trembling all over. I ground my crotch against Jim's face, bottom raised off the seat. The sound of my keening filled the car. The flood kept coming, submerging me over and over again. I was drowning in pleasure. It went on and on, a second and third wave of climax, smaller than the first but still so intense they left me breathless.

Jim eyes watched my face as he rode out my climax. He held onto me as I squirmed and bucked. My foot slid of the seat back and my heel bashed against the window, making a loud bang. There was a gasp and a shuffle from outside and, for the first time, I noticed a woman looking into the car. A cold shiver of excitement slid along my spine. My nipples tingled.

Her mouth was open slightly and the expression on her face conveyed both shock and fascination. She was holding her car key in her hand, still raised as if she'd been just about to use it. The bump as I'd kicked the glass had startled her but she was clearly so involved she couldn't stop watching. Even through the streaky glass I could see two dark little spots of heat on her cheeks.

I spread my legs a little wider and thrust out my chest. I met her gaze. 'Jim. We've got an audience.'

He gave my pussy a final kiss and released me. He turned to look out of the window, wiping away the condensation with his shirtsleeve. The woman gasped and stepped back. She opened her own car, then, with her hand on the door, turned back and mouthed, 'Sorry.'

'If this keeps happening, perhaps we should consider charging an entrance fee.' Jim combed his hair with his fingers then took his handkerchief out of his pocket and wiped his face.

'She could have called the police.' I reached for my dress.

'But she didn't. You're obviously a bit of an exhibitionist on the quiet. We'll have to see what we can do about it.'

'You're scaring me now . . .'

10

We fell into a sort of pattern, seeing each other several times a week. We'd stay at my place and every few weeks we'd drive into London and spend a night or two at Jim's, but I never slept at The Feathers with him because I honestly don't think I'd have been able to have an orgasm with my sister under the same roof.

After we'd been out a few times I realised that he paid for everything in cash. He carried vast quantities of it in his wallet and always seemed to have enough to pay for everything, no matter how unexpected or costly. He once bought himself an expensive cashmere jacket on impulse, then a gold bracelet for me so I didn't feel left out, and still had enough left over to pay for a £100 lunch and a night in a luxury hotel.

Honest people just didn't carry that kind of money, none that I'd ever met anyway. He didn't seem to own a credit card or other plastic and I never saw him take cash out of a hole in the wall. I even began to look carefully at the notes as he handed them over to see if I could tell if the serial numbers ran in sequence as I understood the proceeds of bank robberies did; though I suppose if they did he'd have mixed them up anyway.

I felt stupid for even thinking it, but Jim's continued obfuscations and evasions only added to the problem. If he'd come out one way or the other and stopped being so damned mysterious I'd have felt able to let go. The more I asked, the less he told me and the more pleasure he took in leaving me in the dark.

I was getting ready to meet Jim for dinner one evening when the phone rang. I was in the middle of drying my hair so I dropped the hair dryer and ran to the phone before the machine kicked in.

'Claire, it's Jim.' There was a lot of noise in the background. I could hear garbled tannoy announcements, as if he was in a public place like a railway station.

'Hi. I'm just getting ready.'

'Ah ... that's why I'm calling. I'm going to have to cancel, I'm afraid.'

'Oh, OK. Well never mind, maybe we can do it tomorrow.'

'Not tomorrow. The fact is I've got to go away for a few days. It's business, boring corporate stuff, but I have to go. I should be back by the weekend.' It was hard to make out his voice against the background chaos.

'Where are you?'

'Heathrow. I'm catching a plane.'

I wasn't sure I'd heard him correctly. 'You're catching a plane? Where to?' I pressed the phone hard up against my ear, straining to hear.

'Brussels. We have a small office there.'

'OK. Well, look, why don't I come? You can do what you need to do and then the two of us can have a couple of days together. I love Brussels. What time's the plane? I can be at Heathrow in an hour.'

'I'm sorry, darling, but it won't work. I'm taking off almost immediately. And I'm going to be working solidly. We won't be able to spend any time together at all and you'd just get bored. But next time ...'

'All right. See you at the weekend. I'll miss you.'

'I'll be back before you know it.'

The following Saturday Jim turned up at my house

with the biggest box of Belgian chocolates I had ever seen and a carrier bag full of Continental cheeses. He stacked them neatly in the fridge while I made coffee.

'So how was Brussels?' I tore the cellophane off the chocolates.

'You know how it is – an anonymous hotel room that could be in any city in the world, wall-to-wall meetings, all very uninspiring. I barely had time to eat, let alone see any of the city.'

'Well, you obviously had time to go to the shops for my lovely pressies.' I offered him the box of chocolates. He shook his head. I selected one and popped it into my mouth.

'I'm afraid I sent a minion out for those. Not quite so personal as choosing them myself, I know. But at least it proves I was thinking about you.'

'And I'm very grateful, they're delicious.' The kettle boiled and I poured hot water into the cafetière. 'I thought you were meant to be on sabbatical.'

'I am ... Perhaps I will have a chocolate.' Jim bent over the box, apparently engrossed.

'It must be an important meeting then. If you needed to go even when you're not officially working.'

'It was.' He picked up a chocolate and bit it in half. 'Someone we've wanted as a client for a long time finally asked for a meeting. I had to go.'

'I see ... the personal touch again. Did you pack your knuckleduster?' I pressed down the plunger on the cafetière, deliberately not looking at him.

'No, I didn't. Why the Spanish Inquisition?'

'I'm just curious. Is it true the chambermaid has to make an appointment to clean your room?'

'Who told you that?' He selected another chocolate.

'Who do you think? Bernie.'

'So you've been talking about me?'

'She's my sister and you're my boyfriend. Of course we've talked about you. So is it true?'

He shrugged. 'So what? What does it prove? It's my home from home. I value my privacy and there's a lot of valuable stuff in there. I don't like them messing up my things.'

'It's a bit unusual, isn't it?' I poured the coffee.

'Perhaps, but not necessarily sinister.'

'Not necessarily.'

'But you think it is?'

'I don't know what I think to be honest. But I know you're hiding something.'

'Maybe. But we all have our secrets, don't we? I didn't know until five minutes ago that you'd discussed me with Bernie, for example.' Jim took my hand and kissed the palm. I felt my belly soften and my nipples tingle. 'Sometimes, darling, you let your imagination run away with itself. Come on, let's drink our coffee before it gets cold.'

One Sunday I took Jim to Colin and Bernie's flat for Sunday lunch. Oliver and he fell in love at first sight and, as she watched Jim bounce him on his knee and teach him how to stick out his tongue, I thought my sister was equally smitten.

Jim proved extremely knowledgable about the hotel trade and spent ages talking shop with Colin while Bernie and I put Ollie down for his nap. At the end of the afternoon Jim went down to start the car while I said a last goodbye. I kissed my sister on the cheek and began to walk down the stairs.

'Claire.' I turned to look at her. She was standing in the doorway, one hand on the handle. 'I know Jim's charming and generous, but you will be careful, won't you?'

'Careful? What do you mean?'

'I've been watching him. He's unpredictable, moody: one minute nice as pie, the next he's angry and he's always talking into that mobile phone. He's not being straight with you, I'm sure he's hiding something.'

'You promised you wouldn't do this again. I'm happy, can't you see that?'

'Yes, I can. That's why I'm worried. You're in over your head.' She gazed at me, her eyes pleading. I looked away. 'I probably shouldn't have said anything. It's just that – when you think about it – what do you really know about him?'

'I know everything that I need to.' I trotted down the stairs to join Jim.

Those first weeks of discovery seemed to pass like a dream. If I'd ever felt happier with a man, more intrinsically myself, I honestly couldn't remember it.

My last serious relationship had been with a PhD in medieval literature and the cerebral side had been fantastic but the physical had been as dry and dusty as the manuscripts he was so fond of. The best sex I'd had before Jim was with a financial advisor who'd helped me to arrange my mortgage. Between the sheets he'd been filthy, wild and generous but out of it we simply had nothing to talk about.

Finding both those qualities in Jim was profoundly self-affirming and so exciting I felt as though I was drunk most of the time. Everything seemed half unreal and impossibly perfect, no matter what Bernie thought.

She was right, of course – he was secretive and moody and that was only the half of it. But I couldn't have walked away from him even if I'd wanted to.

A week later I was getting ready to meet Jim when the phone rang.

'I bet you thought I'd forgotten.'

'Hi, Eve. How are you?'

'Fine, thanks, but I've been busy and your little enquiry took me longer than I expected.'

'What did you find out?' There was a slight but unmistakable quaver in my voice and I prayed Eve hadn't noticed.

'Well, he didn't graduate from Trinity, not in English or any other subject. I checked all our records from nineteen-eighty-eight onwards. That's the earliest some-one of his age would normally have graduated. When I didn't find him I went back to nineteen-eighty-five, in case he was one of those prodigies who came up at fifteen and still no luck. So I widened my search to include all the Oxford colleges.'

'Can you do that? I didn't realise.'

'It's a matter of public record, you just have to know where to look. Anyway, the upshot is that no one called James Hyde graduated from any college in Oxford.

'And you checked under Powney too?' My heart was thumping in my chest.

'I did. Same thing. I don't know if that's the answer you're hoping for.'

'Interesting. So he lied to me. Thanks a lot.'

'It all sounds a bit cloak and dagger to me. I'm desperately curious to know the full story.'

'You and me both. I promise to fill you in as soon as I get to the bottom of it.'

We made a lunch date for a few weeks time and I hung up. A hard little knot of tension had settled under my ribs. I felt shivery and weak. So he'd lied to me. And a concrete, direct lie this time. But I still didn't have any concrete answers. Maybe he really was called Hyde but he'd failed his degree or done it elsewhere. And, even if he'd lied about his name, what did that prove? There was far more to Jim's 'secret' than an assumed name.

The next weekend at Jim's house I woke up in the middle of the night to find him gone. I guessed he was in the loo so, as I needed a pee myself, I went off down the hall to the main bathroom, assuming he was using the en suite.

As I passed his study, I saw the door ajar and light spilling into the hall. I was just about to push the door open and say hi when I spotted Jim on his knees with his upper body squeezed uncomfortably under the desk. The absurdity of the position stopped me in my tracks.

Had he dropped something? Or was he trying to plug something into the electrical socket? Then I realised that he was opening a small door to what looked like a cupboard. No, not a cupboard, a safe. The door was thick metal and there was a dial on the front. In the safe, which was about as big as a medium-sized fridge, there were stacks and stacks of paper money. More money than I'd ever seen in one place before.

The piles were uniform, the notes all the same size. Jim picked up a stack about as big as a house brick and I could see they were all purple. Twenty-pound notes. My heart was beating so hard I was worried Jim would be able to hear it. I stood there for several long moments as he counted out money. He shut the safe and it slammed into place with a soft thud. I crept away down the hall and got back in bed.

In the morning Jim woke me with a kiss. 'Come into the bathroom, darling. I need a pee.'

'What do you need me for? Do you want me to hold it for you? I love doing that; the first time I did it I was really surprised how hard it was to control. It feels like you're trying to aim a writhing python.'

'Nobody's ever compared my old man to a python before. Come on.'

I got out of bed and padded after him into the bathroom. Jim sat me on the edge of the bath then lifted the toilet seat. He held his cock in his hand, legs spread in the universal stance of a man about to relieve himself. I watched as he began to pee. The hot liquid tinkled noisily into the water. I could smell the familiar ammonia tang.

I drank in every detail. The arc of the stream, the way that the individual droplets glinted in the overhead light, the way he held it – squashed it almost – between thumb and forefinger as he aimed. The hairs on the back of my neck were erect and tingling. Tension pulled at the base of my belly.

When Jim had finished he shook off the drips and turned to face me. He was stroking himself slowly. 'Why don't you kneel down?' His voice was a throaty whisper.

A wave of heat flashed through me as I realised what he had in mind. I slid onto my knees. My nipples were hard and there was a hot tight feeling between my legs. Neither of us spoke. I looked up into his face. I opened my mouth and tilted back my head like a believer waiting for the Communion wafer.

My bottom lip was only a couple of inches away from him. He was fully erect. He held it at the base, pulling back his foreskin to expose the purple tip. He took a step forwards and slid it into my waiting mouth. I felt the tip of Jim's cock sliding past my lips. I closed my mouth and ran my tongue around the helmet, then dabbled it into the eye.

My heart was pounding. I was trembling all over. He let out a deep moan. He put his hands on my head and began to thrust slowly in and out of my mouth. My crotch was on fire. My skin tingled.

I held onto his thighs and matched my movements to his. I could smell his musky pubes as he thrust into my mouth, feel them scratching my face. Moisture welled between my legs. I felt dizzy and weak.

He was hot and hard in my mouth. He was grunting and panting. I could feel his thigh muscles taut and tense beneath my hands. He banged up against my face on every thrust. My nipples were tingling and stiff. My crotch ached.

With my nose pressed up against his pubes, my breathing sounded snuffly and loud. My mouth made obscene slurping noises as he plunged into me. I reached between his legs and began to stroke his balls, eliciting a soft little moan of pleasure. I fondled them inside their sac, gradually increasing the pressure until I was pulling gently on them.

Jim's thigh muscles began to tremble and his thrusting picked up speed. Sweat filmed my skin. My crotch was tingling and hot. My nipples prickled.

My other hand slid automatically between my legs. My fingers found the groove between my lips. I brushed the tips along the length, dabbling them in the slippery moisture. I stroked my swollen clit and my body gave an involuntary shudder. Icy fingers seemed to slide up my nape and into my hair.

I clamped my hand between my thighs, cupping my mound. My middle finger stroked my aching clit, circling it, establishing a rhythm. I was sweating and breathless. Damp hair clung to my forehead. My nipples burnt with pleasure.

I slid my other hand behind his scrotum and found his arsehole. I ran a fingertip around the edge of the puckered opening. I pressed my sweat-lubricated finger against his hole, exerting firm pressure until it slipped inside. He was warm and tight. His muscles gripped my finger, inviting me in. His body juddered and shook. He let out a long sibilant hiss of pleasure between clenched teeth.

My expert finger worked my clit. My head bobbed. He was hot and hard in my mouth. Pumping muscles and engorged blood. My chest heaved. Tension and heat pulled at the base of my belly. I was quivering all over.

My mouth moved rhythmically. He was riding the edge now, breathing hard and thrusting his hips. He gasped as my finger slid inside him. He watched my face as I sucked him. I was making little noises, groaning and slurping. Waves of pleasure slid along my spine.

'Do you like that?' His voice was practically a whisper. I gazed up at him. His eyes were glowing and intense. His wet lips were dark and plump. My clit was tingling and tense. Blood pounded in my ears. I was rigid with excitement.

Jim's strokes grew shorter and more frenzied. My finger teased his prostate. His hips bucked. His thigh muscles were taut and straining. His fingers grabbed my hair. He was panting and gasping. I pushed my fingertip hard into his prostate.

I worked my clit. My hips rocked, grinding my crotch against my fingers. I was breathless and damp with sweat. My hair fell in my eyes. Heat and excitement pumped around my body. Pressure built. My nipples were swollen and sensitive.

I felt his muscles pulse around my fingers and his body began to quiver. He moaned loudly and he began to throb in my mouth. Sperm pumped onto my tongue. Jim gave a short guttural grunt of pleasure and relief with every volley of come. My crotch burnt with pleasure and excitement.

The pressure at my centre exploded, flooding me with pleasure and release. I was making muffled little mewl-ing noises. I was quivering all over, muscles taut and trembling. My nipples tingled.

I swallowed it all, relishing the salty richness of it. He panted above me, body still trembling. His muscles gripped my finger drawing it inwards. I held on tight, keeping my mouth clamped over his pumping cock. Pleasure surged through me. I was covered in goose pimples. Shivers of excitement prickled my scalp.

He watched me. His cheeks were pink and flushed. He grunted and gave one last thrust, pushing deep into my mouth. I kept sucking, lapping up the last trickles.

Orgasm kept on coming, wave after wave. My skin was alive and sensitive. The hairs on the back of my neck were erect and tingling. My back arched; my body shook.

I licked him clean, not stopping until his cock began to soften in my mouth and I felt his muscles relax and his breathing slow. I gave his shrinking member a final kiss. He pushed my hair out of my face and bent to kiss me.

The next day we slept late. As there was no food in the house, we decided to eat lunch at Nando's in Camden Lock before travelling back to Oxford. We were leaving the restaurant hand in hand when Jim suddenly stopped. He dropped my hand and seemed to stop in his tracks. His face had gone white as if all the blood had drained from it. He seemed to be staring at something. I looked up and down the road, but couldn't see anything out of the ordinary.

'You look as if you've seen a ghost.'

The sound of my voice seemed to galvanise Jim into action. He grabbed my hand and pulled me back into the restaurant. He went straight over to the nearest waiter.

'I realise this sounds melodramatic, but is there a back way out of here.'

The waiter looked confused. 'I'm sorry, sir, customers aren't permitted in the kitchen. It's against our health and safety policy.'

'I appreciate that.' Jim slid his hand into his trouser pocket and pulled out several twenty-pound notes. The waiter's eyes widened. 'You see, I've just spotted someone outside who I really don't want to bump into.' He lowered his voice and leant in confidentially. 'It's my wife, as a matter of fact.' He shrugged as if in apology. 'You know how it is. I'd be ever so grateful if you could help me.' He held the notes between two fingers, inviting the waiter to take them.

The man hesitated. His nostrils seemed to twitch, as if he could smell the money. He stared at it for a long moment then looked at Jim and then at me. His eyes travelled up and down my body and he began to smile.

'I understand your problem, sir.' He snatched the money and pocketed it with the speed of a lizard swallowing a fly. 'Follow me.' He led us through the restaurant and into the steamy kitchen. It was full of gleaming stainless steel and white-jacketed chefs running around as if they were on speed. They didn't even look up as we filed through. We went down a long corridor, picking our way between drums of cooking oil and boxes of provisions. The waiter opened a door which led onto a loading area and car park. He held the door open for us. 'Do you know your way back to the main road?'

'Yes, I think so. Thanks.' Jim brought out several more twenty-pound notes. 'You never saw us. OK?'

'I never saw a thing.' He trousered the money.

'It's really important. My wife's got a really huge brother who'd just love to break my nose.'

'You can rely on me, sir.'

'Good man.'

The waiter went back inside and closed the door.

'What was that about?' I was struggling to keep up with Jim as he dashed across the car park.

'Nothing. Just someone I don't want to bump into.'

I pulled at his sleeve, stopping him. 'I gathered that. Who is it? Are you sure you're not really married?'

Jim chuckled, but the laugh sounded unconvincing and forced. 'I think I'd remember.'

'Well, what then? Who are you hiding from?'

'I'm not hiding from anyone.'

'Then why are you in such a hurry?'

'Believe me, you'd be in a hurry too, if you knew him. He's the most boring man alive. It's just someone I used to know in the army. Last time I bumped into him he bent my ear for half an hour about the best route between Stevenage and Penge. I practically died from the tedium.'

'But you went as white as a sheet. You looked terrified. And you must have given that waiter at least a hundred quid. It doesn't make sense.'

'I was terrified of being bored. The man should carry a government health warning. You ought to thank me. I've saved you from a fate worse than death. Come on.' He took my hand.

A couple of days later Jim called for me at home out of the blue. I opened the door and broke into a huge smile as I realised it was him. 'You're a lovely surprise.'

He stepped inside and kissed me. Even though it was just a peck I felt my nipples stiffen and my crotch grow hot and tight.

'I hope I'm not disturbing you.'

'No, I was just about to make something to eat. Do you want some?'

'Then I arrived just in time. There's somewhere I want to take you. We can eat on the way.'

'I'll get my bag.'

Jim drove to a pub near Abingdon called the Green Man. It was a parody of an English country inn: black beams and horse brasses hanging from rough plastered walls stained dark from nicotine. There were even the obligatory craggy-faced locals standing at the bar chugging on foul-smelling pipes and chatting noisily in the Oxfordshire dialect nobody under seventy spoke any more. Yet the place somehow managed to lack any ambience or cosiness, in spite of its carefully contrived décor.

The lighting was harsh and speakers pumped out pop music so loudly you had to shout to be heard. At one end of the bar was a row of fruit machines which beeped and flickered and clattered out coins every few minutes. And the walls were hung with handwritten notices about five-a-side fixtures and the darts league.

We went through to the lounge bar, which had the advantage of being fruit-machine free and didn't smell of pipe smoke, but it was no less noisy.

'I'm sorry about the lack of authentic atmosphere. I've never been here before but *The Good Pub Guide* says it has great food and it's handy for where we're going.' Jim sat down on the bench beside me.

'You weren't to know. I still don't know where you're taking me.'

'That's right, you don't. What'll it be? Glass of red? I'll bring the menu back with me. Won't be a tick.' He got up and went to the bar.

The meal turned out to be excellent, simple but home cooked. I had calves liver and mashed potatoes and Jim chose steak and oyster pie.

'*The Good Pub Guide* was right about the grub, at least.'

'Yes, but it is a shame about the music, isn't it? Far too loud and I think I'm getting to that age when pop music all sounds the same. I'm beginning to sound like my dad.'

Jim laid down his fork. 'There's a fabulous Baudelaire quote about music, let me see if I can remember it ... ah, yes ... "I love Wagner, but the music I prefer is that of a cat hung up by its tail outside a window and trying to stick to the glass with its claws." Do you know Baudelaire?'

'No, I don't think I do.'

'You should read him. He wrote dark, dark poetry and he was prosecuted for obscenity and blasphemy, which certainly endears him to me. He wrote about the impulse in man to seek God – even those of us without religious beliefs. I can relate to that.'

'He sounds fascinating. I'll have to look him up.'

'He was a very clever man. Intellectual and philosophical yet still had his feet on the ground. He consumed life, lived it absolutely to the full which is probably why he ended up dying from the pox.'

'Do you have a favourite quote?' I sipped my wine.

'Let me think, it's hard to choose. Perhaps "For the merchant, even honesty is a financial speculation." Do you like that?'

'Yes. Very telling.'

Jim smiled and shrugged in mock apology. 'Eat up. We need to get moving.'

Back in the car, we drove through Abingdon. I recognised the soaring stone spire of St Helen's Church and the bridge where the River Ock meets the Thames and I realised we were heading towards the river.

'Are you taking me punting?'

'Not exactly. We're going to a car park near Culham Lock.'

'A car park? Sounds exciting. I should have dressed up.'

Jim laughed. 'It's more a sort of come as you are sort of thing. The emphasis being on come.'

'Now I'm completely confused.'

'Have you heard of dogging?'

'Yes, those places where you go to have sex while other people watch?' My voice came out high and squeaky and I felt instantly foolish.

'Not just to watch. There's a whole complicated code: light off means you want privacy; light on means please watch; windows closed means look don't touch; windows open means join in. That sort of thing.' Jim kept glancing over at me trying to gauge my reaction.

'You seem to know all about it.' My face was tingling and I knew that my cheeks were flushed pink.

'Not really. I looked it up on the internet.'

'They have their own websites?'

'Dozens of them. You should take a look, it's fascinating. I think this is it.'

It was quite dark by now. A dozen or more vehicles were parked, most with the lights on. Most of the cars had at least one watcher. I could see at least four separate sets of legs poking out of one vehicle. The car was rocking and, even from a distance, we could hear the sound of a woman having a thunderous orgasm.

My nipples were painfully sensitive. Every movement of the car rubbed them against the fabric of my T-shirt, making me tingle. There was a hot glow of excitement and arousal at the base of my belly. My crotch felt watery and warm.

Jim parked in the corner and turned on the overhead light.

'Climb in the back. You should be getting quite good at it by now.'

I clambered between the seats into the back of the car. My heart was thumping. My mouth had gone dry and my breathing had grown shallow.

'What now? I hope you're not going to leave the windows down.'

Jim got into the back of the car and put the windows up. 'Don't fret. I'm far too possessive to want anyone else to touch you. We're here to explore your exhibitionism.' He leant forwards and pressed the automatic catch on the driver's side, locking all the doors.

I looked at Jim. His eyes were shining with excitement and intensity. His lips were dark and puffy. He was breathing loudly between parted lips. I could see his chest rising and falling.

My heart was pounding. I could hardly breathe. I could hear the blood pumping in my ears. I looked straight at Jim and began to undress with clumsy fingers, pulling my T-shirt over my head.

'Are you getting naked too?' I unzipped my skirt.

'I don't suppose they're interested in me. But in the spirit of equality, why not?' Jim began to unbutton his shirt.

I threw my skirt and T-shirt on the front seat. I hadn't bothered with underwear since our first outing together. I sat there, naked, watching Jim undress. Already the prickly upholstery had begun to irritate my skin. Jim was half hard and the sight of him naked in such inappropriate surroundings was arousing and perverse.

My nipples were hard and dark and my pussy was tingling. The air conditioning had gone off when Jim had switched off the engine and it had already grown warm in the car.

'Lie down.' His voice was urgent and breathy.

I slid onto my back along the seat and rested one leg along the back of the headrest. I put my other foot on top of the driver's seat. Jim reached out and stroked my pussy with a fingertip. I shivered all over.

'You've given me a raging hard-on. Can you see?' Jim handled his cock, exposing the swollen purple helmet. 'And we've already got an audience.' He nodded towards the window behind him where I could see two white faces pressed up against the glass.

'Why don't we give them something exciting to look at, then?' I could hardly believe my own boldness.

'Make yourself come. I think they'd like that.'

A hot rush of excitement flashed over me like a slap in the face. I lowered my hands to my crotch and pulled my lips apart, stretching myself wide for their eager gaze. I hoped they could see the moisture shining in the light and I imagined them looking at my swollen tense clit.

Jim slid a finger along my moist pussy and I gasped. He slowly pushed two fingers inside me, turning his hand upwards to locate my G-spot. He pressed hard on it with the tips of his curled fingers and I almost came. I let out a high cry of alarm and arousal and my whole body shuddered.

He slipped his fingers out and held them up for our audience to see. They were shiny, even in the dim light of the overhead lamp. He brought them to my lips and I sucked them clean, never taking my eyes off his face. My crotch was tingling and congested. My nipples burnt.

I held myself open and circled my clit with my index finger. I rested my left foot against the driver's headrest, tensing my leg and lifting my bottom slightly off the seat. I stroked my sweet spot.

My body seemed to be vibrating with sensation – extreme, intense and powerfully erotic. Jim's eyes never left me. He stroked his cock lazily. Behind him, I could see other eyes watching me. The steamy window distorted their faces, making them seem ghostly and indistinct. But the expression in their eyes was unmistakable: pure naked lust. I felt absolutely wanton. Waves of endorphin flooded over me, making me feel dizzy and weak.

Heat and excitement pumped around my blood, enlivening every pore and particle with arousal. I could see my chest rising and falling as I breathed and the sound of it seemed to fill the car. My pussy felt tingly and moist.

Condensation trickled down the windows. I imagined the men outside watching me, noticing every tiny movement and gasp. I pictured them, cocks in hand, pressed up against each other in eagerness to see. Did they have a good view or was the glass too steamy? Could they see the pooled moisture at my opening? Could they see how my crotch had swollen and darkened with arousal? And could they see the little twitch my clit gave every so often?

I was rocking my hips, creating a rhythm. My foot was pressed against the headrest, my leg rigid. My thigh muscles had begun to quiver. My breasts were an inferno of sensation, throbbing, aching and tingling. My finger moved frantically. I was riding the razor's edge, on the brink of orgasm.

I became aware of sounds from outside the car: grunting, groaning and excited breathing. They were wound up with excitement, ready to burst, and all because of me. It was my body that was turning them on, my sexuality that was driving them wild. More than anything, I wanted to come for them. I worked my clit, thighs taut and trembling, hips rocking.

I was panting and trembling. My nipples were hard and sensitive. My fingers moved constantly. My thigh muscles quivered, utterly beyond control. A ball of pleasure and tension had settled in my pelvis and little electric shocks of delight spread through me like lightning.

I circled the swollen bead of my clit. My back was damp against the seat. I could hear Jim's excited breathing as he watched me.

I was on the edge. Blood pounded in my ears. Heat throbbed in my groin. I rocked my hips, rubbing myself against my fingers. My legs thrashed and my body trembled. I was breathing hard. My heart beat like a drum. Every nerve ending, pore and sinew was alive and working overtime. Pleasure seeped through my veins.

Adrenaline and endorphins gushed around my bloodstream, providing a rush as intense and intoxicating as any narcotic. The sensation was so intense and overpowering that I felt overwhelmed, almost afraid of it though I never wanted it to stop.

My orgasm erupted like a volcano. I was screaming. The car rocked. The tingling in my breasts focused into tingling, electric jolts of pleasure. My whole body was trembling. I was covered in sweat. And they were watching me, looking on, cocks in hand, as I made myself come for them. Were they shooting their spunk as my body shook and juddered? Were their eyes on my engorged crotch? I howled and panted, riding it out.

My bottom was raised off the seat, hips rocking obscenely. Pleasure pumped around my body. My fingers ached from holding myself open, and I had cramp in my thigh. My finger circled my clit, coaxing out every last shred of pleasure.

The screaming stopped and my breathing slowed. I bent my knee and massaged away the cramp with both hands. Jim gripped my thighs and pulled me round until my bottom was at the edge of my seat. He put my legs over his shoulders and slid his cock home in one short thrust. My body juddered with pleasure and I moaned.

He wrapped his arms around my legs and began to thrust. The seat underneath my back was rough and prickly. My head banged against the backrest on each stroke. He gazed down at me. His mouth was on the edge of a smile. His hair was damp and drooping over his forehead. His chest was slick against the back of my thighs.

Outside, the watchers were a constant presence, more than I could count now, surrounding the car. I could feel their eyes moving over my body like ghostly caresses. I felt alive, sexy, powerful. My crotch was tingling.

I gripped the edge of the seat with both hands, bracing myself against his thrusts. The sound of Jim's urgent breathing mingled with the grunts and heavy breathing from outside.

My breasts were burning, my crotch liquid. Jim was rigid inside me. He began to moan. He was breathing through clenched teeth, lips drawn back. He was thick and hard and he fitted inside me as if he was meant to be there. I rocked my hips, rubbing my clit deliciously against his scratchy pubes.

I looked up at him. His hair was dishevelled and damp. Sweat gleamed on his face. His neck and upper chest were blotched and red. His nipples stood out hard and dark, he was breathing through his open mouth. His lips were rosy and plump and the expression in his eyes was intense and passionate.

He reached down and stroked both my breasts. His thumbs found my nipples and brushed across their swollen tips, making me gasp. I laid my hands over his, holding them in place. His hips were pumping rhythmically. He moved inside me, slow and deep. On each stroke my clit rubbed against his pubic bone, his wiry hairs providing friction.

I could feel eyes on my body, burning into my skin. I tightened and relaxed my thigh muscles as Jim slid up and down inside me. I sighed as he moved, relishing the sensation of his hardness sliding past the ring of contracted muscles. When he hit my bottom I gave a little forwards movement of my hips to rub myself against his pubes.

I was getting close again and I knew Jim was too. He was panting hard, his chest rising and falling visibly as he moved. The red stain on his neck had spread and converged, covering his throat with a veil of scarlet. His nipples were erect and taut, a tiny circle of dark pinpricks standing out around their perimeter. His eyes were half closed and he looked at me through slitted lids.

Pale indistinct faces gazed in at us through the steamy windows. Cold shivers shot up and down my spine. The hair on the back of my neck was standing on end. Inside me, he was as hard as steel and as hot as a furnace. Jim fingered my nipples, making them tingle. I ground my crotch against his, providing the rhythm and friction I needed to come.

My orgasm took me by surprise, beginning with a sudden little clutch in the belly then bursting in my groin like a bomb. I rubbed myself against him, riding out wave after wave of shivery, tingly pleasure. I was moaning and gasping. I leant forwards, supporting my weight on my hands as I ground my crotch against his.

His strokes grew shorter. My feet banged up against his ears, my head bashed the seat. Jim gave one deep stab of his hips. He ground his crotch against mine. His head was bent back and he howled at the roof of the car. He pumped out sperm inside me, holding onto my thighs.

The watchers began to disperse when they realised the show was over, moving on, no doubt, to the next exhibition. I dressed with trembling hands and climbed into the passenger seat beside Jim.

We didn't talk much on the way home; Jim seemed content to drive in silence. He smiled over at me from time to time and I was far too sated and exhausted for conversation. He pulled up the car outside my house. He stopped the engine and turned to me.

'I hope you know how much I care for you.' He cupped my face and kissed me.

'I think I do.'

I opened the door to get out but he caught my arm, holding me back.

'There's one more thing I want you to do before you go in.' He got out of the car and I followed. He opened the boot and took out a yellow duster and a bottle of spray cleaner. He held them out to me, smiling.

Hot blood rushed to my face. I took the cleaner and cloth silently. Jim got back into the car. He'd parked under a streetlamp so it was fairly easy to see the streaks of sperm on the paintwork. Some of it had dribbled down onto the bumper, some had splashed onto the windows and roof.

My nipples tingled. I could still feel Jim's cock inside me. I sprayed the cleaner onto the patches of semen and polished the bodywork clean with the duster. I was thoroughly ashamed and utterly excited. I felt as though it was me who had soiled the car's pristine paintwork.

Not personally, of course, but I was in no doubt that my depravity had been the cause. Cleaning the car seemed only fair, a right and fitting punishment for my sin and my shame.

I don't know how long it took me but when I was finished my arm was aching and I was out of breath. I opened the boot myself to put the cleaner away then walked round to the driver's side to say goodbye to Jim. He pressed the button to lower the window. He handed me my handbag.

'Thank you. I'll call you tomorrow.' He began to raise the window then stopped halfway. 'I almost forgot to pay you.' He took a few coins out of his pocket and handed them to me. The window slid up and he drove away. Inside the house I counted out the coins. There was £2.50.

11

Jim invited me on a short camping holiday to Europe. When he said 'camping' I'd pictured a tent and a backpack, but it turned out he'd borrowed a camper van – a huge American Winnebago, more luxuriously appointed than most five-star hotels so we'd hardly be roughing it.

The van, borrowed from 'a friend', somehow unsettled me. In our first intoxicating weeks together, I was greedy for his company and barely even noticed that we never socialised. I wouldn't have wanted to share him anyway. But, gradually, I'd begun to feel as if he was deliberately compartmentalising, keeping our relationship separate from the rest of his world.

Men often did this, I knew – arranging their lives and their feelings into separate areas like provinces in a kingdom, all of them making up the whole but each having a distinct identity and set of rules. It was, I'd always thought, a way of organising things, of giving them the illusion of control and mastery over their fates.

But Jim's motives seemed to me a little different. The provinces in his kingdom had high walls around them and armed soldiers guarding the gates. And I'd begun to feel like a princess in a tower, cut off, isolated and powerless.

The loan of the van seemed to imply he had current live friendships and an entire other life I was not privy to. When I asked who owned it, he was deliberately mysterious, as I'd known he would be. I hadn't expected any answer that would satisfy my curiosity; in fact I'd have been shocked and disappointed if I'd got it. Almost as if I'd asked only to confirm what I already suspected, piling up proof.

We spent a night in a Travelodge on the outskirts of Dover and got up early to catch a ferry to Calais. We stood at the bow and watched England shrink into the distance. It promised to be another hot day. The ship's wake churned up spray, cooling us.

'Look, Claire. Home will be out of sight soon. Can you imagine how early seafarers must have felt when they sailed away? They didn't even know if there was even anything out there. I always feel a bit like that when I cross water, as if there are limitless possibilities over the horizon, whole worlds waiting to be discovered. It makes me feel like ... oh, I don't know ... a Viking, or Marco Polo.'

'Marco Polo, perhaps. You're too dark to be a Viking.'

'Doesn't it get to you? The excitement, the possibilities, the adventures? I'm getting the beginnings of an erection just thinking about it.'

'You've always got the beginnings of an erection as far as I can tell. But I know what you mean. The first time I went abroad I got the Magic Bus to Greece after I finished university. I remember I stood on the deck watching the white cliffs growing smaller and smaller and, for a moment, I was terrified. I literally had no idea what was going to happen next. But almost as soon as the thought came into my head I realised that not knowing meant I was truly free.' I turned to look at Jim, leaning on the rail.

He smiled. 'It must have felt good.'

'Yes. Until that moment my whole life had been mapped out for me by other people. I'd known exactly what was expected of me and who I was supposed to be. The clever girl, the dutiful daughter, the good Catholic. But now no one expected anything of me; nobody even knew who I was. I could be who I wanted, do what I wanted. It was utterly liberating.'

'I bet. So did you let your hair down? Go wild? Please tell me you did.'

'Certainly did. I made up for lost time. I think I slept with every bloke in our group and every waiter, beach bum or Australian backpacker who wasn't gay and probably a few who were – I wouldn't take no for an answer in those days. I had a fabulous time. Until I got appendicitis in Crete and had to be flown home. Then in the autumn I started my Masters. I like to think of it as my summer of love.'

Jim took my arm and led me towards a bench. 'Sun, sea, sand and shagging? That's just the kind of itinerary I have planned for us. Except for the backpackers and waiters; mixed doubles rather than a team event.'

'Sounds good to me. I assume you've sown a few wild oats yourself?'

'Fields and fields of them, but what man hasn't?'

'I bet you slept with whores when you were in the army, didn't you?' My voice came out all sort of high and strangled.

'A couple. Everyone does it. Some of my mates got quite addicted to it. But it never really worked for me. The thing that turns me on about fucking a woman is the knowledge that she wants it as much as I do. It was pretty clear that the tarts saw it as a chore, even though some of them put on quite a show of enjoying themselves.' Jim looked at me. 'Are you shocked?'

'No, not at all.'

'Well, you sounded it.'

'Quite the opposite really. I'm envious in a way. You really are open to anything, aren't you?'

'Envious? Why?'

'I haven't believed in God for years, but if I'd done what you did, I'd still be convinced I was going to hell.'

'All the more reason to do it, don't you think? And didn't anyone ever tell you that the road to hell is paved with Australian backpackers and Greek waiters?'

I laughed. 'I suppose when you put it like that.'

'No, if you ask me when you and those Bangkok whores I fucked turn up at the Pearly Gates it won't take St Peter long to decide which of you to let in.'

'And it wouldn't be me?'

'Would you let you in?'

'Probably not. But then, like Groucho Marx, I'm not sure I actually want to belong to a club that's prepared to have me in it.'

'That's the spirit. We're outcasts, you and I – outsiders. We make our own rules and what we want we take. The rules and roles society sets so much store by aren't for us; they're just another kind of prison. We might be lost, Claire, but at least we're free.'

We drove south, skirting Paris, and stopped in Chartres to visit the cathedral. Much to my surprise, I discovered that Jim spoke the language like a native, using rapid colloquial French I couldn't keep up with, and I realised that my own rusty A-level French was so formal and theoretical that it barely equipped me to communicate.

We ate lunch in a Chinese restaurant, but it was a fancy Frenchified version of Chinese food unlike anything I'd ever eaten at home. We walked around the city, following a map we'd picked up in the tourist office. Towards the end of the route, we got lost and found ourselves in the Arab quarter. We bought halva and sweet pastries in a dingy little grocery store and stumbled across a jazz pianist rehearsing in a deserted bar.

Jim persuaded the mustachioed patron to allow us to listen and did such a good job of charming him that he brought us coffee after coffee on the house. When we left, the big man clapped Jim on the back and said something I couldn't follow. When I asked for a translation he said in heavily accented English: 'I told him he speaks French like an Arab. It's a compliment; believe me, no Arab, would want to speak it like a Frenchman.'

We made our way back to where we'd parked the camper, finding our way more by luck than anything else. We put our purchases in the back and set off. Instead of heading for the main road Jim drove to the town centre and parked.

'I just need to pop into the bank. No need for you to come in. I won't be long.' He smiled at me and got out of the camper.

I watched him go into the Banque Populaire du Nord. I assumed he wanted to buy some euros. I reached into the glove compartment for a copy of *Paris Match* I'd bought at the ferry terminal and began to read in the vain hope that it might improve my French.

A church bell tolled four o'clock and I looked up. I'd lost track of time. Jim had been in the bank for at least twenty minutes. I considered getting out of the camper and going in after him but he'd taken the keys with him and, with all our possessions in the back, I couldn't risk leaving it unlocked.

I stared at the entrance to the bank as if I could make him come through the doors by act of will alone. As if in answer, it opened and he stepped out into the street but, instead of heading for the car, he crossed the road and went into the Crédit Agricole.

I gazed at the door long after he'd disappeared trying to work out why a man who never went near a bank at home would need to visit two French ones in the same afternoon. If he was exchanging currency, any bank would have done it, so why two? And, anyway, he'd already bought five-hundred pounds' worth of euros at the bureau de change in Dover, the same as I had.

A cold wave of unease washed over me. He may have accounts there, I supposed, spreading his money around. Maybe he was even hiding it from the taxman. But, no, people who did that put it in proper offshore accounts where it earned high interest and was safe from prying eyes. Whatever the reason, I was certain that asking Jim for an explanation would be a waste of breath. There might have been a legitimate reason, but I couldn't think of one.

After fifteen minutes he came back out into the street. Instead of making straight for the car he walked around the corner. A few minutes later he reappeared carrying a small paper carrier bag. He climbed into the car and handed it to me.

'A little present for keeping you waiting.' He buckled his seat belt.

I tossed my magazine in the back and opened the bag. Inside there was a small gold box, wrapped in a piece of ribbon. I took it out of the bag, undid the bow and lifted the lid. Nestled inside were half-a-dozen exquisitely beautiful chocolates. There was a delicious aroma of cocoa and alcohol.

'They're handmade. Eat up.'

I selected a chocolate. 'Do you want one?' I held out the box.

Jim shook his head. 'They're all for you.' He started the car.

We drove onto Saumur and I saw the castle for the first time, like something out of a fairy tale. We booked into a small hotel above a *tabac* filled with taciturn old men smoking Gauloises and watching football on a tiny TV above the zinc-topped bar. As we trooped across the room with our bags they fell silent and sullen, turning their eyes away from the screen to watch us. As the door closed behind us, the hubbub resumed.

In the hallway behind the bar there was red-flock wallpaper and dark gleaming wood everywhere. The proprietor led us up a broad staircase so highly polished, that stepping on it was like flirting with death. I hung onto the banisters and walked up slowly. When I got to the top undamaged, I realised I'd been holding my breath.

Our host opened the door to our room and pushed it wide with the flourish of a conjurer opening his magic cabinet. He handed Jim the keys and left us to it. After such a build up, the room couldn't help but be a disappointment. Decorated by the same interior designer as the hall, it was dark, oppressive and gloomy. The sun had faded the flock paper and the furniture, though highly polished, was all clearly old, giving the room an aura of neglect and penny pinching.

The bed was a huge belle époque affair with an elaborately carved headboard. I sat on the mattress and the iron bedstead squeaked under my weight. The window looked down on the courtyard where we'd parked the van. There were a pile of crates and a group of dustbins outside the kitchen and a huge bored-looking dog, tied up beside a kennel – hardly a romantic view.

'The bastard's cheated us.' Jim was reading the notice of charges on the back of the door, set by the local council and intended to prevent overcharging. 'The official rate is a hundred and fifty euros; he charged me one hundred and seventy.'

'Cheap at half the price.' I struggled to open the window.

'Let me do that. Do you want a bath? Assuming there's any hot water.'

'I don't think so. I'll just go and take off my make-up and clean my teeth.' I heaved my suitcase onto the bed and unzipped it. I stepped out of my shoes and padded off to the bathroom. 'It's clean anyway, even if it is a bit basic. But why do the French always have this horrible corrugated toilet paper? I should have brought up a roll of Andrex from the van.'

I squeezed toothpaste onto my brush. Jim came into the bathroom and lifted the toilet seat. He unzipped and began to pee.

'When in Saumur, Claire . . .' He flushed and the plumbing rumbled into life. 'Shall we see what we've got left to eat?'

We ate a meal of bread, tomatoes and ham, bought from a street market in one of the villages we'd driven through on the way, and the pastries from the Arab grocery store. We shared a bottle of wine, drinking directly from the bottle in the absence of glasses. We spread the food out on the bed, using paper bags for a tablecloth and Jim's pocket knife for cutlery. The bread was crisp, the tomatoes soft and sweet and the ham salty and tender. We fought over the wine, then held it by the neck and glugged it down.

I gathered up the wrappings and the empty bottle and dumped them all in the wastepaper bin while Jim closed the shutters. I was shaking crumbs off the bedspread when he came up behind me as I bent over the bed.

'Don't move.' He flipped up my skirt and pushed it up to my waist. He ran his hands over my naked buttocks, making me tremble. I could feel his palms on my buttocks as his thumbs explored my pussy, pulling the lips apart. I felt his face close to my skin and heard him inhale. I tingled all over.

He flipped my skirt back down. I sat down on the bed. Jim went over to where he'd left his suitcase and began rummaging through the contents. He found what he was looking for, brought it back to the bed and held it up for me to see. It was a pair of metal handcuffs. Jim was holding one of the cuffs and the other swung on its chain, glinting in the light.

'I brought these from home. Why don't you take your dress off and kneel on the bed?'

I got up and pulled my dress off over my head. Without waiting to be told, I stuck both arms out in front of me and watched as Jim fitted the cuffs. The metal was cold and heavy against my wrists. My breathing had grown shallow and my nipples were erect. I waited in my shackles, my heart pounding.

Jim tugged on the chain, pulling me forwards. He cupped my face with his free hand and bent to kiss me. His mouth was hot and hungry, his breathing noisy and erratic. I was kneeling on my haunches, my knuckles pressed into the mattress for support. He kissed my neck. I could feel his breath, hot on my skin, as his mouth slid down my throat.

'Move into the middle and bend over.' His voice was throaty with urgency.

I moved across the bed on all fours, like an eager puppy. I positioned myself in the centre of the bed, my naked arse thrust up into the air. I could hear Jim undressing, then the mattress shifted as he climbed up on the bed and got behind me. I felt his fingertips trailing over my buttocks and thighs. The contact made me skin instantly goose-pimply and quivery little tingles slid up my spine and over my scalp.

I heard the bed creak under Jim's weight and he used his thumbs to pull apart my lips. I felt his moist breath, then his hot slippery tongue. The delicious shock of it made me jolt forwards and bash my head against the headboard. I felt Jim's mouth withdraw.

'Careful, Claire, or I'll be carting you down to casualty with concussion.'

I laughed. 'What a lovely alliterative sentence ... "carting Claire down to casualty with concussion". I like it.'

'Quiet –' he gave my bottom a playful pat '– some of us are trying to work here.' I felt his mouth against my opening as his thumbs stretched apart my lips. His tongue circled my clit.

The intimate heat of it made me tingle. My thigh muscles were quivering and my breathing had grown noisy. My nipples were hard and sensitive, responding to each sensation Jim's eager mouth created.

I felt his tongue pushing into me, opening me and slipping inside. I shifted my weight to my elbows and rocked my hips, rubbing myself against his face. His mouth drew away, then I felt his tongue sliding up the length of my slit.

I could feel his beard stubble scratching my sensitive flesh. I could hear him panting behind me. Was his cock hard? I wondered. Did it stand out in front of him, purple and proud as he mouthed my crotch? Was it aching and painful? Maybe there was even a bead of moisture glistening in its single eye.

His mouth found my clit and he sucked on it, then slid upwards and dabbled at my hole. I could hear the moisture there, squelching as he moved his tongue against me. I felt his hand on my hip and the bed creaking under his weight as he straightened up. He shuffled forwards on his knees and I felt the moist tip of his cock sliding up and down my pussy. He used the weight of his hips to enter me. The first moment of pleasure as he slid into me was breathtaking. I arched my back, lifted up my head and exhaled noisily.

He bent over my back and supported himself with one hand. He slid the other in front of me and between my legs. I gasped as his fingers located my clit. My hair was falling in my face. Jim's balls bashed up against me on every thrust. The bed creaked under us.

I looked down at the metal cuffs encircling my wrists; they glinted in the light. I could feel their weight. When I moved they were cold against my skin. I could see the tiny keyholes and I hoped Jim could remember where he'd left the keys.

Jim gave a particularly deep thrust and knocked me forwards. I put out one hand to grab the top of the headboard, but the cuff tugged on its chain and pulled my other hand out from under me and I toppled over. I grabbed onto the headboard, hands side by side.

Damp hair was clinging to my face. My nipples were prickling with pleasure. My crotch was liquid and tingling. Jim's fingers worked my clit. He always seemed to have just the right touch – not too much direct contact at first, then building to a rhythm when I began to respond.

His body slid against my back. He felt hot and hard and thick inside me. His breathing was laboured and noisy. Every so often he'd give a satisfied little grunt of pleasure and exertion.

I could feel the familiar heat and tension building in my pelvis. My nipples were aching and sensitive. Occasionally, they would brush against the bedclothes as I moved, eliciting a wave of shivery pleasure.

Jim's fingers squelched as he fingered me. The noise seemed animal and obscene, like the slapping of his balls against me and sliding of our sweat-slick bodies. He was pounding me hard. His fingers worked my clit. I held onto the headboard and pushed back against him, matching his rhythm.

My nipples rubbed against the rumpled bedding. The bed creaked and hit the wall in rhythm with our thrusting. The bedclothes rustled; the cuff's chain clanked as I repositioned my hands. Excited breathing and guttural moans of pleasure seemed to hang in the air.

Pressure was building to a pitch. Jim was bent over my back, his belly and chest slick against my skin. His strokes had grown shorter and more urgent. He bent to kiss my shoulder and I felt hot air gushing out of his nose like dragon's breath.

He was rigid inside me. My crotch was tight and tingling, my nipples ached. Every millimetre of my skin felt sensitised. I held onto the headboard with both hands, my knuckles white. The cuffs dug into my wrists. My knees hurt.

Jim jabbed his hips in short staccato stabs. He was panting and groaning, his mouth right beside my ear. My body was on fire. He gave one deep, fierce thrust and circled his hips. He let out a deep grunt of joy and release.

His orgasm was all it took to tip me over the edge. I held onto the bed and arched my back. Sensation overwhelmed me. Electric jolts of exquisite pleasure rocketed up and down my spine. My scalp prickled.

His fingers circled my clit, coaxing the orgasm out of me. Blood pounded in my ears; I was dizzy and trembling. My muscles gripped him as he came inside me. I was sobbing and moaning.

The hairs on the back of my neck were erect and prickly. I seemed to be vibrating with pleasure. Tremors radiated outwards from my crotch and pumped around my bloodstream. My nipples were hard and tingly.

In the yard below the dog began to howl. Someone started to bang on the other side of the wall and I could hear angry French voices telling us to shut up. I let out a final wail of satisfaction as the last peak consumed me. I ground my crotch against Jim's hand, wringing out the last shreds of pleasure

Jim lay panting over my back. I could feel his wet hair against my skin. His chest heaved. His moist breath warmed my skin. I could feel his thighs quivering against mine.

The handcuffs were digging into my wrists and cutting off my circulation. My fingers were beginning to go numb. My knees ached. Jim was heavy against my back.

I felt him soften inside me and his thigh muscles relax. He stopped fingering my clit and cupped my pussy in his hand. He kissed my neck, then rolled over onto the bed beside me.

'Naked and handcuffed, every man's fantasy.' He looked up at me.

I let go of the headboard and lay down beside him, resting my shackled hands on my belly. 'Not every man. Some of them fantasise about being on the receiving end, you know.'

'Tempting, but no thanks.' He went over to his suitcase to retrieve the key. I held out my wrists for him to unlock the handcuffs. 'Slowly does it. The feeling will come back quickly enough.' He rubbed my wrists. 'You looked absolutely beautiful lying there unable to move.'

'Thanks. I loved it. It was ... do you know, I'm lost for words. It was indescribable.'

Jim climbed into bed. He shook his head. 'A professor of English, lost for words ...'

'I'm not a professor, actually.'

'Not yet. As a matter of fact, I rather like the idea of fucking a professor. Somehow it makes the sense of defilement seem all the more delicious.'

'I know what you mean. One of my ex-boyfriends liked to say, "May I fuck you now, Dr McAdam?" It was so wicked.'

'Of course. I knew you were a PhD but somehow it never occurred to me that made you a doctor. How wonderful. I feel thoroughly depraved now.' He leant over and kissed me. 'I love you, Dr McAdam.'

'Well, now I really am lost for words.'

Some time during the night, I was woken by Jim's phone ringing. He sat up in bed and fumbled for the light switch. I covered my eyes with my hand as the light hit them. He rushed over to the chair where he'd left his clothes and rummaged through his pockets for the phone. He looked at the display then pressed the button to answer.

'Yes . . . Oh no. Is there much damage? . . . Smashed? . . . All of them?'

I sat up in bed. 'What is it, Jim?'

He waved his hand to silence me. 'But you'd done what I asked? . . . That's good. OK. We were expecting it. You've called the police? . . . Ring the insurance company first thing in the morning. OK, keep me informed.' He hung up and sat down on the chair on top of his rumpled clothes.

I climbed out of bed and walked over to him. I stroked his hair. He looked up at me and smiled.

'Something's happened?'

'There's been a break-in at my office. Nothing missing as far as they can tell but lots of damage. They've snapped every single computer disk in two and smashed everything.'

'Oh, Jim. I'm sorry. Do you need to go back?'

He shook his head. 'No. My staff can handle it. And, fortunately, we're well insured so it'll be OK.' He smiled at me again but, in spite of his reassurance, I could see the concern in his eyes. 'Let's go back to bed. We've got a long drive in the morning.'

In the morning, before we left the city, Jim visited the Crédit Lyonnais and the Banque de France while I waited in the camper. Curiosity burnt inside me so strongly I could almost taste it but I knew better than to ask and, in any case, I wasn't at all sure I could handle the answer. When Jim climbed in beside me, I just smiled at him as though nothing was wrong and started the engine.

We drove south, seeing the sights and stopping in campsites on the way. We saw the walled city of Carcasonne and spent a day in Arles. In every major town, Jim visited banks but he never offered an explanation and I never asked for one.

We crossed the border into Italy, heading for Florence. My Italian turned out to be much better than Jim's and, after our experience in France, I was disproportionately proud. Though he understood the basics, he couldn't keep up with the speed of colloquial Italian so it was always me who bartered with shopkeepers or asked for directions.

We arrived after dark and booked into a campsite just outside the city. We were too tired from driving to do anything other than eat a quick meal and go to bed. In the morning, I was woken by Jim, standing by the open doorway of the van calling to me.

'Claire, come and look at this.'

I hauled myself up onto my elbows, thick headed. 'What time is it?'

'I'm not sure. Early. I got up for a pee and on my way back from the toilet block I spotted the view. You've got to have a look.'

'But I'm naked.'

'Put something on.'

'OK, OK.'

I climbed out of bed and slipped into the dress I had taken off the previous evening, then padded over to Jim. He took my hand and led me out onto the dew-wet grass. In the valley below, Florence was spread out like a model village. Its bridges, spires and domes gleamed in the sun. At the horizon, the sky was still stained with pink and orange. In the distance, we could hear a church bell tolling.

'Isn't it incredible? That's the cathedral.' He pointed. 'There's the Uffizi and that square building with the tower, that's the Palazzo Vecchio. Can you imagine waking up to that view every day? Aren't we lucky?' Jim squeezed my hand.

'It's beautiful.'

'Am I forgiven for waking you up?'

'Oh yes, I wouldn't have wanted to miss this.'

'There's a wonderful little café by the Uffizi, where I used to go every morning. We can have our breakfast there.'

'Are they open at this hour? I bet we're the only people in the whole of Italy who're awake.'

'No, they're probably not. We'll have to wait a few hours.'

'Well, I'm wide awake now. How are we going to pass the time?'

'Come back to bed, I'm sure I can think of something.'

* * *

Florence was like a living museum, everywhere you looked there was some famous artwork or piece of architecture. After lunch, Jim took me to see Donatello's *David* at the Bargello. Once a barracks and prison, its origins were clearly obvious. In comparison with most of the spectacular architecture that surrounded us, the building's high fortified walls seemed austere and sinister. But inside, it was packed with room after room of breathtaking art. I couldn't quite mesh the two versions of the place: the exterior unadorned and forbidding and the interior ornate and full of beauty. It was almost as if its present role was somehow atoning for its past cruelty.

'It's just up here, I think; it's a long time since I was last here.' He held my hand as we walked up the stairs. 'Yes, here it is.' His voice was practically a whisper.

The statue was life size, tiny in comparison with Michelangelo's version, which we'd seen that morning. Michelangelo's *David* was a muscular giant any man would have feared, but Donatello had sculpted him as the boy he was. His body was not yet fully muscled and his chest still bore the plump softness of childhood. His decorated hat made him seem playful and boyish, like a child pretending to be a warrior. Only the head of Goliath, under David's raised foot told the viewer that this was really the giant killer.

'It's wonderful.' I gazed at the figure.

'Did you know that for a thousand years all sculptures had been reliefs, carved into a flat panel, like a wall? Not since antiquity had anyone conceived a figure like this, fully in the round. Can you imagine how shocking it must have been?'

'I can. It really takes your breath away, doesn't it?'

'I knew you'd love it. I just had to bring you here. What men they must have been, Michelangelo and

Donatello. To spend years painting a ceiling or to create something no one had done for a millennium. What vision they must have had, what courage.'

'I can see it appeals to the iconoclast in you.'

'Yes, it does, I suppose. The Spanish have a saying: "Take what you want and pay for it, because if you don't you won't have what you want but you'll end up paying for it anyway." That speaks to me.'

'Yes, I think I'm beginning to see that. Thanks to you.'

'My depraved influence you mean?'

'If you like. But whatever it is, I seem to be developing a taste for it.'

'At last . . . my work is done.'

We drove back towards the border. I grew used to Jim visiting banks in each of the major towns we passed, while I waited patiently for him in the van and never offered any comment. We spent the night in a farmer's field somewhere near the frontier amid grazing sheep. I woke up to see Jim sitting on the edge of the bed, putting on his trousers. It was still dark outside and he hadn't turned on the light in the van.

'What's up?' I propped myself up on one elbow.

'Shhhh! I think I heard someone outside.'

'You can't have, we're in the middle of nowhere.' I kept my voice to a whisper. I wasn't sure which of us I was trying to convince. My stomach felt as though it had turned to lead and my heart was beating double time.

Jim stood up and stepped into his shoes. He reached into an overhead locker and rummaged under a pile of towels. He spoke over his shoulder.

'I'm going to go outside and see what's going on. I want you to stay here.'

'I'm not staying here on my own. You might be in danger.'

'Stay here, I said.' Jim pulled a cloth bag out of the locker and tipped its contents onto the bed.

'A gun! Where did you get that?'

'I bought it in France.' He began to load bullets into the handgun.

'Whatever for?'

'For our protection. And it's proved necessary, hasn't it?'

'But a gun ...'

'This is the real world, Claire. It can be dangerous out here. It's not punting on the Isis, or a picnic by the canal.'

'There's no need to patronise me.'

'Do you want to have an argument or shall I go outside and find out what's going on?'

'Sorry. But I'm coming with you.' I slithered over the bed and began to dress.

'Suit yourself, but you stay behind me, OK?' Jim opened the door and we stepped out just in time to see a young man carrying a knife in one hand and a crowbar in the other coming around the front of the van. Though clearly as startled as we were, the man didn't pause but kept coming towards us brandishing the knife.

'Stay still and you won't get hurt.' The man spoke in Italian.

Jim was holding the gun down by his thigh on the man's blind side. He raised it and pointed it directly at him. 'Tell him to drop the knife of I'll blow his fucking head off, then ask him how many of them there are.' Jim never took his eyes off the man.

Before I could translate the man dropped his weapons

and put his hands up. 'No problem, pal, I leave now. Just me and my brother Aldo. We not hurt you. We leave now, OK?' Though putting on a show of bravery, the man couldn't keep still and he never took his eyes off the gun.

'What's your name?'

'Mauro. Mauro Biagi.'

'And where is Aldo?' Jim took a step closer and pointed the gun directly at the man's groin. The man's hands instinctively shot down to cover his genitals but, realising the movement could be construed as threatening, he raised them again. He was shaking visibly now.

'He's in the car. I get him.'

'No you don't. We'll all go. You can lead the way. And, just so you know, I was in the army and I'm an excellent shot, so don't even think about making a run for it.'

'No, pal, I no run. We go now.' He led us round the van towards the road. There was an elderly battered Cinquecento parked under a tree with a young man sitting smoking behind the wheel. When he saw us, he got out of the car, smiling and walking towards Mauro, clearly assuming his mission had been successful and we were his hostages. When he spotted Jim's gun, he turned on his heel and was on the point of running, when the knifeman called out in Italian: 'Stay there, or he'll kill us.'

Aldo stopped in his tracks and stood motionless until we reached him.

'In a moment I'm going to let you get in the car and drive away.' Jim cocked the gun. 'If you even think about coming back, I'll kill you. If I ever see your miserable faces again, I'll kill you. If you go to the police, I'll kill you. And I doubt you'll be going to the police anyway, otherwise you'll have to explain what you were doing here in the dead of night with a fucking great knife. Do I make myself clear?'

'Yes, we understand. We won't go to police. We go now, OK?' Mauro was nodding manically and pointing down the road towards the nearest village.

'Get in the car.'

The men climbed into the car and Jim bent down and poked the gun through the open window.

'I could have shot you both if I'd wanted to and I still can. Go straight home.'

Jim straightened up and lowered the gun. The car started and sped off down the road. Jim stood and watched it until it was out of sight and I stood and watched him. His lips were set into a hard line and I could see the muscles in his jaw working as he clenched and unclenched his teeth. His body was rigid, on alert.

My gaze travelled down his right arm to the gun in his hand. I don't think I'd ever seen one in real life before. They were something I associated with American drug dealers and gangsters but that was so far away they were barely real to me. I didn't, for a moment, think he'd have carried through on his threat to kill them, but if I'd been on the other end of the gun, I'd definitely have been scared.

When the car disappeared over the horizon, Jim cracked open the gun and tipped the bullets into his palm. He pocketed the ammunition and reached out to hold my hand.

'Are you all right?' His voice was soft and concerned.

'I'm in one piece but I wouldn't say I'm all right.'

Jim led me back towards the van. 'It's just the shock, you'll be OK after a good night's sleep.'

'You think I can sleep after that?'

'I understand, but you're safe now.'

We got into the van and Jim shut the door behind us, then paused to lock it. I stripped off my clothes and climbed into bed, suddenly cold. I huddled under the covers.

'I can't believe you brought a gun on holiday with us.'

Jim shrugged. 'I got it in one of those hunting shops in France. Rural Italy can be dangerous. I wanted to be prepared. I know you're upset, but it's not a big deal.'

'Not a big deal? How do you intend to get it past security in Calais?'

'I don't. I'm going to get rid of it as soon as we get back over the French border.'

'You can't just dump a gun. Someone might find it and use it, a kid even.'

'Relax. I'm going to dismantle it and get rid of it in bits. No one will get hurt and neither did we, that's the main thing.'

On the way back to Calais, Jim dumped a component of the gun in every town we passed, wrapping it in newspaper and dropping it into a rubbish bin. He threw the bullets into the Loire, standing on a bridge and skimming each one across the water like stones.

12

When we got back home I holed myself up in my house, not answering the phone. I was restless and edgy. The first few days I tried to work on my book but my concentration kept wandering. I sat in front of the television, flicking from one channel to another in search of anything to distract me. Eventually I turned to my DVD collection because it offered hours of guaranteed diversion. I watched one after another, curled up under my favourite blanket. When I got to the end, I began at the beginning again, finding comfort and reassurance in their familiar plots and dialogue.

I ate out of the freezer when the fresh food ran out, having spare ribs for breakfast and half a chocolate cheesecake for dinner. At night I read into the small hours, immersing myself in imaginary lives and fictional worlds where other people made the decisions and I was only an onlooker.

At first, Jim rang every day, leaving friendly, jokey messages asking me to ring. It seemed to gradually dawn on him that something was wrong and the messages grew increasingly concerned, his voice urgent.

I ran to the machine each time the phone rang, my heart pounding, while I listened for the greeting to end and the beep to sound. I'd hear Jim's voice and something would pull at my gut and I'd experience an involuntary shudder of pleasure as I remembered his fingers on my body or his eyes looking into mine while we made love. But I didn't trust myself to answer.

Eventually, Bernie began to call, alerted by Jim that something was up. But I still didn't pick up the phone. I couldn't face explanations or commiserations. Her messages grew increasingly concerned and, after three or four days, anger and hysteria began to creep in. Didn't I realise how worried she was? Was I ill? Had I had an accident? I turned down the volume on the answerphone.

I was sitting in front of the TV, still in my pyjamas, when I heard a key turn in the lock. I heard the door creak but the safety chain prevented it from opening fully.

'Claire! It's Bernie. Let me in.'

I turned up the volume.

'I know you're in there, otherwise the safety chain wouldn't be on. Let me in.' She rattled the door. 'I've got a key to the back door too, remember.'

'It's bolted,' I shouted.

'Let me in, otherwise I'll have to break a window. Please, I'm worried about you.'

I clicked off the TV and got up to let her in. I slammed the door closed and unhooked the chain then went back into the living room. I sat down on the sofa and covered my knees with the blanket. Bernie opened the door with her key and came into the room. She was carrying Ollie in his car seat in one hand and his changing bag in the other. She dropped the bag on the floor and plonked the baby carrier down on the coffee table.

'I'm beginning to regret giving you a key.' I didn't even look at her.

'You can have it back if you like.' She tossed it onto the table.

'It's only for emergencies.'

'What do you call this?'

'I'm alive and well. You can go home now.'

'But you're *not* well. I bet you haven't washed for days. Your hair's all greasy and your pyjamas are covered in food. Do you even know what time it is?' She sat down beside me and laid a hand on my knee, the first human contact I'd had for days. I looked down at her hand because seeing her face would have made me cry.

'I'm all right. Or at least I will be. You know how it is.'

Her hand was soft and heavy. I could feel her body heat soaking into me. 'It's Jim, isn't it? Did you fight?'

I shook my head. 'No, nothing so straightforward.' I still couldn't meet her eyes.

'What then? Did something happen on holiday?'

The baby began to cry and wriggle. Bernie unstrapped him and picked him up. She laid him across her shoulder and bounced him, rubbing his back until he grew quiet and sleepy.

'It's not any one thing. It's one little incident on top of another ... and he'll never tell me anything. I have to piece everything together like a puzzle and I'm still not sure I know what's going on. If only he wasn't so bloody secretive.'

'I knew –'

'Don't you dare say I told you so. I'm too exhausted and fragile for it today.'

'That isn't what I meant. I didn't come here to crow. I'm worried about you. Please tell me what's wrong.'

'Oh, Bern. Please don't be nice to me or I'll cry.'

She put out a hand to hug me and I shuffled across the sofa but the baby got in the way and we couldn't manage it. I took him from her, carefully sliding him across from her shoulder to mine, sleepy and heavy. I bent my head and smelt his sweet, powdery baby smell.

I began to cry, silently, as I held him. Huge hot tears ran down my face. I stroked his back through his sleepsuit as his tiny heart beat against mine.

When there was nothing left in the freezer except frozen peas and ice cubes, I did an internet grocery order, spending a fortune on luxuries and titbits I'd never normally allow myself. Jars of marinated olives, half a dozen Continental cheeses, butter, Belgian chocolate and gourmet microwave meals the puritan in me usually considered too expensive and indulgent.

I finally dragged myself to the shower while I was waiting for the delivery though my motive was to kill time rather than get clean. There was an obscure comfort in wearing the same clothes day after day, softened and shaped by wear and smelling of me.

I was in my dressing gown, towelling off my hair, when the doorbell rang. I went downstairs eager to unload my groceries and make something delicious for lunch but, when I opened the door, it was Jim. I thought about closing it in his face but he must have seen it in my eyes because he put out a hand and grabbed the edge of the door and pushed it wide open. He stepped into the hall and shut it behind him.

'Well, you look OK. Aren't you going to invite me in?' He was dressed in my favourite dusky-pink shirt and a pair of linen trousers. I could smell his aftershave. I took a step back.

'You seem to have invited yourself.' I didn't move.

'Talk to me, Claire. Do you know what I've been through? First I thought you were ill or lying at the bottom of the stairs dead. Bernie and I have both been frantic.'

'Yes, she came here. You shouldn't have bothered her, she's got enough on her plate.'

'Why are you being like this? Don't be angry with me. When Bernie told me you were OK, I was so relieved, but there's obviously something wrong.'

'You know there is.' I was conscious of my nakedness under the thin gown. I tightened the belt and folded my arms across my breasts.

'I'm not a mind-reader. Is it the gun? ... I knew you were upset.'

'Not just the gun. The other things.'

'What things?'

'Don't pretend you don't know what I'm talking about. There's something going on and I want to know what it is.'

'I don't know what you mean.'

'No? The mysterious phone calls you won't explain. The knuckleduster. The prison remark. Thinking we're being followed then changing your car – it can't have been a coincidence. The unexplained business trip even though you're not working? Why did you need to visit all those banks when we were away? And you've got a safe full of twenty-pound notes. I've seen it myself. I don't think I've ever seen that much money in one place before. I could go on but what's the point? None of it makes sense unless you're hiding something.'

'You've seen my safe? When?' His face had gone white.

'One night at your house. I wasn't spying. I was on my way to the loo. What are you, Jim? A bank robber? A drug dealer? A gun runner?'

'None of those things, I promise you.'

'What then? I want to believe you, really I do, but I need answers.'

'I understand. But I can't give them to you – not yet. I need you to trust me, Claire. Soon I'll tell you everything and, I promise, it isn't half as sinister as you imagine. I just need to sort a few things out first.'

I focused on his chest because his eyes would have broken me. I could see a dark curl of hair poking out at the top of his shirt and a fading love bite on his throat. I remembered giving it to him in Florence when we made love after watching the dawn and the recollection softened my crotch and made my heart lurch. I looked away.

'I don't know if I can do that.'

'Will you think about it? Please?'

I nodded. He reached out and cupped my cheek in his palm. His skin was soft and warm and his hand seemed to mould to the contours of my face.

'Look at me.' His voice was pleading and tentative. 'Don't you know how much I want you?'

I met his gaze. He smiled and I felt my nipples tingle.

'Yes, I do. But it's not about how much we want each other.'

'OK. I won't chase you. If you need time, you can have it. I promise, I'll tell you everything in the end and, in the meantime, I'm asking for your trust. But I want you ... I need you ... and you know where to find me.' He bent to kiss me softly on the lips. I stood there, motionless, with my eyes closed, trying to memorise the smell of him, the taste of him. He straightened up and smiled at me, then turned and opened the door. It closed behind him.

'Goodbye,' I whispered.

I ate my way through my gourmet groceries, nibbling treats as I watched my DVDs or sitting up in bed surrounded by goodies as I read long into the night. I was growing fat, so I dug out my baggy old pyjamas and tracksuit bottoms. I registered my growing waistband dispassionately, as a fact that needed to be noted but was no cause for concern.

I reread all my favourite books, piling them up beside my bed so that I could begin a new one the moment I'd turned the final page. I read until my eyes drooped and the book dropped out of my hand.

The phone rang less often now but I seldom bothered to listen to the messages. Days ran into one another and became meaningless. I cooked huge meals in the middle of the night then slept all day, waking up in bright daylight with no idea what time it was. I'd have bouts of angry cleaning, dusting, tidying and hoovering the house from top to bottom. I'd do load after load of laundry then run out of interest before I got round to hanging it out to dry.

It was days before I realised that I'd stopped sleeping. There was a pile of dirty crockery by my bed and the floor was littered with discarded books. I sorted them into piles, those I'd finished with and those waiting to be read, and I realised I'd read a dozen books over the previous three days. I counted them again, but it was right and it dawned on me that I couldn't remember the last time I'd slept.

I looked round at the chaos of my room then down at my clothes, suddenly disgusted. I stripped out of my dirty pyjamas and tossed them at the laundry bin. As I sat down on the bed, I caught a glimpse of myself in the dressing-table mirror. I gazed at my reflection, noticing every detail, with the same guilty pleasure as a voyeur peering through the curtains into a stranger's life.

My hair was dull and tangled, my shoulders drooped and my eyes were dark rimmed. Books and food wrappers were scattered all over the bed; the pillows were piled up in a heap against the headboard. The bottom sheet had come loose at the corner, exposing the mattress. There was a big coffee stain in the middle of the duvet.

I was making myself ill. Something had to change. Jim's loss pulled at my gut like hunger. He'd promised me answers, if only I could wait. Could I live with that? I sat for ages, staring into the mirror but the only answer I could find was that I couldn't live without him. I crawled up the bed and climbed under the covers.

I don't know how long I slept but when I woke it was light outside and the sun was shining. I opened the curtains for the first time in days then threw the windows open. I stood under the shower for ages, scrubbing my body and shampooing my hair twice to get it clean. Afterwards I put on some proper clothes then changed the bedlinen and put away all the books.

When my room was restored to its customary order I picked up the phone and dialled Jim's mobile number. It rang and rang. I waited for the voicemail to kick in so I could leave a message but it just kept on ringing. I ended the call and dialled The Feathers' familiar number. As I listened to it ring, I could feel my heart thumping and a glow of anticipation warming my face.

'The Feathers Hotel.'

'Hi, can you put me through to Jim Hyde, please.'

'I'm sorry, Mr Hyde is no longer staying with us. Is that you, Claire?'

'Yes. Who's that?'

'It's Trish. Let me put you through to Bernie. I think Mr Hyde left a message for you.'

She put me on hold and a tinny version of 'Ode to Joy' tinkled into life. I waited for what seemed like ages taking long deep breaths in a futile attempt to calm myself. Finally, the line clicked and the music stopped.

'Claire. How are you?'

'Better, thanks. But what happened to Jim? Trish says he's gone.' I could hear the baby crying in the background.

'Yes, a couple of nights ago. It was quite strange, actually.'

'What happened?'

'Well, he had a phone call, which is unusual in itself. Apart from you I don't think anyone's ever called him here before.'

'No, he always uses the mobile.'

'And this call was in the middle of the night, which is even stranger – no one makes a social call in the middle of the night, do they? It had to be an emergency. The night manager put him through. Anyway, half an hour later, he goes down to reception and says he's checking out and pays his bill.'

'But he left a message for me?'

'Yes, I'm getting to that. He came up to the flat and banged on the door. As it happened, I was up feeding Ollie so I answered it. He apologised for disturbing me and said there had been an emergency and he had to move on, then he handed me a note for you. He made me promise that I'd give it to you personally, not to post it or anything.'

'I'll come straight over.' I hung up before Bernie had time to say goodbye and I was halfway down the path to the car before I realised I hadn't even bothered to bring my house keys.

I ran every red light between my house and The Feathers and parked on the drive. I dashed up the stairs to Bernie's flat, bounding up the steps two at a time. When I knocked at her door, I was breathless and sweating.

She opened the door with the baby on her hip. 'Well, you look better, at least. Come in.'

I shook my head. 'I haven't got time. I've got to find Jim.'

Her eyes gave a little flicker, but I could tell she was trying hard to suppress her disapproval. She picked up an envelope from the hall table. 'Here.' She handed it to me.

'Can I borrow your keys to my house? I left mine at home.'

'Of course.' She rummaged in a bowl of keys on the table and gave them to me.

'Thanks.' I turned to leave.

'Call me or maybe I can come over to see you with Ollie . . .'

But I was already halfway down the stairs.

Back in the car I looked at the envelope. It was heavyweight cream paper, obviously expensive. I turned it over in my hands. There was an embossed circle in the flap bearing the maker's name. I slit the envelope open with my car key, tearing the paper. Inside was a single sheet of the same paper, folded in four. I opened it. It was a mobile phone number, nothing else, not even a signature.

I got out my phone and checked my contact list to see if the number was for Jim's mobile, but they didn't match. I punched in the digits and pressed the send button. It was answered after the first ring.

'Claire. I was so happy when I saw your name on the display. How are you?' His voice sounded like home.

'I'm OK, thanks. New phone?'

'Yes, I had to get rid of the old one.'

'Why?' I nestled the phone against my cheek.

'Problems. But never mind that.'

'Where are you?'

'Another hotel. You've been here with me. Do you

know where I mean?' There was an edge in his voice that told me not to name it.

'Yes, I remember. In the same suite?'

'That's right.'

'I'll come over. It shouldn't take me too long.'

'See you soon.'

I drove home and hurriedly packed a bag. I crammed in all my toiletries and as many clean clothes as I could find, not knowing when I'd be home again. I tossed the case and my laptop into the boot and headed for the nearest garage to fill the tank. As I queued to pay for the petrol, I realised I was starving, so I grabbed bags of crisps, chocolate, packaged flapjacks and bottles of water and dumped them all down on the counter.

I ate as I drove, swallowing down the trashy snacks with trembling hands, not stopping until I began to feel sick. I switched on the radio, but the jangly pop music made me feel too edgy so I switched between stations until I found a Handel oratorio on Radio 3.

I let the sacred music wash over me, consciously slowing my breathing. I forced myself to stick to the speed limit and I tried not to get annoyed when the car in front refused to go above 30 mph or a motorcyclist overtook on the inside.

When I arrived at the hotel, my heart was throbbing and my crotch ached with heat and hunger. I parked and struggled up the steps with my luggage.

'Good afternoon, Dr McAdam – Mr Hyde told me to expect you. May I help you with your bags?'

I shook my head. 'I'm in a hurry. Thank you.'

'If you'd like to leave your luggage, I can bring it up later.'

I dropped everything except my handbag.

'Thanks,' I called over my shoulder as I dashed inside.

When I reached Jim's suite he was standing in the doorway waiting for me.

'Hello, darling. Reception told me you were on your way up. Come in.' He stepped aside. He followed me inside and shut the door behind me.

'It's so good to see you. I'm sorry I ran away.' I opened my arms and he stepped into them. I laid my head against his broad chest. He gripped me tight in an enormous bear hug, almost knocking the breath out of me. He nuzzled his face into my hair and I heard him inhale. His hands stroked my back.

I lifted my face for a kiss and he cupped my cheeks in his hands and brought his lips to mine. Little jolts of electric pleasure shot up and down my spine. My scalp was tingly and sensitive. My crotch tightened.

I could feel hot breath gushing out of his nostrils, heating my skin. His lips were soft and warm and he tasted of coffee and brandy. His hard body was pressed up against mine, the bulge of his crotch pushing against my belly. His lips moved down my neck, nibbling and kissing. I sighed.

'As I recall,' he whispered between kisses, 'last time you were here you never got to see my bedroom.'

'That's right.' I ran my hands over his back, feeling his muscles.

'Come with me.' He took my hand and led me across the room to the bedroom. Inside he unbuttoned his trousers and unzipped his fly. 'Look.' He pushed his trousers and pants down a few inches and released his erection.

I got to my knees and looked up at him. He was smiling down at me, his rigid cock stood out proudly between us. I stroked the underside with one finger. I touched his balls and he let out a long sigh. Slowly, I slid back his foreskin, exposing his dark helmet. He moaned. I pushed it all the way down, creating tension on the little strip of skin that joined it to the head. Jim made a soft little grunt of pleasure. A shiver of excitement ran down my spine.

I put out my tongue, looking up into his face. He watched with rapt attention as I licked up a bead of moisture from the eye and ran my tongue under the ridge of his helmet. His hands balled into fists and his thigh muscles began to quiver. I felt my nipples crinkling and hardening inside my clothes.

I opened my mouth and swallowed him to the root. It felt smooth and silky. I loved the feel of the hard muscle and blood pumping under the skin. I felt his hands on my head, stroking my hair. I shivered. My head bobbed. My mouth slid along his shaft.

My nose bumped against his pubes on each down stroke. I loved the way he stretched my mouth and made my jaw ache. I loved feeling the tip pressing at the back of my mouth. I was beginning to sweat. My T-shirt clung uncomfortably to my body. I was panting, breathing noisily through my nose.

One of Jim's hands cupped the back of my neck. The other stroked my face. His fingers were soft and warm. I tingled under their touch. He'd begun to move his hips, pumping in and out of my mouth. He was breathing hard, letting out an urgent little grunt every time he exhaled. His erection twitched on my tongue.

'We'd better stop.' Jim's hips stopped pumping. 'Otherwise I'm going to come in your mouth.'

I released him. 'Would that be such a bad thing? You know I love doing it.'

'I can tell. And I love that look of pure pleasure on a your face as I watch you swallow. But I'm not interested in a quick blow job. I want to make love to you properly.' He dropped to his knees and cupped my face. He stroked my lips with his thumb. He started pulling my T-shirt up, trying to get it off. I helped him, pulling it over my head and tossing it aside. Underneath I was naked; my nipples were already hard and red.

He kissed my neck, making me moan. Jim reached behind me and unzipped my skirt and pulled it down over my hips, taking my knickers with it, bunching them up around my knees. He ran his hands up the back of my naked body from my thighs to my shoulders. My skin tingled with heat and desire where his finger-tips made contact. I bent back my head and moaned.

Jim helped me up and we climbed onto the bed. He rolled me over onto my back and pulled my skirt and underwear down my legs, freeing them. He threw them aside and sat back on his heels, smiling and out of breath.

I opened my legs and Jim lay down between them and began slowly kissing along the length of each inner thigh. Starting at the knee, he drew ever closer to my aching cleft. He took his time to kiss my thigh, moving agonisingly near to my very wet crotch, but never actually touching it. I thrust my groin up at him, hoping he would get the idea, but he just went on tonguing the groove between pussy and thigh.

He blew on me, his breath cooling the moist folds. To tease me, he stuck out his tongue and lightly licked the length of my pussy. I closed my eyes and relaxed back against the bed. I concentrated on the sensation his mouth was creating. My heart thumped in my chest. I was goose-pimply all over. The hairs on the back of my neck were erect and tingling.

Jim's tongue bathed my plump lips, wetting and warming them. He sucked one of my swollen labia into his mouth and nibbled on it softly. I moaned and arched my back. His tongue moved constantly, exploring every millimetre, and then he began to concentrate on my clit. He circled the engorged bud, lapped at it.

He flicked my clit with his tongue then sucked it into his mouth. He nibbled it. My body juddered and my nipples tingled. He slid one finger, then two, inside me and I gasped in delight as they filled me. Jim found my G-spot easily and began to massage it as his mouth expertly worked on my swollen bud.

His fingers moved inside me. My crotch ached. I looked down at him as he licked me. His eyes were closed and I could tell that all his attention was focused on pleasuring me. I thrust my crotch against his warm mouth.

My hips were rocking to a rhythm dictated by the fire in my groin. My muscles gripped his fingers. My thighs began to tremble and twitch. My nipples were tingling and sensitive.

Jim's fingers slid inside me. The pressure of his fingertips against my G-spot sent out waves of delight, which pumped round my bloodstream. Tension and excitement built in my belly. The nape of my neck prickled with pinpricks of pleasure.

I pressed my heels down into the mattress, raising my hips up off the bed as I rode Jim's face. Heat and congestion burnt between my legs. My heart was racing. Blood pounded in my ears. I was moaning softly; my breath hissed as it escaped between taut lips.

My nipples were swollen and dark, standing out against my pale skin like ripe berries. Every flutter and tingle in my excited crotch seemed to be transmitted directly to them, making them throb with pleasure.

My hair was damp and matted against the pillow. The duvet beneath me was wrinkled and damp. I was wound up with arousal and tension, aching and urgent. My skin was shivery and alive. Jim worked my clit as his fingers moved inside me.

I ground my crotch against Jim's eager face. I could feel his beard stubble against my sensitive flesh. His hot breath gushed out of his nose as he licked me. He circled his fingers inside me and I arched my back. I was moaning constantly, the sounds reaching a pitch as my excitement grew.

Every muscle in my body was taut and rigid. My legs trembled with involuntary excitement. I could hear Jim's excited breathing as he licked me. His hair was damp under my palms. My moans had grown high and urgent. My body was rigid and trembling. A warm rush of pleasure began to spread out from my belly.

I was coming. A wild, primal, animal scream escaped my throat. My muscles gripped Jim's invading fingers as wave after wave of orgasm overwhelmed me.

He wrapped his free arm round my hip and held on tight, riding out the waves. I pressed my feet into the mattress and thrust myself into his face one last time, calling out his name. Panting and sweaty, I lifted my head off the pillow and smiled at him.

He gave my pussy one final kiss then looked up at me. 'Will you get on your knees for me? I want to do it from behind.' He stroked his cock with one hand. He scrabbled to his feet and kicked off his shoes. He pushed his trousers and pants all the way down and stepped out of them. He unbuttoned his shirt and pulled it off.

I got down on all fours and looked over my shoulder. Jim climbed onto the bed behind me and positioned himself. He stroked my buttocks with both hands, making me tingle.

Jim ran his rigid cock along the length of my pussy,

making me moan. He leant his weight forwards and slid home, filling me. I sighed. It slid past my muscles, coaxing them to open for him. He circled his hips, letting me feel it inside me. I moaned.

I loved the reassuring weight of him behind me and the manly feel of his hairy thighs against my skin. I loved the feel of him inside me, where he belonged. He held on to my hips and began to move. We quickly found a rhythm which suited us both. He pounded me urgently, panting hard.

I turned my head and looked into his face. His blue eyes met mine. They seemed bottomless and deep. They held me, hypnotised me almost. His full lips were curved into a smile. I smiled back.

Jim withdrew and, for a moment, I felt bereft. Then I felt him pressing against the tight bud of my arsehole. He held on to my hips and pushed inside. I grunted in shock as he entered me. I breathed deeply as my muscles grew used to the invasion.

'You bad boy, that feels so good,' I said over my shoulder.

Jim smiled. He rocked his hips, sliding inside me.

I moaned softly as he moved inside me. He bent over my back and kissed me on the shoulder. He rubbed his cheek against my back and his face was damp with perspiration, his hair wet. He reached round with one hand and began fingering my clit.

He pumped me hard. I rocked my hips, meeting his thrusts. My nipples rubbed against the duvet. Jim's expert fingers worked my clit. His other hand gripped my shoulder, providing leverage for his thrusting cock.

My long hair fell in my eyes. It clung to my face in damp strands. My breathing was erratic and loud. I dug my fingers into the duvet, my muscles rigid. Heat coursed through my arteries, it pumped inside my brain. The tingle of tension between my legs that signalled an imminent orgasm was impossible to ignore.

Jim was grunting and gasping. He pounded my arse, jerking my body forwards on each thrust. His thighs felt damp and slippery against my legs. He gripped my shoulder, pulling me onto him. His nails dug into my flesh.

I was getting close again and I could tell from his erratic breathing that Jim was too. Both of us were slick with sweat. He moved inside me. Every nerve ending was alive; I felt nothing but pleasure.

Jim's body began to tremble behind me. He moaned, a low growl that began in his throat and built until it filled the room. I rocked my hips, rubbing my clit against his moving fingers. I was nearly there. I was going to come.

Sweat filmed my body. Damp hair fell over my face and clung to my back. Jim's fingers rubbed my clit. I pressed back against his hand, intensifying the pleasure. I was gasping for breath.

I dug my nails into the duvet and ground my crotch against his hand. Coils of ecstasy spread out from my groin. I cried out. We were coming together. My muscles gripped his cock as orgasm overwhelmed me. My nipples throbbed with pleasure.

He leapt and twitched inside me. He thrust his hips in long slow strokes, emptying his seed into me. I was trembling all over, muscles taut and straining.

I looked over my shoulder at him. His eyes were closed. He was smiling to himself, his lips drawn back, exposing his white teeth. Sweat ran down his face. His body shook and trembled as he came inside me. He collapsed over my back and kissed my neck. His ragged breathing was loud against my ear. His damp hair was cold against my face.

After we'd come Jim stayed inside me, holding me from behind, his sweat-slick body pressing against my back. I felt him soften and plop out of me and he lay down on the bed beside me and brushed my damp hair out of my face. When I got my breath back I turned to him and whispered, 'I've missed you.'

Jim and I never did talk about my absence or the events that had led up to it. He'd promised to tell me everything when he was ready and by going back to him I'd implicitly accepted his terms, even though patience had never come naturally to me.

As the days went on it mattered less and less. It gradually faded like a bad memory or a half-forgotten dream. The gun, the phone calls, the assumed name and the unexplained visits to foreign banks all seemed to fuse into a single shadowy recollection; like an incident from childhood when memory merges with mythology and half-formed emotions and you can no longer trust it.

We stayed at the hotel for a week, barely getting out of bed except to eat. We made love so often that we both got sore and, when the sheets got too sweaty, we'd do it on the sofa or in the bath.

Several times a day Jim's phone would ring and he'd go into the other room to take the call and, when he came back, neither of us would mention the interruption. We'd eat in our room, sitting on the carpet and scoffing the elaborate food as if we were on a picnic. We drank champagne every night, falling asleep slightly tipsy with our lips raw from kissing.

One morning we were just getting out of the shower

when a mobile phone rang in the other room. I raised my eyebrows at Jim and gave a fake sigh.

'It's not mine this time, Claire.'

I ran naked into the sitting room, having no clue where to find my phone. I finally located it in the pocket of my laptop bag, but by the time I managed to find it, it had stopped ringing. I looked at the display. It had been Bernie.

I pressed the button to return the call and sat down on the sofa.

'Hi. Sorry, I couldn't find the phone.'

'That's OK. How are you?' Bernie's voice sounded uncharacteristically tentative.

'Fine. Never better.'

'You're with Jim.'

'Yes. Why?' I rubbed my wet hair with the towel.

There was a long pause. 'Well, as long as you're all right.'

'How's Ollie?'

'Wonderful. He misses you.'

My stomach gave a little flutter. 'I'll see you soon, Bernie. I promise.' I hung up and went back to the bathroom, where Jim was shaving. He used an old-fashioned safety razor and proper soap with a brush. I watched as he slid the blade up his throat, sweeping away the foam.

'Everything OK?' He rinsed the blade in the sink.

I looked at him, my face stern. The phone call agreement clearly didn't extend to mine. 'It was Bernie.'

'What did she want?' He shaved his upper lip and I could hear the blade rasping against the bristles.

I shrugged. 'Nothing. She said Ollie misses me.'

'How sweet.'

I shook my head. 'No, it's code. When we were kids and I came for the holidays, Bernie would always tell me that Bobo – her teddy – had missed me. She was far too self-reliant to tell me she'd missed me herself. She was the big sister and she'd have died rather than admit a vulnerability. I should go home.'

'Of course. I've been greedy.' Jim splashed water onto his shaved face. 'But you'll come back soon?'

'Try to stop me.'

13

I drove back to Oxford and spent a week visiting Bernie and the baby and catching up with work. I went out with friends I hadn't seen for ages and I finally got round to having lunch with Eve. I kept myself busy. I even had fun. But there was a hole in my gut with Jim's name on it.

His absence filled every dusty corner of my life, poisoning every pleasure. I felt incomplete and pointless without him. We spoke every night at eleven and I looked forward to the phone calls like a man with terminal cancer waiting for his dose of morphine. We talked for hours but he never spoke of his 'problems' and I never asked.

He told me he had to spend a few days in London and he invited me to join him for the weekend. He'd booked a suite at a hotel in Kensington, one of those modern, minimalist places which win design awards but completely lack any character. Of course, I wondered why we couldn't stay at his house, but not asking questions had become a habit and a comfort.

I drove up on Friday evening and went straight to the hotel. Jim surprised me by telling me we were going out.

'It's a masked costume ball. A charity thing. I go every year.'

'But we've got nothing to wear.'

'I hired outfits for us. They're in the other room. Shall we go and look.' Jim took my hand and led me through to the bedroom.

Laid out on the bed was an old-fashioned brocade dress in a deep-bronze colour. It had a corseted bodice and a wide skirt. It was the kind of thing Nell Gwynne might have worn.

I reached out and stroked the fabric. 'It's beautiful. Where's yours?'

Jim opened the wardrobe and brought out an outfit on a hanger. 'The theme is characters from fiction. I'm Mr Darcy and you're Moll Flanders. Shall we get dressed?'

'I think I'll do my make-up and hair first. It'll be easier without that heavy dress on.'

In the bathroom I made up my face and put my hair up in a high chignon, leaving half of my curls free to tumble around my face. With my eyeliner pencil, I drew on a couple of beauty spots.

When I got back to the bedroom, Jim was already dressed and was tying his cravat in the mirror. His tight white breeches and frock coat seemed to emphasise his height and physique. His dark hair and masculine features gave the effete clothes an edge of danger, making him look like the archetypal wicked romantic hero.

'How do I look?' He fitted his mask and turned to me for approval.

'Dashing and dangerous, like Flashman or Mr Rochester.'

'Thanks. I like what you've done with your hair. Do you want a hand with the dress?'

I shook my head. 'No, thanks. Why don't you go and sit in the other room and I'll come out when I'm ready.'

Jim left the room and I stripped off my clothes. The outfit had no proper underwear, just a short white chemise and a pair of stockings which were held up with garters. I put them on and picked up the corseted bodice, trying to work out how to put it on. It laced at the back, but I'd never have been able to do it up myself. Then I noticed a row of tiny hooks and eyes at the front, concealed under a flap. They probably weren't very authentic but they were practical.

Getting them done up on my own was quite an operation. At first, I thought they weren't even going to meet, but I pulled hard, stretching the elastic until the bottom hooks were aligned and gradually repeated the procedure until it was fastened all the way up.

The corset reached from under my bust to my hips and it gripped me like a lover's tight embrace. There was a pair of kitten-heeled ankle boots that fastened with a row of buttons at the side. I bent down to put them on and I instantly realised that putting the corset on first had been a mistake. I was constricted so much around the middle that I just couldn't bend far enough without my breathing being inhibited. I tried it over and over again but just succeeded in making myself overheated and breathless. Eventually I undid half a dozen of the hooks at the bottom of the corset to enable me to bend in the middle. I put on the boots before refastening the corset.

I really wanted to look at myself in the corset, stockings and boots before I put the dress on but there was no mirror in the room. I picked up the skirt and went through to the bathroom to use the full-length mirror.

The boots seemed to elongate my legs and the corset nipped in my waist. Though full breasted, I'd never had much of a waist but the corset gave me a perfect hourglass figure. My body reminded me of Gina Lollobrigida in her circus costume in *Trapeze*, or maybe Marilyn Monroe in *Bus Stop*. I'd never really seen myself in that way before; there was always something too Irish, too wholesome about me. But in the mirror, I looked utterly right, utterly myself in the clothes, as if, by manipulating my body, they'd somehow freed the true me.

A thump from next door interrupted my reverie. I began to struggle into the skirt. First I had to put on a stiff padded underpinning. It tied around my waist with a ribbon and stood out on either side of my body, making it look as though I had enormous, projecting hips. The skirt fitted over the top. It was thick and stiff and quite difficult to handle and, when I'd finally got it fastened, I could feel its weight.

I looked at my reflection. I looked incredible. The skirt swung as I moved. My breasts were pushed up over the corseted bodice, covered only by the thin cotton of the chemise. I fitted the final item of my costume: a plain black mask. When I walked into the living room, Jim whistled and got to his feet.

'You look so gorgeous I'm tempted to call off our night out and ravage you instead. But we should go. We don't want to be late.'

'Where are we going anyway?' I asked as we entered the lift.

'Do you know Kenwood House?'

'On Hampstead Heath?'

'That's right. It's for the Friends of London's Museums. You know the sort of thing.'

'The great and the good all dressed up to the nines and vying to get their photo taken for the *Tatler*?'

'Exactly. But it's fun. And where else would you get the opportunity to go out dressed like that?' The lift doors opened. 'Come on, there's a taxi waiting for us outside.'

The taxi dropped us of in the car park, a short walk away from Kenwood House. We could hear the distant rumble of music. All around us extravagantly costumed couples made their way along the narrow path. Ahead of us a woman in a voluminous crinoline and a forty-something man in an American cavalry uniform and sword picked their way along the lane. The woman was using both hands to squash her skirts so as not to get them caught on the bushes either side. The man walked behind her with his hand on the hilt of his sword.

'Scarlett and Rhett,' Jim whispered.

We turned a corner and the house came into view. It was lit up by floodlights. In front of it two enormous marquees had been erected. Amplified music spilt out of the nearest tent. Jim took my hand and led me across the grass.

In the first marquee a small band played on a platform. Beside the stage a handful of costumed couples were dancing to a waltz. A camera-bedecked photographer wandered around, snapping pictures of the partygoers.

The second marquee was laid out with tables covered in glistening white cloths. Candles in frosted glasses twinkled in the centre of each table beside a bowl of roses. There was a bar at one end and a buffet beside it manned by white-shirted waiting staff. We piled up our plates with food and carried them over to a table. Jim went off to the bar to get our drinks.

I was tucking into a tempura prawn when the man we had seen earlier came over to me. Without waiting for an invitation he sat down beside me. His shoulders were so broad beneath his blue, military jacket that I was pretty certain they were heavily padded. He was even sporting a Clark Gable moustache and I tried to work out if it was genuine or glued on.

'I hope you don't mind me interrupting. Allow me to introduce myself –'

'Pleased to meet you, Mr Butler.'

He laughed. 'I can be him, if you like. But who are you? I've been trying to work it out.'

'Moll Flanders.'

'Of course. And you look delightful.' He smiled.

It was odd talking to someone with half of his face covered by a mask and I realised how much of communication is visual rather than verbal.

'Thank you. Where's Scarlett?'

'She's powdering her nose. And where is your escort?'

'I'm here.'

I'd seen Jim approaching, but he was behind Rhett, out of his eye line. Rhett got to his feet.

'I won't keep you, then.' He executed a small formal bow and walked away.

'An admirer?' Jim sat down.

'Yes, I think so.'

'Well, I'm hardly surprised. You look gorgeous.'

'You're not jealous?'

He shook his head. 'I doubt if there's a man here who wouldn't like to go to bed with you. The difference is, I'm the one who does.'

After we'd eaten we went to watch the dancing. Exotically dressed couples whirled around the floor in outfits from all eras. I looked around the floor trying to identify the characters. Most were impossible to work out, but some were obvious. There were several Draculas, half a dozen Guinevere and Lancelots and a Nancy and Bill from *Oliver Twist*. A man in knee breeches and a peasant shirt open at the throat was doing an enthusiastic foxtrot with a woman in a velvet dress and I thought they were probably Heathcliff and Cathy. I turned to Jim.

'Shouldn't I be Lizzie Bennet if you're Mr Darcy?'

'You should.' Jim had to shout to be heard over the

music. 'But, to tell you the truth, I wanted to see you in a corset. Do you mind?'

I laughed. 'Not at all. I love the outfit.'

'Let's dance.' Jim took my hand and led me onto the dance floor. We managed a waltz without major accident, but when the music changed to a quickstep I became totally lost, in spite of Jim's guidance. I couldn't follow the beat or keep up with the steps. When we finally admitted defeat I was breathless and overheated.

'You obviously paid attention to those dancing lessons at Sandhurst. I seem to have two left feet.'

'Never mind.' He bent his head and put his ear right beside mine. His hot breath on my neck made me tingle. 'Why don't we find ourselves somewhere secluded for a private dancing lesson?' He kissed my neck and a flurry of feather-light shivers slid along my spine.

'Where do you have in mind? There are an awful lot of people about.'

'I'm sure we'll find somewhere.' He took my hand and led me out of the tent and across the garden. In the distance the lake gleamed silver in the moonlight. We walked away from the house. The music grew quieter and more distant as we neared the lake. Jim led me behind a tree, a huge oak, and pressed me up against the trunk. I could feel its gnarled bark against my naked shoulders, cold and hard.

Jim cupped my face between both hands and kissed me. I closed my eyes. My crotch seemed to soften and grow warm. My breasts were pressed up against his chest with only the thin covering of my cotton chemise between us. My nipples were crinkled and sensitive. His lips slid down my throat and I sighed.

His hands pulled down my chemise, uncovering my breasts. I gasped as he kneaded them and his fingers found my swollen nipples. My heart was pounding. My breathing had quickened and grown shallow. My skin was goose-pimply and alive with pleasure.

Jim bent his head and sucked on a nipple. His mouth was hot and wet, his breathing noisy. I tingled all over and my legs turned weak. I leant against the tree trunk for support. He began to tug at the front of my skirts, his hands clumsy with urgency. I pulled them up, using both hands to bunch them up around my waist. The cool air felt delicious and wicked against my naked pussy. My chest was heaving. My crotch was hot and tight.

I watched as Jim fumbled with the front of his breeches. There was no fly, so the only way to free his erection was to pull them down. He slid them down to his knees and his arousal was obvious, standing out in front of him, purple and proud. Jim took a step forwards and slid his hands under my skirt. He cupped a buttock in each hand and lifted me up. I held onto his shoulders and wrapped my legs around him.

I was rigid with excitement and anticipation. I was breathless and hot. My skirts were bunched uncomfortably round my waist and my nipples were rubbing against Jim's clothes. Between my legs I was liquid and tingling. Jim reached between us with one hand, positioning himself. He pushed forwards with his hips and began to slide into me.

I moaned as he entered me. I could feel him stretching my muscles, filling me. I was trembling all over. My nipples prickled with pleasure.

Jim began to jab his hips, each thrust ramming me back against the tree. I wrapped myself around him, arms over his shoulders and ankles crossed behind him. I tilted my pelvis up to meet his thrusts, matching his rhythm and grinding my clit against his scratchy pubes.

My nipples ached. A hot fist of tension was pulling at

the base of my belly. My breathing was rapid and shallow. My chest heaved.

He was hot and hard inside me. His thighs muscles were taut and straining. Warm breath hissed out between taut lips, heating my skin. I could feel his heart beating against mine.

Our bodies moved as one. Our hips pumped.

Damp hair clung to my face. Sweat filmed my skin. My nipples rubbed against the coarse material of his coat, making them tingle. Heat and excitement pumped around my body. My crotch ached.

Jim's fingers dug into my buttocks. Each stab of his hips thrust my body upwards. My back rubbed against the rough tree bark. Music rumbled in the distance. A bird twittered overhead. The sound of our excited breathing seemed to hang in the air.

I was tingling all over. Shivery tingles crept up my nape and over my scalp. My nipples prickled with pleasure. Blood pumped in my ears.

I saw something move at the edge of my vision. I turned my head to look. About a hundred yards away, Rhett Butler stood watching us. My stomach seemed to flutter and leap. A wave of heat crashed over my face.

'We've got a spectator, to your right.' My voice was an excited whisper. Jim turned his head to look, hips still pumping.

'He must have followed us.' He repositioned his hands, getting a firmer grip. 'But you always seem to like an audience, don't you?'

'Maybe.' I imagined Rhett's eyes on my body, taking in every detail, consuming me with his gaze. The taut muscles in my thighs, Jim's fingers digging into my buttocks. My curls dancing and falling in my face in rhythm with Jim's thrusting hips, my wobbling, rosy-tipped breasts.

My pussy tingled. My nipples burnt. I gripped Jim with my legs, pulling him into me. I ground my clit against his pubes.

Jim was grunting from exertion and excitement. He was rigid inside me, thick and pumped with blood. His hips pistoned. I held on tight, pulling down hard on his shoulders and bringing up my pelvis to meet him, matching his rhythm.

I was hot and uncomfortable inside the heavy clothes. My skirts were bunched and tangled around my waist. The top of the corset chafed my skin. Sweat ran down my body. Jim's thighs were damp and itchy against my skin. My crotch burnt with heat and pressure.

Jim stepped up the pace, thrusting his hips in short sharp jabs. His weight pinned me against the tree, thrusting me up and down, rubbing my naked buttocks against the rough bark. I was panting and moaning. I was quivering all over, muscles taut and straining.

I held on tight, pulling in with my legs to match his thrusts. I rubbed myself against his pubes, hips moving frantically. Tension built. Pleasure pumped around my bloodstream. The hairs on the back of my neck were erect and tingling. Shivers slid up my spine.

I looked over at our voyeur. He'd moved closer. He stood with one hand on the hilt of his sword, the other clenched into a fist. He was directly in a shaft of moonlight and I could clearly see that he was smiling.

I imagined standing in his place watching us. Could he see that Jim was beginning to lose control? Had he noticed me gripping him with my legs, pulling him into me? Could he see how aroused I was? Riding the knife-edge of orgasm, ready to tip over the brink?

I watched him watching me, keeping my eyes focused on his face. I was sure he knew I could see him, but he didn't move. Was his heart pounding in his chest?

Was his cock hard? Was his breathing thready and shallow?

My nipples throbbed, my crotch ached. Jim's strokes grew short and frantic. His hips pumped. His arm muscles were taut and quivering. His fingers dug into my buttocks. His face was filmed with sweat. His hair clung to his forehead. He was grunting and panting.

I was moaning and sobbing. Tension was building to a pitch. My crotch was on fire. Jim gave a final deep thrust. His body juddered and shook. He tipped back his head and groaned into the night.

I pulled in my legs and rocked my hips, grinding my aching clit against him. Orgasm shot through me like a drug rush. Pleasure shot up my spine. I tingled all over, my muscles trembled.

I sobbed and screamed. Jim was breathing like a steam train, pressing his body up against mine as he came inside me. It kept on coming. I was breathless and weak. I shivered all over. My thigh muscles were taut and straining. I ground my crotch against Jim, wringing out every shred of pleasure.

I was light headed and dizzy, blood thundered inside my skull. I clung onto Jim, riding it out. Sweat trickled down my face. I was alive with pleasure. My scalp prickled.

It went on and on. My heart hammered. My body shook. My legs trembled. I could feel Jim's balls pressing up against me as he came inside me. His weight pressed me against the tree, holding me in place. He watched my face, a half-smile on his lips, his eyes glowing and intense.

We stayed like that long after it was over and he'd softened and slipped out of me. His body was hot and heavy. His clothes scratched my skin and made it itch. His skin against mine was damp and slippery.

'Is he still watching?'

'Yes. He saw it all.'

Jim laughed, softly. 'Let me put you down.'

I straightened my legs and Jim lowered me to the ground. He took a step back, trousers still round his knees, and waved to our voyeur. Rhett raised both hands and mimed applause then bowed and walked away.

Back at the hotel, I went into the bathroom to take off my make-up. When I came out Jim was already in bed. I undressed, tossing my clothes on a chair. I climbed in beside him and he pulled me close. He ran his fingers along my spine. I could hear him inhaling, smelling my hair. Already my crotch was hot and tingly. My breathing had grown thready and rapid. I could feel a pulse throbbing in my throat.

Jim sat up and slid his hand under his pillow. He pulled out a length of rope in a coil. 'Why don't you lie down and put your hands above your head?' His voice was thick with arousal.

I slid over to the middle of the bed, pulling across my pillow to support my head. I raised my arms over my head. Jim looped the rope around one of the bed's brass rails then used the free ends to tie my wrists. When he was finished, he pulled on the rope, making sure I was firmly restrained. It was hard and itchy against my skin. Shivery tingles spread up my body, making my nipples tingle.

Jim pushed back the covers. I could see that he already had an erection. He clambered across the bed and knelt between my legs. The rope pulled on my upper arms, stretching them above my head. My ribcage was elongated and stretched. My heart was pounding. I could hear my own rapid breathing.

He stroked the length of my pussy with his thumb.

My body was rigid with tension. My crotch was aching and painful. He pushed my thighs apart. Jim ran his finger along the length of my pussy. He stroked my clit, circling it with his fingertip, teasing me. My body shuddered and my nipples peaked.

The fine hairs on my nape were at attention, prickling with pleasure. My skin was alive, tingling with pleasure and excitement. Jim's fingers stroked me. Tension and warmth throbbed in my crotch. Blood was rushing to my head. Endorphins were coursing round my bloodstream, making me feel dizzy and intoxicated.

Every throb and flutter of my crotch seemed to be directly transmitted to my erect nipples. They burnt and tingled. My crotch was tight. Heat and excitement pumped around my body.

Jim began to stroke my clit directly. I moaned. I rocked my hips, establishing a rhythm. I'd begun to pant. My chest rose visibly as I breathed.

I lifted my head and looked down at Jim. It pulled on my arms and the rope dug into my wrists. He was sitting cross-legged, gazing at my crotch. I could see a fine sheen of sweat on his upper lip. His eyes were shining and intense. His lips were slightly parted and the tip of his tongue was visible, glistening and pink. Between his legs, his erection stood proud.

I relaxed back against the pillow. My crotch was tingling. I was covered in goose pimples. Jim slid two fingers into me and I gasped. My nipples prickled with pleasure. He curled the fingers inside me and began to press them against my G-spot. I gave an involuntary jerk as he located it. He began to push the tips of his fingers hard into the sensitive spot, at the same time rubbing my clit with his thumb. Sweat trickled out of my hair and ran down my face. I gripped the bedspread, arching my back and rocking my hips.

Jim slid his fingers in and out slowly, pressing the tips into my G-spot on the in-stroke. His thumb never left my clit. Each stroke of Jim's thumb brought me to a new pitch of arousal. The pillow felt solid under my head. My bound arms ached. The sheet was slippery and crumpled beneath me. It was stuffy and humid in the room with the windows closed and I was sweaty and damp.

My nipples prickled with pleasure and heat. The hairs on the back of my neck were erect and tingling. My crotch felt liquid and tight. My breathing was shallow and erratic and I'd begun to moan. I mewled and sobbed constantly, each little tremble and throb eliciting a new exclamation of pleasure.

Jim dug his fingers hard into my G-spot and I screamed. The shock and pleasure of it made my body jerk backwards. My head hit the headboard and it crashed against the wall. He did it again, but this time I was ready for it. I let out a long deep moan.

The feeling seemed to focus all my sensation to my crotch and was so intense it was almost, but not quite, an orgasm. Every time he did it, my arousal seemed to step up a gear. I'd never been so wound up with excitement or tension and I knew that when the dam burst it would be incredible.

I looked at Jim. Sweat glistened on his brow. His cheeks were flushed pink and his lips were full and dark. From time to time, he let out a little grunt of exertion as he pushed his fingers into me. I could see the muscles and tendons in his forearm moving as he worked. Seeing me watching him, he smiled and dipped his head and sucked hard on my clit a couple of times.

As his hot mouth made contact, my thigh muscles quivered and a hot gush of excitement rushed over my neck and face. Jim straightened up. His fingers stretched me open, pulling on my lips and creating delicious tension on my clit. I was sweaty and exhausted. Damp hair clung to my face. The pillow under my head felt like wood and my neck ached.

My crotch felt wet and slippery. Jim was stroking my clit with his free hand. My nipples were crinkled and tingly. My heart was beating so hard that I thought if I looked down I'd be able to see it. There was a hot coil of pleasure and excitement nestled at the base of my belly.

I was rocking my hips, thrusting them rhythmically up and down. I dug my heels into the mattress. The bed was creaking and screeching. The headboard banged against the wall.

There were tears in my eyes; I could feel them running down the side of my face and into my hair. Sensation and heat were all that existed for me. I was a pounding heart, an aching crotch, taut nipples.

The pleasure was coming in waves, each new peak larger than before. The coil of excitement in my belly had focused and intensified. My back was arched, my hips pistoned. I could hear moaning and sobbing, but it seemed far away and unimportant. The headboard banged against the wall like a bass beat; the springs squealed. My clit was rigid and tingling.

Jim curled his fingers inside me and circled his thumb hard against my clit. It was all it took to push me over the edge. My body shook. I was writhing about on the bed, back arched and muscles taut. Jolts of pleasure spread out from my crotch like lightning. My toes curled, I pressed my head into the hard pillow, my bottom came up off the bed.

I heard myself screaming, crying and laughing. It was so loud that it hurt my ears. Blood boomed in my head. Pleasure rocketed through me. Tingles slid up and down my spine. I could feel myself coming.

My body was rigid. I was panting and screaming. Sweat poured off me. The sheet underneath me was damp and creased. My hair was dripping. I just kept on coming, gripping Jim's fingers like a vice. My breasts tingled; every throb of orgasm seemed to travel directly from my clit to my nipples.

I could hear Jim panting and groaning as I came. He held onto my thigh with his free hand. I was trembling all over. I gasped for breath. My throat hurt.

I relaxed back against the bed. I was shattered. My chest heaved. My muscles ached. Every so often my crotch gave a little butterfly flutter as my muscles adjusted. I felt sweaty and filthy. I heaved myself up as far as I could and looked down at Jim.

He smiled. Slowly, he slid his fingers out of me. He lay down on top of me, supporting his weight on one elbow and using his other hand to position his cock. I could feel his hot wine-scented breath on my face as he pushed his erection up against me. It was hot and wet and slippery. It began to slide inside, stretching me and spreading my lips. I was trembling all over. My crotch tingled.

Jim put a hand on either side of my body and straightened his arms, locking them at the elbow, like a man just about to do press-ups. He rolled his hips upwards, pressing himself into me.

I let out a long deep sigh as he slid into me. I felt him slipping past my muscles, thick and hard. He was stretching and filling me. I spread my legs wider and brought my hips up to meet him. I could feel my clit rubbing against his pubic hair as we moved, providing delicious friction. My clit was swollen and sensitive. The hairs on the back of my neck prickled with pleasure.

His face was transformed by lust. His eyes were glassy. Breath hissed between his teeth. The scratchy rope dug into my wrists and made them sweat. Jim moved inside me. A red flush of arousal was visible on Jim's chest and throat. He began to move his hips, thrusting in short violent stabs. He let out a little grunt on each stab, like a boxer delivering an uppercut, or a tennis player returning a serve.

My hair was trapped beneath my shoulders. My body jerked with each thrust, rubbing my head against the bed. A ball of heat throbbed in my belly. I was covered in goose pimples.

Jim lowered himself onto his elbows and dipped his head to suck on my nipple. I gave a high gasp of shock and pleasure. He sucked on the distended bud, lavishing it with his tongue. His mouth was fiery hot. Breath hissed out of his nostrils, warming my skin.

Jim began to nibble, using his teeth to pull on my nipple, elongating my breast. His hips pumped. I could feel his pubes scratching my naked labia and rubbing against my clit. His balls bashed up against the top of my buttocks.

Exquisite pleasure burnt in my nipple. My crotch ached. Tickly little tingles of excitement slid up and down my spine. My arm muscles were stretched and beginning to ache. Jim's damp hair had fallen in his face. His back shone in the light. He was grunting and moaning as he worked my nipple.

Jim began to kiss my breasts. He lavished my hot flesh with his tongue. He sucked on it, and I felt my skin being drawn into his mouth, then between his teeth as he began to nibble. A warm thrilling rush crept up my neck. My crotch was hot and tight. I could feel it gripping Jim, pulling him into me. His teeth dug into the meat of my breast and I began to moan, throwing back my head and groaning at the ceiling.

Pressure and heat and pain seemed to throb into me

from Jim's mouth. I could hear obscene, wet squishy noises as he sucked on my flesh. His hips moved rhythmically, on autopilot.

The bed was complaining loudly, creaking and groaning beneath us, shaking and rocking as if it was on the verge of collapse. Jim stepped up the pace and the headboard began to bash against the wall on every thrust.

He nibbled my breast. I cried out, a single high cry of pleasure. Jim gave my breast a final kiss and straightened up, looking down at me. I was rigid with excitement, my back arched. My crotch ached.

The headboard banged, the bed squealed. I looked up at his face. He was close to coming; I knew the signs. His eyes narrowed and flickered, his lips were full and dark. Every so often, he moistened his dry lips with his tongue.

Some men look aggressive when they fuck you, their faces transformed by power and momentum, but not Jim. He always looked like a musician lost in a moment of musical ecstasy or maybe, I thought, like a saint in one of those old master paintings, in the throes of some divine epiphany.

His thrusts were pushing me up the bed. My nipples tingled; tension and pleasure burnt in my belly. Having already reached orgasm I knew it wouldn't take long for me to come again. Jim slid his hands down the bed and under my buttocks. He gripped a cheek in each hand for leverage and gave several short hard thrusts. I wrapped my legs around him, locking my feet behind his knees. His wet face rested on my breasts and I longed to be able to take it in my hands and kiss it all over.

His fingers dug into my buttocks. His body began to buck and tremble. He was grunting between clenched teeth as he breathed. The bed rattled and shook, the headboard clanging against the wall. Tension and heat built in my gut. My skin prickled with pleasure. Watery shivers of excitement slid along my spine. My nipples burnt.

Jim was thrusting in short urgent strokes. I matched his rhythm, pressing down with my feet and bringing my hips up to meet him. Blood throbbed in my ears. Our sweat-slick bodies slid against each other. Damp hair clung to my face.

He was grunting and panting. His hair was damp against my breasts. His hips pistoned. I was on the edge. Heat and excitement flooded through me. I was tingling all over. My crotch was liquid and constricted. My thigh muscles were quivering.

'God!' Jim gave a final deep thrust and lifted his head to look at me. His body seemed to quiver. His blue eyes gazed into mine, shining and intense. I felt him come inside me and imagined the creamy sperm filling me.

The tension shattered. Pleasure jolted up my spine like a lightning strike. I was tingling all over. Jim was motionless apart from his heaving chest and the trembling he seemed powerless to control. His arms were locked at the elbow, his fingers pressed into my buttocks. I was panting and sobbing. My head thrashed against the pillow. Orgasm flooded through me. My nipples tingled, my skin prickled.

It kept on coming, crashing over me like a flood. I was alive with pleasure and excitement. I was trembling all over. Damp hair clung to my face. My body was rigid, my back arched. I shuddered as the final peak possessed me. I let out a long involuntary moan, a long note of pleasure and excitement.

Jim's body was heavy, his skin clammy. His breathing began to slow. I felt my muscles soften and relax. I was suddenly exhausted. He let go of my buttocks and reached up to untie my wrists. I lowered my arms gingerly and wrapped them around him. Jim lay there for several minutes with his head on my chest, stroking my back and occasionally turning his head to kiss my throat. Finally, he spoke. 'Would you do me a favour and get something out of my jacket for me? It's a black velvet box.' He lifted his head and looked at me. He was smiling; his eyes seemed to sparkle in the light.

I got up and went over to the chair where Jim had left his clothes. 'Is this it?' I held up a flat square plush-covered box.

'That's it, bring it over here.'

I carried it back to the bed and handed it over. 'What's in it? Is it for me? It's not even my birthday.' I knelt down beside the bed.

'Patience.' Jim opened the box and held it out to me. Inside, nestled in a blue velvet lining, was a thick silver necklace like a torque, which seemed to be formed of a single flat piece of metal. But, as I looked closer, I could see a small hinge in the centre of the back and in the front it fastened with a tiny silver padlock. Inside the circle formed by the necklace there was a heavy silver chain with an ornate key hanging from it. 'There's an inscription on the back.'

I picked up the torque. It twinkled in the light as I turned it over in my hands. I read the inscription aloud. '"To Claire with all my love, Jim. Without the slave the master is nothing." Jim, it's beautiful. Shall I put it on?'

'Let me. We'll have to unlock it first.' Jim took the box and used the key to release the tiny padlock. He put the torque around my neck and fitted the padlock. When it snapped shut an icy shiver of excitement slid down my spine. Jim fastened the chain with the key around his own neck.

'It's lovely. I'll never take it off.'

'Obviously not.' Jim lifted the key on its chain and waved it at me. 'You know, I'm getting tired of this rootless life I've been leading. I'm thinking of going back to work. But first, I think I'd like to do some more travelling. Our little jaunt to Europe has given me a taste for it and I'd like it very much if you'd come with me. There's almost a month before term starts. Please say yes.'

'I'd love to, but I've got a lot of work to do before October. I'll have to see how much time I've got available. Though I must admit, I've rather missed the van. It's like travelling around in your own little cocoon.'

'I know what you mean. I spent six months in it, driving all over Europe. I grew to think of it as my turtle shell. But I thought we'd push the boat out a little this time – hire a car, stay in hotels. Money's no problem, so why not?' Jim pulled back the covers and I climbed in beside him. 'I had this friend once, called Terry. He was a proper scally. Nothing seemed to frighten him. He'd break into building sites and climb to the top of the scaffold, then prance around up there like a tightrope walker.' He reached down and stroked the surface of my collar.

'He sounds like fun.'

'He was. Terry always used to say you should live as if you expected to die the very next day. I didn't understand what he meant at the time. I thought I was immortal then. Though when you get to our age, you know that death lurks around every corner. It wasn't until I grew up that I realised Terry had learnt that lesson young. His mum died of cancer when he was seven. And a few weeks later, his dad went down to the railway line and threw himself under a train. Terry knew then something it's taken me all my life to learn.'

'Eat, drink and be merry, for tomorrow we may die.'

'Except I've always thought it ought to be "Eat, fuck and be merry"; put two fingers up to the grim reaper by celebrating life. Please say you'll come with me. It wouldn't be the same without you.'

'As long as I'm back in time for the start of term, I'd love to come.'

Next morning I woke up to find Jim gone. I could hear the shower running in the en suite bathroom. I sat up, intending to surprise him by climbing in beside him when I spotted his wallet lying on the bedside table. I shuffled across the bed and picked it up with trembling hands.

Inside there was the usual fat wad of cash and several credit cards. I carefully slid out the first one and looked at it: 'Mr James Griffin'. I pulled out another at random – it was a company American Express card in the name of Specialised Security Services Limited. I held the cards in my hand, paralysed and confused. I'd suspected he was using a false name but somehow finding proof of it was shocking. I didn't know what to think, what I should do.

The water stopped and I heard the shower door slide open. I put the cards away and replaced the wallet.

14

On Monday, back in Oxford, I rang Eve and quickly discovered that James William Griffin had graduated from Trinity in 1989. I went online and typed Specialised Security Services into Google and the first item on the list was the company website. I felt like a traitor as I waited for the page to load but, if Jim wouldn't tell me the truth, I had to find it myself.

His company, it appeared, specialised in personal security in high-risk situations but was distinctly vague on details except that it operated extensively in the Middle East. So that explained why he spoke French like an Arab. Jim was listed as founder and director of operations.

After two more hours of fruitless searching my back ached and my eyes stung. I went downstairs to make some coffee and accidentally knocked a cup into the sink as I was filling the kettle. Clumsiness was a sure sign that something was wrong. As I made the coffee I tried to work out what I should do about my discoveries. It seemed that honesty was a one-way street with Jim keeping rigid control over the direction of the traffic. He demanded that I prove my trust even though he refused to return the favour.

Though I knew every millimetre of his body and had shared his most intimate thoughts, there were whole territories of his soul I was a stranger to. If he had nothing to hide then why had he hidden it? It's only our shame and our sin that we take such pains to make secrets of. Surely he didn't think I would judge him?

Sometimes I felt as though he actually wanted me to fear the worst. I'd never found out how he'd got his scar. I'd assumed he'd been wounded in combat but, for all I knew, it could have been a fight in a pub. Or the prison remark – deliberately piquing my interest and then leaving me hanging as if he relished my shock and confusion.

And yet I'd never felt so safe as when I was with Jim. I'd never once felt in danger with him, not even when the two incompetent thieves had tried to break into the camper. And I didn't for a moment think it was the gun in his hand that had made me feel safe. It was Jim, his presence, his confidence and that odd blend of strength and gentleness that he seemed to embody. Paradox was woven through his personality like the blue veins in a slice of Stilton.

I'd promised him I would wait for answers but I couldn't ignore things any more. I knew I had to do something but how could I even bring up the subject without owning up to going through his wallet and instantly putting myself in the wrong? In any case, did I even want to know the truth? There was comfort and familiarity in denial and pretence.

I carried my coffee through to the conservatory and drank it looking out onto the garden. The grass was long and the beds weedy and overgrown. I'd been neglecting things since I'd met Jim.

Disorder had always paralysed me. The untidier my surroundings grew the more frozen I became. The external confusion somehow seemed to seep inside me and eat away at my ability to focus. Taming the chaos in my environment was the only way of banishing the chaos inside. It seldom failed me.

I finished my coffee then put on my gardening clothes and went out to tackle the jungle. The garden tamed, I turned my attention to the house. I dusted and hoovered from top to bottom, changed the bedding, put the ironing away. When I'd finished, I felt dirty and hot so I ran a bath and lay in the tub with my eyes closed until the water began to cool. As I dried myself it struck me that the answer had been obvious all along.

The next day Jim picked me up and we drove to Heathrow. He hadn't been exaggerating when he'd promised me a luxury holiday. We flew first class to Paris, hired a convertible Mercedes at the airport and booked ourselves into the Ritz.

After dinner we got ready for bed. When I came out of the bathroom Jim was sitting up reading in bed. He looked at me over the top of his glasses, a gesture that, for some reason, I always found irresistible. He took them off and put them on the bedside table then threw back the covers and patted the mattress. He opened his arms for me and I laid my head on his chest.

'Claire, forgive me if I'm mistaken, but it seems to me you've been acting a little strange all day. Sort of distracted and withdrawn. You hardly spoke to me on the flight. Is there something wrong?'

If I'd been able to see his face I don't think I'd have been able to answer but lying like this I felt somehow cocooned and protected.

'Yes, there is, now you come to mention it.' I stroked his belly with my fingertips, running them along the hard tendrils of his scar. 'You remember the night we went to the ball?'

'Of course.'

'Well, the next morning when you were in the shower I noticed your wallet on the bedside table so I looked inside.' My heart felt as if it had leapt into my throat.

'I see. Helped ourselves to a little cash, did we?' Jim's tone was light, jokey almost.

'No, of course not. I'm not a thief.'

'That would sound much more convincing if you hadn't just admitted to going through my wallet.' His voice remained neutral. He kissed me on the top of the head.

'Are you angry?' I daren't look up at him.

'Do I sound it?'

'No, you don't actually. I would be.'

'It's only natural, Claire. I can hardly blame you. And what did you find out?' He stroked my hair.

'Your real name. So, when I got home, I rang up my friend – who happens to be registrar at Trinity – and she found your graduation details.'

'I see. And I assume that you'd already done the same for Jim Hyde and discovered he doesn't exist?' His hand stroked my back.

'Yes.' I waited for a response, my heart pounding, but Jim remained silent. 'So then I Googled the name of your company and found the website.'

'And now you want an explanation?'

'I know I promised I'd wait, but I'm frightened, Jim. Only, this time, I'm not running away. I tried burying my head in the sand, but it didn't work. I need the truth now. You've asked me for total trust and I've given it over and over again. But you've given me nothing in return except this strange life we lead when we're together – as if there's no past and no future, just now, just us.'

'I thought you enjoyed being with me?'

'I do. I love it. I love you. But it's not quite real, is it? You've got a whole other life that I'm locked out of.

There's something going on and I need to know what it is. Why can't you trust me?' I sat up.

Jim was leaning against a pile of pillows, his body turned towards me. His hands were loosely clasped and I noticed a pale band where he usually wore his watch. His scars were just visible above the bedclothes – a chaotic mass of raised red ropes which pulled and distorted his skin. I could see his chest rising and falling as he breathed. He looked straight at me, his lips formed into a half-smile. Somehow, the stripe across his wrist and his war wound seemed to make him seem vulnerable and to fill me with tenderness.

'You're right,' he said finally. He reached out and took my hand. 'I should apologise. I've been so concerned about keeping my secrets that it never even occurred to me I could trust you with them. I hope you can forgive me.'

'Of course I can. But I can't put up with this secrecy any longer. If I don't get the truth – right here, right now – I honestly don't think we can go on.'

I saw alarm in Jim's eyes.

'I couldn't bear it if you left me again. When you shut yourself away I felt utterly lost and alone. I knew then I should tell you the truth, but I wasn't ready.'

'But you'll tell me now?'

Jim nodded. 'I'll tell you everything. Right from the beginning.' He began to tell me his story. At first it was tentative and faltering, like picking at a scab. He told me of his penny-pinching childhood in a home without love where school was his refuge and salvation and he'd gone to university as a deliberate act of escape.

He told me that he'd joined the army right after graduation. He'd worked in intelligence with Special Forces and had nearly died when a bomb exploded beside him in the first Gulf War – so that explained the scars.

After that, he'd been a mercenary in Africa, then had seen a gap in the market so he'd started the business. Most of his clients were Middle East governments. It was specialised work, not all of it strictly legal and even some of the legal stuff was morally dubious. He talked long into the night as we sat in the dark holding hands, filling in details, facts and feelings. Eventually, we both grew too tired to carry on and we turned out the light and fell asleep in each other's arms.

We spent two days exploring Paris then drove south, heading for Spain. In Monaco we stayed at the Hermitage, with its belle époque exterior and then the Grande Hotel in Cap Ferrat where we walked in the footsteps of Somerset Maugham and Churchill.

Each night after dinner Jim would tell me part of his story. I learnt he'd married the daughter of his senior officer and they'd argued about children – he'd wanted them, she hadn't. I learnt the names of his lovers, how he'd felt when his parents had died.

Night after night he'd share another instalment of his past. He began to grow hungry for it, rushing through dinner so that we could sit side by side sharing his secrets. The words tumbled out like floodwater breaching a dam.

Every few days we moved on to another city and another hotel. Our fellow residents were an odd mix of those born to money and those who had acquired obscene quantities of it. We rubbed shoulders with dukes, American heiresses and media celebrities. The former looked down on the latter and Jim and I couldn't help looking down on them all.

There was a sense of unreality about everything – the

lifestyle, the picture-postcard locations and Jim's nightly confessions. I began to sense that, for him, our journey represented something more. A final fling or even some kind of extended wake. I listened to each halting confession silently, never commenting or judging. His story seemed to be building towards a climax and I knew that his secret was at its heart.

Near Barcelona, at Alcañiz, we stayed at Castillo Calatravos. It stood on a hill above the town, its Gothic, fortress-like walls forming a natural defence and providing spectacular views. After dinner Jim took me for a walk in the grounds and we sat down on a bench beneath a tree. We sat silently for a while, watching the sun dip behind the castillo, staining the sky lilac. Cicadas trilled in the woods behind us.

'Do you remember me telling you about Terry?'

I nodded. 'Your friend, the scally.'

'That's right. After I did my A levels I worked in a pub. I was supposed to go up to Oxford in the autumn, only that's not how it happened. One night someone left their credit card behind and I pocketed it and had a bit of a spree.'

'Like that Fry guy?'

'Exactly. I don't know why I did it. It seemed harmless at the time ... not even real money. Anyway, I ended up in prison. That's where I met Terry and, afterwards, we stayed friends. Do you remember a bank robbery about ten years ago? It was in all the papers. The gang managed to intercept a consignment of used notes on their way to being destroyed.'

'Yes, I do. Did they catch them in the end? I can't remember.'

'No, they didn't. Well, Terry was part of the gang. If it had been me, I'd have taken the proceeds and gone to Rio or wherever and lived quietly on it for the rest of my life. But Terry ... I suppose it was his childhood, but no matter how much money he had he always wanted more. Anyway, he went to prison for another robbery and spent the next seven years inside. When he came out he got cancer and died within months.'

'I'm sorry. You were obviously fond of him. What happened to his money?'

'He left it to me. Before he'd gone inside he'd left me a locked briefcase and asked me to look after it. We were pals so I never asked any questions. After he died I opened it.'

'And it was the money?'

Jim laughed. 'No. You can't fit that much money in a briefcase. It was details of where he'd stashed it and a letter saying that if anything happened to him he wanted me to have it.'

'So that's what you've been living on?'

'Mostly. But there's more. Terry had a partner-in-crime. His real name's Kenneth but everyone calls him Taxi because of his big ears. He was inside when Terry died but when he came out he wanted his share.'

'And he knew Terry had given it to you?'

'I don't know how he found out, but he did.'

'And he's after you?'

'Right. So I left the country and spent months travelling about in the camper van. I took the cash with me and, in every town I passed –'

'You put it in the bank.'

'Not exactly. I opened a safe deposit box and put some of the money in it.'

'So it was Taxi who broke into your office?'

'Yes. Looking for me. I'd covered my tracks, of course, and I didn't think he'd be able to find me but then he broke into my house –'

'That's when you left The Feathers?'

'Right. I knew it would only be a matter of time, so I tossed my mobile and moved on.'

'And that's why you've come abroad again? To get away?'

'No ... no ... I've decided to stop running. I'm going to give him the money. Money made a prisoner of Terry; I don't want that happening to me. So that's it. My whole sordid story. Are you shocked?'

I smiled at him and slowly shook my head. 'So you've got a past, we all have. And Terry stole it, not you. It doesn't change a thing. In fact, if I'm totally honest, it's part of what I like about you. Your darker side, your contradictory nature, is a big part of your appeal.'

'I'm glad you think so. That's why I chose to call myself "Mr Hyde" actually.'

'Of course, Dr Jekyll's sinister alter ego. How apt. I can definitely relate to that. I know there's something dark and hidden inside me longing to be expressed. Does that make sense?'

'It does. Baudelaire said, "I have felt the wind from the wing of madness." I think we should all taste madness occasionally. Look it in the eye and see what it can teach us. Otherwise we're only living half a life.' Jim took my hand. 'So you still love me?'

'Of course I do.'

He smiled. 'I just needed to hear you say it.' He took my hand. 'Come with me.'

I allowed him to lead me into the tall pine trees. Twigs crackled underfoot and the moist air smelt of compost. It was growing dark. I bumped into an overhanging branch.

'Where are we going? I can't see a thing.'

'This ought to do.' Jim dropped my hand and took off his jacket. He laid it down on the ground like Walter

Raleigh flinging down his cloak. 'Lie down there. I assume you're knickerless, as usual?'

'I am, but –'

'Just lie down. The minute I uncover my arse every gnat for miles around is going to come and feast on it. The quicker we are the better.'

'What about me? They'll bite me too.' I sat down on the jacket and then lay down.

'I promise I'll massage calamine lotion into every single bite.' Jim knelt on the ground. He leant forwards and lifted my legs, bending them at the knees. I felt the night air on my naked pussy. I could feel bumps and prickles through his jacket.

He lifted my skirt up to my waist, folding it neatly out of the way. Then he did the same with my strappy T-shirt, uncovering my breasts. My nipples crinkled as the cool air hit them, making them tingle. I leant up on my elbows and watched as Jim unzipped his trousers and pulled them and his boxers down to his knees.

'Mmmmm ... you're already hard.' I could see the purple tip of his helmet peeking out from the foreskin cowl.

Jim reached between my legs and slid a finger along my slit. 'And you're already wet.'

He got on top of me, supporting his weight on one elbow, and used his other hand to position himself. I gave a deep sigh of satisfaction as I felt him sliding inside me.

The air felt slightly moist against my skin. I could hear small animals scampering nearby and orchestral music in the distance, coming from the hotel restaurant. Jim's weight felt solid and reassuring on top of me. He bent his head and sucked on a nipple. Tingly fingers trailed up my spine. The hairs on the back of my neck stood up.

My nipples were hard and sensitive. Jim's sucked one swollen bud into his hot mouth and ran his tongue across the tip.

I reached down and laced my fingers through his hair. His hips moved slowly, each tiny movement eliciting a wave of pleasure.

I could feel Jim's balls pressing against my bottom each time his cock hit home. His scratchy pubes rubbed against my clit. I wrapped my legs around him and rocked my hips, matching his movements. I could feel sharp foliage sticking into me through the linen of Jim's jacket. My crotch was hot and aching. I was covered in goose pimples.

Jim stepped up the pace, moving his hips rhythmically and jabbing his cock home. The exposed parts of his body had grown clammy and hot. I could hear him panting and grunting as he pleasured my nipples. Hot breath hissed out of his nostrils, warming my skin.

Tension pulsated in my belly. My nipples were alive and prickling with pleasure, responding to every tingle and throb in my pussy. I moved my hips, grinding my clit against Jim's pubes. Above us, a nightingale had begun to sing.

Jim kissed my neck, sliding his tongue along my throat. I tilted back my head, lengthening my neck. His mouth was hot, his breathing erratic. He kissed the sweet spot beneath my ear and I let out a long sigh of appreciation.

I'd begun to sweat; my skin felt clammy and hot. Damp hair clung to my forehead. My clothes felt restrictive and uncomfortable. Jim's body felt slick and slippery against mine. Foliage crackled and rustled underneath us as we moved. I was tingling all over.

He felt thick and hard inside me, stretching and filling me. My excited crotch rubbed against his pubes.

My taut nipples brushed against Jim's shirt as our bodies moved in rhythm.

The front of Jim's hair had fallen over his forehead. He supported himself on his elbows and looked into my eyes. His hips pumped. Our bellies made slippery noises as they slid against each other.

He bent his head to kiss me. His lips were full and soft and he tasted of wine. His tongue slipped between my lips. My crotch was on fire. Pleasure snaked through my veins. My nipples were hypersensitive and responsive. As they rubbed against Jim's shirt, electric tendrils of pleasure multiplied and spread through my body.

Jim's neck and chest were flushed red. His lips were dark and swollen. Sweat glistened on his brow. I could feel the tense muscles in his thighs as his hips pumped. His balls slapped loudly against my arse on every thrust.

The nightingale sang. The sound mingled and harmonised with the music drifting from the restaurant. The undergrowth crackled underneath us. Our breathing was loud and jagged. I'd begun to mewl and sob and Jim was grunting noisily in rhythm with each thrust.

My crotch was tight and tingling. My thigh muscles were quivering uncontrollably. I rocked my hips, rubbing my clit against Jim's wiry pubes on every thrust. My body was filmed with sweat. I held onto his buttocks, pulling him into me.

Jim's strokes had grown short and urgent. His body was tense above me, his thigh muscles rigid. He was grunting and moaning, making guttural, animal noises. His eyes flickered beneath narrowed lids. His lips were parted and dark.

Blood pounded in my ears. I was trembling all over. Heat and tension throbbed in my pelvis, building to a pitch. I was gasping and sobbing, almost screaming.

Jim's wet hair was clinging to his forehead. His eyes

shone with passion and tenderness. His shirt was creased and damp against my skin. He was hammering me hard. I was hovering on the brink, riding the precipice – a few more strokes and the roller coaster would tip over the edge and hurtle downhill. Sensation built. I was wound up with tension and excitement, waiting for release.

I used my legs for leverage and moved my hips, grinding my tingling crotch against Jim. My fingers dug into his buttocks. My breathing was frenzied and noisy. Tears welled in my eyes. I could feel him hot and thick inside me. I gazed into his eyes.

The pressure reached its limit. I felt the tension fracture and pleasure explode inside me. Heat and satisfaction coursed through my body. I arched my back. My head thrashed from side to side, foliage clung to my hair.

Jim gave several shallow thrusts then pushed his hips forwards in a final deep stab. His head was raised, his neck extended. He let out a long sigh of pleasure and release. I felt him pumping sperm inside me. I wrapped my arms around him, stroking his back as he came.

Orgasm pumped around my bloodstream. My body quivered and shook. My nipples tingled. Sweat dropped off Jim's face into mine. His thigh muscles were taut and tense. He circled his hips, wringing out the last shreds of pleasure.

When it was over, his body relaxed and he lay with his cheek resting on my chest. He turned his head and kissed my naked breast, then took my nipple into his mouth and sucked on it. We lay like that for a long time, his head on my chest and me stroking his hair. Neither of us wanted to break the spell.

The sweat had cooled on my body, making me feel chilly and dirty. My hair was matted with foliage and there were thorns and twigs sticking into me through Jim's jacket. I could hear insects buzzing around and I was pretty certain that my exposed flesh was covered in bites.

It was pitch black now, even blacker in the woods with the canopy of trees overhead. Jim helped me up and we sorted out our rumpled clothes. He held my hand and led me out of the wood. As we stepped back into the garden I looked up at the stars. The castle's high walls were lit up with floodlights and the forbidding structure was silhouetted against the dark tent of the sky.

It had grown cool and Jim wrapped his jacket around my shoulders. The orchestra had stopped playing and the night was silent except for the cicadas and some muted voices coming from the terrace.

'Look.' Jim pointed at the sky. I looked up just in time to see a shooting star or a comet streak across the sky like a silver bullet.

15

The next day we drove to Barcelona and booked into the Hotel Majestic. We spent the morning exploring the city and, after a quick lunch, went to the cathedral to meet Taxi.

We sat on the steps waiting for him. Terry's briefcase rested between Jim's knees and it was hard to imagine that such a mundane object contained the key to such an enormous fortune. If Jim was anxious he didn't show it but I was worried enough for both of us. Maybe I'd watched too many movies but I couldn't believe that handing over the money would end it.

'What time are we supposed to be meeting him?' I leant close to Jim and lowered my voice.

'One-thirty. And there's no need to whisper.'

'Sorry. I'm nervous.' I looked at my watch. It was almost half past.

'Don't be.' He reached for my hand. 'There he is.'

I scanned the crowds looking for anyone who might look like a bank robber.

It took me a couple of seconds to spot him, but the moment I did I knew it had to be him. He was middle aged with closely cropped hair and enormous ears. They stood out from his head at right angles, huge and pink.

Even without the ears I'd have known it was him. There was no mistaking his nationality. His face bore the lobster hue of the unaccustomed sunbather and he moved with a sort of stoical lassitude as if the heat was an ordeal which had to be borne.

He was wearing a formal suit, in spite of the weather, and moved with the broad-shouldered menace of a nightclub bouncer. He walked up the steps towards us, his expression unreadable behind mirrored sunglasses. Jim got to his feet and I did the same.

'Taxi.' Jim held out his hand and the man shook it.

'Good to see you at last. Is that it?' He nodded towards the briefcase.

The moment I heard him speak I knew he was the man who'd rung the hotel asking for Mr Powney. His voice was quiet and had a sort of rasping quality to it, like someone with laryngitis.

'Yes.' Jim picked it up and handed it over. He dipped his hand into his pocket and brought out the key.

'Everything you need is inside. Keys to the safe deposit boxes, the addresses, how much is in each.'

'And it's the amount we agreed?' Taxi pocketed the key to the briefcase.

'Yes. Exactly half of it. And you'll keep your part of the bargain?'

'Of course I will. I only ever wanted the money.' He extended his hand for a farewell handshake. He nodded in my direction. 'Goodbye, Dr McAdam. It was a pleasure meeting you.' He turned and walked away.

I turned to Jim. 'It was Taxi who rang The Feathers asking for Mr Powney, wasn't it? That's why you asked me about his voice.'

Jim nodded. 'He was in an accident when he was a kid. Tried to hang himself after he saw a lynching on an episode of *Bonanza*, it damaged his vocal chords.'

'And who's Mr Powney?'

'Nobody. It was my mother's maiden name. He knew I was using an alias.'

'I see. It makes sense now. What's his half of the bargain? To leave you alone?'

'Something like that.'

'But how can you be sure he will?'

'Because he wants his freedom. I can put him inside for the rest of his life, don't forget, if I go to the police.'

'What are you going to do with Terry's half?'

'I've decided to start a charity for young offenders. I'm going to call it the Terry Jenkins Foundation.' Jim took my hand. 'Come on. We'll have some coffee then go exploring.'

A few days later, back in London, Jim took me to his company's office. We went up in a glass and chrome lift and he led me through the open-plan office to the board-room. The room gleamed with polished wood. A huge window looked out over the city. Jim sat down at the head of the long table and I took the seat beside him.

'Are you going to tell me what we're doing here now?'

'I'm selling the company to my management team. We're signing the papers today.'

Before I could answer, the door opened and four suited men entered the room followed by a woman with a notebook. They sat down.

'Good morning gentlemen, good morning, Carole.' Jim stood up. 'I want to introduce you all to Dr Claire McAdam.' He introduced each of them by name and we all shook hands. 'So, gentlemen, shall we get on?'

The man opposite me, who I thought I remembered was Mike, the finance director, opened a folder and laid it in front of Jim.

'If you'll sign here and here, I'll sign on behalf of the new board and then it's official. The bank transfer is already arranged. The settlement should be in your account this afternoon.' He took out a Mont Blanc pen from his pocket and handed it to Jim.

Jim signed his name then slid the folder across the

desk to Mike. He signed with a flourish and there was a small round of applause. Mike got up and went over to a sideboard where champagne in an ice bucket and a tray of glasses were laid out. He opened the bottle and gave us each a glass.

'I'd like to propose a toast.' Jim raised his glass. 'To new beginnings.'

When I woke up it was dark and I had a raging thirst. It took me a couple of seconds to remember where I was. I sat up and the familiar shapes of Jim's bedroom slowly came into focus. My head began to throb and I remembered Jim and I polishing off a second bottle of champagne when we got home from the meeting. We'd drunk it in bed and afterwards we'd made love. I didn't even remember falling asleep.

His side of the bed was empty. I padded through to the en suite and turned on the shower. I was drying my hair with a towel when Jim came in wearing a fluffy bathrobe. His hair was spiky and messy from sleep and I could see the beginnings of a five o'clock shadow. He sat down on the edge of the bath.

'Hello, darling. You were sleeping so peacefully when I woke up that I didn't want to disturb you. I made some coffee when I heard you moving around. It's downstairs when you're ready.'

'Thanks. I think I'll need a couple of aspirin with it.'

'Hangover? We did rather overdo the bubbly.'

'Headache. I'm hoping it will go away once I get moving. What are you going to do, Jim? Now that you're unemployed.' I wrapped the towel around my head like a turban.

'Hardly unemployed. I made several million when I signed that piece of paper so I don't really need to worry.'

'So you won't work any more?' I squeezed toothpaste onto my brush.

'Eventually I will. I just need to work out what I want to do.'

'Any ideas? Will you start another company?'

Jim shook his head. 'The settlement forbids me from setting up a rival business and I sold it because my heart wasn't in it any more, anyway. No, I'll do something new. I've thought about opening a restaurant, and I've got Terry's charity to organise remember. But I probably won't do anything for a while.'

'How do you feel?' I closed the toilet lid and sat down, facing Jim.

'Well, on the one hand, I'm a bit nervous I think. No, who am I kidding? I'm terrified. Uprooted, in unknown territory. But mainly I feel utterly liberated. Lighter somehow as if a whole new world of possibility is open to me.'

'You know what that reminds me of? The phoenix. Your old life is in ashes and, here you are, rising out of the flames ready to face your future.'

Jim laughed. 'Actually I've always thought of myself as more of a peacock.'

'Yes, I can see that ... your smart suits and expensive shirts.'

'Do you know the interesting thing about peacocks?'

'I don't think so.'

'They mate for life.' He reached out a fingertip and stroked the surface of my collar. I felt something inside me soften and a shivery tingle slid up my spine.

'I tell you what,' I said when I trusted myself to speak, 'why don't we do something special tonight? To mark the occasion – the beginning of your – our – new life?'

'Sounds wonderful. I'll go and put on my best peacock

suit and why don't you wear that red dress you look so beautiful in?'

I dried my hair, leaving the curls natural, and did my make-up. Jim sat on the bed watching me get ready. It had only taken him minutes to shave and dress. He wore a silk shirt beneath his best suit and he looked irresistible. I put on my earrings and turned to him for approval.

'You look unbelievable.' He got to his feet. 'We've come a long way, haven't we?' He lowered his head and kissed my neck.

'A million miles. Every step a pleasure.'

'Come on. The taxi's waiting.' Jim took my hand and led me downstairs.

'Browns Hotel, please, mate.'

'Right you are, guv.'

It was a warm evening, but already there was a hint of autumn in the air. The trees were turning auburn and leaves gathered on the pavement. We snaked through busy London traffic.

The taxi paused at a pedestrian crossing and two teenaged lads caught sight of us. Instead of crossing the road when the green man began to flash, they stood like statues, paused in mid-step staring into the car. One of them laid his hand on his crotch and wolf whistled. The lights changed and their heads swivelled after us as we pulled away.

Visit the Black Lace website at
www.black-lace-books.com

LOOK OUT FOR THE ALL-NEW BLACK LACE BOOKS – AVAILABLE NOW!

All books priced £7.99 in the UK. Please note publication dates apply to the UK only. For other territories, please contact your retailer.

THE TOP OF HER GAME
Emma Holly
ISBN 978 0 352 34116 7

It's not only Julia's professional acumen that has men quaking in their shoes – she also has a taste for keeping men in line after office hours. With an impressive collection of whips and high heels to her name, she sure has some kinky ways of showing affection. But Julia's been searching all her life for a man who won't be tamed too quickly – and when she meets rugged dude rancher Zach on a business get-together in Montana, she thinks she might have found him.

He may be a simple countryman, but he's not about to take any nonsense from uppity city women like Julia. Zach's full of surprises: where she thinks he's tough, he turns out to be gentle; she's confident she's got this particular cowboy broken in, he turns the tables on her. Has she locked horns with an animal too wild even for her? When it comes to sex, Zach doesn't go for half measures. Underneath the big sky of Montana, has the steely Ms Mueller finally met her match?

Coming in May 2007

BRIGHT FIRE
Maya Hess
ISBN 978 0 352 34104 4

Jenna Bright's light aircraft crash lands en-route to Scotland, hurtling her out of her hectic modern life as a courier pilot and back in time over two thousand years. Leaving behind her fiancé Mick, who's more interested in bedding Jenna's friends than planning his wedding, Jenna faces iron-age Britain and is revered as a goddess by the Celtic villagers she encounters.

Having no choice but to adapt while trying to find a way home, Jenna encounters mystery, magic and a sexual hunger equalled only by the powerful urge to survive. Caught in an erotic tangle between Brogan and Cathan, two of the village's most powerful men, Jenna finally glimpses a way home but, having never felt so sexually free and adored by so many, she's not sure she's quite ready to go back to her old life.

VELVET GLOVE
Emma Holly
ISBN 978 0 352 34115 0

Audrey Popkin realises she has bitten off more than she can chew when she gets embroiled with icy-cool banker, Sterling Foster. His ideas about how to have fun are more bizarre than any English Literature graduate should have to put up with! One morning she packs her bags and walks out of his luxury Florida apartment, heading back to Washington DC in search of a more regular deal with a more regular guy. But, for a girl like Audrey, this is not as easy as it sounds.

When Patrick Dugan, the charismatic owner of an old-world bar with a talent for mixing the smoothest cocktails, fixes Audrey in his sights, some strange alliances are about to be formed. Within a week Audrey talks her way into a job at Patrick's bar and a room in the apartment he shares with a drag queen jazz singer called Basil – who has a great line in platinum wigs. Audrey soon realises that Patrick is not all he seems. Why is he pretending to be gay? And what is he covering up for his father, a pillar of the local community? Audrey is so besotted with the enigmatic barman that she doesn't realise they are connected by a mutual adversary – a steely, cold-hearted son of a bitch who will take them all down if he doesn't get his little plaything back.

Coming in June 2007

SUITE SEVENTEEN
Portia Da Costa
ISBN 978 0 352 34109 9

When vibrant, forty-something widow Annie Conroy spies her new neighbours having kinky sex in their back garden, she decides it's time that she too woke up and smelt the erotic roses. And where better to begin her daring adventures than the luxurious Waverley Grange Country Hotel, and its hidden den of iniquity, the chintz-clad but wickedly pervy Suite Seventeen? Under the stern but playful eye of exotic master Valentino, Annie quickly discovers the shocking hidden depths of her own sensuality, and surrenders herself body and soul to his outrageous games of power. But when the Waverley's entire future hangs in the balance, and Annie has the means to help save it, dare she gamble on going one step further . . . and giving her heart to the mysterious man who's come to control her?

IN THE FLESH
Emma Holly
ISBN 978 0 352 34117 4

Surely there has never been a woman more sensual, more irresistible, than svelte dancer Chloe Dubois. She is a heady combination of innocence and sultry seduction, and Japanese-American businessman David Imakita will risk everything he has to keep her: his career, his friends, even his integrity, such is her power over him.

But who is this temptress and what does she want? Is it money, prestige or just love? David's ex-Sumo bodyguard, Sato, believes Chloe will cause havoc in their ordered lives, and turns up information on her that is far from pretty. The warning signs are there, but it is already too late for David, who is under her spell and besotted. Will this unrepentant temptress overturn her wild ways and accept the opportunity to change her life for the better, or will the dark family secrets of her past resurface and destroy them both?

Black Lace Booklist

Information is correct at time of printing. To avoid disappointment, check availability before ordering. Go to www.black-lace-books.com. All books are priced £7.99 unless another price is given.

BLACK LACE BOOKS WITH A CONTEMPORARY SETTING

☐ ALWAYS THE BRIDEGROOM Tesni Morgan	ISBN 978 0 352 33855 6	£6.99
☐ THE ANGELS' SHARE Maya Hess	ISBN 978 0 352 34043 6	
☐ ARIA APPASSIONATA Julie Hastings	ISBN 978 0 352 33056 7	£6.99
☐ ASKING FOR TROUBLE Kristina Lloyd	ISBN 978 0 352 33362 9	
☐ BLACK LIPSTICK KISSES Monica Belle	ISBN 978 0 352 33885 3	£6.99
☐ BONDED Fleur Reynolds	ISBN 978 0 352 33192 2	£6.99
☐ THE BOSS Monica Belle	ISBN 978 0 352 34088 7	
☐ BOUND IN BLUE Monica Belle	ISBN 978 0 352 34012 2	
☐ CAMPAIGN HEAT Gabrielle Marcola	ISBN 978 0 352 33941 6	
☐ CAT SCRATCH FEVER Sophie Mouette	ISBN 978 0 352 34021 4	
☐ CIRCUS EXCITE Nikki Magennis	ISBN 978 0 352 34033 7	
☐ CLUB CRÈME Primula Bond	ISBN 978 0 352 33907 2	£6.99
☐ COMING ROUND THE MOUNTAIN Tabitha Flyte	ISBN 978 0 352 33873 0	£6.99
☐ CONFESSIONAL Judith Roycroft	ISBN 978 0 352 33421 3	
☐ CONTINUUM Portia Da Costa	ISBN 978 0 352 33120 5	
☐ COOKING UP A STORM Emma Holly	ISBN 978 0 352 34114 3	
☐ DANGEROUS CONSEQUENCES Pamela Rochford	ISBN 978 0 352 33185 4	
☐ DARK DESIGNS Madelynne Ellis	ISBN 978 0 352 34075 7	
☐ THE DEVIL INSIDE Portia Da Costa	ISBN 978 0 352 32993 6	
☐ EDEN'S FLESH Robyn Russell	ISBN 978 0 352 33923 2	£6.99
☐ ENTERTAINING MR STONE Portia Da Costa	ISBN 978 0 352 34029 0	
☐ EQUAL OPPORTUNITIES Mathilde Madden	ISBN 978 0 352 34070 2	
☐ FERMININE WILES Karina Moore	ISBN 978 0 352 33874 7	
☐ FIRE AND ICE Laura Hamilton	ISBN 978 0 352 33486 2	
☐ GOING DEEP Kimberly Dean	ISBN 978 0 352 33876 1	£6.99
☐ GOING TOO FAR Laura Hamilton	ISBN 978 0 352 33657 6	£6.99

☐ GONE WILD Maria Eppie   ISBN 978 0 352 33670 5

☐ IN PURSUIT OF ANNA Natasha Rostova   ISBN 978 0 352 34060 3

☐ MAD ABOUT THE BOY Mathilde Madden   ISBN 978 0 352 34001 6

☐ MAKE YOU A MAN Anna Clare   ISBN 978 0 352 34006 1

☐ MAN HUNT Cathleen Ross   ISBN 978 0 352 33583 8

☐ THE MASTER OF SHILDEN Lucinda Carrington   ISBN 978 0 352 33140 3

☐ MÉNAGE Emma Holly   ISBN 978 0 352 34118 1

☐ MIXED DOUBLES Zoe le Verdier   ISBN 978 0 352 33312 4   £6.99

☐ MIXED SIGNALS Anna Clare   ISBN 978 0 352 33889 1   £6.99

☐ MS BEHAVIOUR Mini Lee   ISBN 978 0 352 33962 1

☐ PACKING HEAT Karina Moore   ISBN 978 0 352 33356 8   £6.99

☐ PAGAN HEAT Monica Belle   ISBN 978 0 352 33974 4

☐ PASSION OF ISIS Madelynne Ellis   ISBN 978 0 352 33993 5

☐ PEEP SHOW Mathilde Madden   ISBN 978 0 352 33924 9

☐ THE POWER GAME Carrera Devonshire   ISBN 978 0 352 33990 4

☐ THE PRIVATE UNDOING OF A PUBLIC SERVANT   ISBN 978 0 352 34066 5
     Leonie Martel

☐ RELEASE ME Suki Cunningham   ISBN 978 0 352 33671 2   £6.99

☐ RUDE AWAKENING Pamela Kyle   ISBN 978 0 352 33036 9

☐ SAUCE FOR THE GOOSE Mary Rose Maxwell   ISBN 978 0 352 33492 3

☐ SLAVE TO SUCCESS Kimberley Raines   ISBN 978 0 352 33687 3   £6.99

☐ SLEAZY RIDER Karen S. Smith   ISBN 978 0 352 33964 5

☐ STELLA DOES HOLLYWOOD Stella Black   ISBN 978 0 352 33588 3

☐ THE STRANGER Portia Da Costa   ISBN 978 0 352 33211 0

☐ SUMMER FEVER Anna Ricci   ISBN 978 0 352 33625 5   £6.99

☐ SWITCHING HANDS Alaine Hood   ISBN 978 0 352 33896 9   £6.99

☐ SYMPHONY X Jasmine Stone   ISBN 978 0 352 33629 3   £6.99

☐ THE TOP OF HER GAME Emma Holly   ISBN 978 0 352 34116 7

☐ TONGUE IN CHEEK Tabitha Flyte   ISBN 978 0 352 33484 8

☐ TWO WEEKS IN TANGIER Annabel Lee   ISBN 978 0 352 33599 9   £6.99

☐ UNNATURAL SELECTION Alaine Hood   ISBN 978 0 352 33963 8

☐ VILLAGE OF SECRETS Mercedes Kelly   ISBN 978 0 352 33344 5

☐ WILD BY NATURE Monica Belle   ISBN 978 0 352 33915 7   £6.99

☐ WILD CARD Madeline Moore   ISBN 978 0 352 34038 2

☐ WING OF MADNESS Mae Nixon   ISBN 978 0 352 34099 3

BLACK LACE BOOKS WITH AN HISTORICAL SETTING

☐ THE AMULET Lisette Allen ISBN 978 0 352 33019 2 £6.99

☐ THE BARBARIAN GEISHA Charlotte Royal ISBN 978 0 352 33267 7

☐ BARBARIAN PRIZE Deanna Ashford ISBN 978 0 352 34017 7

☐ DANCE OF OBSESSION Olivia Christie ISBN 978 0 352 33101 4

☐ DARKER THAN LOVE Kristina Lloyd ISBN 978 0 352 33279 0

☐ ELENA'S DESTINY Lisette Allen ISBN 978 0 352 33218 9

☐ FRENCH MANNERS Olivia Christie ISBN 978 0 352 33214 1

☐ LORD WRAXALL'S FANCY Anna Lieff Saxby ISBN 978 0 352 33080 2

☐ NICOLE'S REVENGE Lisette Allen ISBN 978 0 352 32984 4

☐ THE SENSES BEJEWELLED Cleo Cordell ISBN 978 0 352 32904 2 £6.99

☐ THE SOCIETY OF SIN Sian Lacey Taylder ISBN 978 0 352 34080 1

☐ UNDRESSING THE DEVIL Angel Strand ISBN 978 0 352 33938 6

☐ WHITE ROSE ENSNARED Juliet Hastings ISBN 978 0 352 33052 9 £6.99

BLACK LACE BOOKS WITH A PARANORMAL THEME

☐ BURNING BRIGHT Janine Ashbless ISBN 978 0 352 34085 6

☐ CRUEL ENCHANTMENT Janine Ashbless ISBN 978 0 352 33483 1

☐ FLOOD Anna Clare ISBN 978 0 352 34094 8

☐ GOTHIC BLUE Portia Da Costa ISBN 978 0 352 33075 8

☐ THE PRIDE Edie Bingham ISBN 978 0 352 33997 3

BLACK LACE ANTHOLOGIES

☐ BLACK LACE QUICKIES 1 ISBN 978 0 352 34126 6 £2.99

☐ BLACK LACE QUICKIES 2 ISBN 978 0 352 34127 3 £2.99

☐ MORE WICKED WORDS Various ISBN 978 0 352 33487 9 £6.99

☐ WICKED WORDS 3 Various ISBN 978 0 352 33522 7 £6.99

☐ WICKED WORDS 4 Various ISBN 978 0 352 33603 3 £6.99

☐ WICKED WORDS 5 Various ISBN 978 0 352 33642 2 £6.99

☐ WICKED WORDS 6 Various ISBN 978 0 352 33690 3 £6.99

☐ WICKED WORDS 7 Various ISBN 978 0 352 33743 6 £6.99

☐ WICKED WORDS 8 Various ISBN 978 0 352 33787 0 £6.99

☐ WICKED WORDS 9 Various ISBN 978 0 352 33860 0

☐ WICKED WORDS 10 Various ISBN 978 0 352 33893 8

☐ THE BEST OF BLACK LACE 2 Various ISBN 978 0 352 33718 4

☐ WICKED WORDS: SEX IN THE OFFICE Various ISBN 978 0 352 33944 7

☐ WICKED WORDS: SEX AT THE SPORTS CLUB   ISBN 978 0 352 33991 1
    Various

☐ WICKED WORDS: SEX ON HOLIDAY Various   ISBN 978 0 352 33961 4

☐ WICKED WORDS: SEX IN UNIFORM Various   ISBN 978 0 352 34002 3

☐ WICKED WORDS: SEX IN THE KITCHEN Various   ISBN 978 0 352 34018 4

☐ WICKED WORDS: SEX ON THE MOVE Various   ISBN 978 0 352 34034 4

☐ WICKED WORDS: SEX AND MUSIC Various   ISBN 978 0 352 34061 0

☐ WICKED WORDS: SEX AND SHOPPING Various   ISBN 978 0 352 34076 4

☐ SEX IN PUBLIC Various   ISBN 978 0 352 34089 4

BLACK LACE NON-FICTION

☐ THE BLACK LACE BOOK OF WOMEN'S SEXUAL   ISBN 978 0 352 33793 1   £6.99
    FANTASIES Edited by Kerri Sharp

To find out the latest information about Black Lace titles, check out the website: www.black-lace-books.com or send for a booklist with complete synopses by writing to:

> Black Lace Booklist, Virgin Books Ltd
> Thames Wharf Studios
> Rainville Road
> London W6 9HA

Please include an SAE of decent size. Please note only British stamps are valid.

Our privacy policy
We will not disclose information you supply us to any other parties. We will not disclose any information which identifies you personally to any person without your express consent.

From time to time we may send out information about Black Lace books and special offers. Please tick here if you do <u>not</u> wish to receive Black Lace information.   ☐

Please send me the books I have ticked above.

Name ....

Address ....

....

....

....

Post Code ....

Send to: Virgin Books Cash Sales, Thames Wharf Studios, Rainville Road, London W6 9HA.

US customers: for prices and details of how to order books for delivery by mail, call 888-330-8477.

Please enclose a cheque or postal order, made payable to Virgin Books Ltd, to the value of the books you have ordered plus postage and packing costs as follows:

UK and BFPO – £1.00 for the first book, 50p for each subsequent book.

Overseas (including Republic of Ireland) – £2.00 for the first book, £1.00 for each subsequent book.

If you would prefer to pay by VISA, ACCESS/MASTERCARD, DINERS CLUB, AMEX or SWITCH, please write your card number and expiry date here:

....

Signature ....

Please allow up to 28 days for delivery.